I dedicate my book to other writers who like myself, found the time, had the discipline and made sacrifices to write and self-publish their first novel...I tip my hat to you all.

Slider's Challenge

ONE

Inside his head, the pain was like that of a train somewhere in the far-off distance, with the sound of its rumbling getting ever closer and louder … Soon, it was deafening. His eyes were still closed as he gently coughed and placed the palms of his hands across his weary face, with his fingers just touching his ears. He let out a long, smooth breath and slowly his eyes opened.

Slider turned his head to look across the white-fringe pillow to his left, where the red illumination on the clock showed 06:45. He reached for the small table lamp which sat atop the bedside cabinet and switched it on, his body taking a few seconds to adjust to its light. He wondered for a moment just how bad today's head pain was going to be. Slowly, he pushed the duvet back and moved his legs gently out of the bed, placing his bare feet on the red Persian rug that covered the mock herringbone flooring. Sitting upright, he arched his spine a few times, then reached across for his Nortriptyline tablets. From the small white plastic container he tapped out a few into the well of his palm, and washed them down with some water which was left in his glass from the previous night. After a long yawn, he gently lay back on the mattress, closed his eyes, and tried to grab just a few extra minutes of rest.

The door creaked and Becky, his nine-year-old daughter, entered the bedroom. 'How's your head today Dad?' she inquired, holding a spongy finger biscuit in one hand and a glass of milk in the other.

'I think I can go to work today,' he said, yawning again. 'Is Andy awake yet?' Slider had been diagnosed with a tension headache many years ago and had his good days and his bad days. The Amitriptyline and Duloxetine tablets didn't have much effect, apart from giving him a dry throat, and sensitivity to light was always an issue. Now he'd moved on to Nortriptyline, but they didn't seem to help much either. Recently he'd come across an article in a daily newspaper about doctors who had been testing a new drug called Erenumab. He'd made a note of this new drug and would mention it to his neurologist, Dr Lombardi, the next time he saw her.

Becky moved her head around the panelled door, observing her father getting dressed. 'He's on the computer. Dad, can I play the piano for a bit?'

'It's a bit early, angel, we don't want to annoy the neighbours at this time of the morning. Wait till I come home tonight, and we can both play.' His daughter pursed her lips and blew out a draught of air. 'I'll tell you what, darling, we can both play our favourite piece of music tonight.' Slider was forty-two years old, four years older than his wife Lily, and was trying to learn to play the piano, but time was against him and at his age it didn't come easily. The same could be said for him using his laptop. 'Thank God for Andy,' he would say when problems occurred.

Becky had finished her biscuit and was leaning against the edge of the door with both arms crossed in front of her stomach. She sighed, 'But Dad, you know you can't, it's too difficult for you!'

Matthew Slider looked at her, smiled, and winked. 'One day, Becky, one day.' He finished dressing in his black and red chequered shirt and customary black jeans and walked a few steps across the open landing and up the single step to his son's room. Andy was a talented eleven-year-old, with a flair for computers and gadgets. On the outside of his door was a No Entry sign. Slider used the knuckle on his index finger to knock on the door. He opened it slowly and observed his son on his laptop.

Andy was still in his Doctor Who dressing gown and using his favourite yellow and black headphones, which were a Christmas present from his mother. A recovering alcoholic, she'd gone to Hereford for a few days to visit her sister Rose. Andy slipped off his headphones and removed his black-rimmed glasses, which his father thought made him look a little like Harry Potter, and placed them on top of an exercise book. Gazing at his father, he yawned, stretched his arms, and asked, 'How's the head today, Dad?'

'So, so,' he responded. Slider went downstairs. It was seven thirty and time to start work. Matthew Slider had been a private hire taxi driver in Cardiff for sixteen years. He relished the job and the freedom that it gave him, and the variety of passengers he carried ensured that every day was different and a challenge. His first stop today was to pick up two brothers, Keith and Robert, who was happier being called Bob. They always put a smile on Slider's face because no one could ever understand how these two boys could be so different: Keith was short and tubby with fair hair, while Bob, who was very tall for his age, had jet black hair and wore black-rimmed glasses.

As the car rolled back off the driveway, Becky and Andy were in the upstairs bedroom window waving to their father. Becky put her lips to the glass and crossed her eyes. Her brother looked at her and moved his head upwards as if to sigh. Slider smiled and held up his watch to the windscreen and tapped it. Andy nodded in approval. It meant "Be ready to go when I get back." The traffic on this May morning was starting to build, the sun was starting to rise, and it was going to be a beautiful day. It took about fifteen minutes to get to the boys' house, and as the car pulled up, he could see Keith was eating a piece of toast. It was one of his pet hates that people would bring food into his car and eat it, so he deliberately drove past their house and did a U-turn in the road. This gave him an extra minute or so to delay the boys getting into his car. As they got in, Slider turned on the music system and the Led Zeppelin song 'Kashmir' reverberated throughout the car. Immediately he started to move his head in time to the beat.

'No, not today, Slider, we've got exams!' shouted Keith.

'You boys are definitely no fun today,' he said, glancing over his shoulder.

'Sorry,' added Bob, who was covering his ears.

As he drove into the school grounds, he imagined what the future was going to be like for these young people. This was 2018 and the use of artificial intelligence was rising. What would it be like in a decade, he thought? In fact, he worried about what life would be like for his own children too.

It was ten past eight when he got back. As he drove up the driveway to the front of his house, he noticed that the rose bushes in front of the bay windows were starting to produce buds. In fact, most of the front garden was coming alive with perennials and other unknown varieties of plants. He sounded the horn as he stopped. Becky opened the front door and Sooty, their tortoiseshell cat, leapt out and straight onto the bonnet of his car. He had only had his Skoda Superb for nine months and this was another pet hate of his. Slider grinned as he thought of the pun. He liked to look after his car and pussy claw marks were a definite no-no. 'Has somebody fed this cat today?'

'Yes, Dad,' Becky said as she adjusted the plaits in her black hair. 'I also gave her some nuts and clean water.'

Slider raced up the stairs and into the toilet. He lifted the seat and had a welcome pee. 'Andy, are you nearly ready yet?' his father yelled. The boy was always slow in the mornings, a little bit like his father when he was young, but this little-known fact had never been mentioned. As he came down the stairs, he stared through the spindles at Sooty, who was in the kitchen crunching on her food. Hearing him, she looked up. Their eyes met as he said, 'If I catch you on my car again, there's going to be trouble.'

Becky, who was sat at the breakfast bar, overheard this remark and said, 'Dad, she's only a cat.'

He stopped and looked at the cat purposely. 'Watch it, girl.' Sooty finished eating, turned and walked towards the cat flap, and she was gone. Andy slithered down the stairs at 8:26 a.m. and walked through the kitchen door and into the garden. His father had his usual mug of coffee in hand and was staring into the fishpond. He put his coffee mug down onto a small square plastic table and went into the garden shed to fetch the fish food. He took off the top and threw a few handfuls into the water. The goldfish immediately rose to the surface.

'Dad, it's time to go!' Becky was right: it was half past eight.

Slider knew the traffic would be bad if they left it much later. He returned the fish food to his shed, locked the marigold-coloured door, and walked back into the kitchen. 'Have we all got everything?' Their father always had to say this because someone always forgot something.

They nodded.

'Is everything turned off?' Again, they both gestured yes. Andy opened the front door and they all filed out. Slider was the last to leave. He turned and had a quick look around, and at that precise moment the cat bolted back through the cat flap and stood frozen upon seeing him: 'And I will see you tonight.' He closed the front door, deadlocked it, and walked to the car.

Becky and her brother always took it in turns to ride shotgun in the front of the car, but because Andy was feeling so tired today, he immediately went for the back so that he could sprawl across the three seats. His sister had a large grin on her face as she put her seat belt on.

'Thanks, Andy.' He gave a large yawn and said something that neither of them understood.

'Son, you're going to have to go to bed a bit earlier; I can't have you like this every morning.' Their father knew the exam season was looming and how important they would be to his children. Something will have to change, he thought. Perhaps we all could do with a weekend away, he mused. 'Perhaps a few days in Weston-super-Mare and some sea air,' he whispered to himself.

TWO

They had only been gone a few minutes when Becky said, 'Dad, you've forgotten your bottles of water.' He felt the cup holders, and his daughter gave a wry smile as she looked out the side window.

'There is always something!' he moaned. 'Always something!' Their father usually took two half-litres of water to keep himself hydrated. His mind was working fast now, trying to think what to do. He could go back, which would make his children late, or he could go to Elmer's Café – a café in the Cathays suburb of Cardiff where taxi drivers went for breakfast – and pick up a few bottles. He decided instead to press on and take his kids to school, reaching the school just in time. 'I'll pick you up at the usual time,' he said after giving his daughter a hug and ruffling his son's hair.

Slider logged on for work and drove past Roath Park Lake, which he had fished in when he was a teenager. The lake was now in a poor condition, with green algae covering over half the surface area. The bottom of the lake had a large build-up of silt, which prevented rowing boats from using the whole of the lake. He could remember when Cardiff City Council had machines dredging the silt off the bottom, but that was many years ago when councils had money to look after their parks. This was 2018, and unfortunately there was no spare money for luxuries like that. After a short wait, he received his first call of the day from Carver. He had only been working for the company since last September and it was like a breath of fresh air compared to his previous employer. The job was to pick up Jena from the concourse of the University Hospital of Wales. As he approached the pick-up point, he could see a woman in green fatigues. She saw him as he drew nearer and raised her arm. He stopped next to her, and she got into the back of the car. 'Jena?'

'Yes,' she said, smothering a yawn.

The job was to take Jena to the University Hospital Llandough. The journey was an easy one, but his mind was more on where to buy some water. From her uniform, he could make out that Jena was an ambulance driver, either starting or finishing her shift. Considering her tiredness, he deduced that she must have just finished work. After dropping his passenger off and clearing the fare, he turned on the radio and just caught the start of the ten o'clock news. He sat still in the car with his eyes closed and took a few deep breaths. The sun had broken through the clouds en route to the hospital, and his head pain was a gathering force. 'Why me,' he muttered. 'Why does this happen to me?' After a few moments he opened his eyes and said to himself, 'Penarth Pier.' The pier was only a ten-minute drive away, and with most of the heavy traffic heading back into Cardiff the roads should be clear. A bacon roll and a cup of coffee sounded very inviting considering that he hadn't eaten anything yet. So he pushed the red button on his smartphone and logged off from work.

As he was leaving the hospital grounds, he noticed a bright yellow restored Ford escort in a parking space. This put a large smile on his face and brought back fond memories of the time when he and Lily did their courting in his old two-tone cream and grey car. Out on the main road a concrete lorry was dispensing its load slowly along the road where new kerbstones were being laid. As he drew up close to the lorry, he lowered the side window and shouted across to a worker, 'You must have a job for life working on the roads!'

The road worker lowered his head, looked at him, and after exhaling his cigarette smoke, coughed, and said, 'Well you'll never be out of work driving your taxi!' The men laughed, and Slider's car moved slowly away.

* * *

Penarth is situated just four miles southwest of Cardiff. It's a vibrant town with lots of modern restaurants and bars, as well as some traditional Victorian and Edwardian buildings. Driving down the hill towards the pier, he could see that the tide was unusually high that morning, with a large swell on the sea. As the hill bottomed out, he spotted two empty parking spaces opposite the entrance to the pier. He drove just past the first and reversed neatly into the adjoining space. Slider turned off the engine and sat quietly looking at the sea.

The sun was now fully out and shining in his face. He closed his eyes once again, moved the seat back, and took some long, deep breaths. When he reopened his eyes a large container ship had appeared from out of nowhere and was heading towards the docks in Cardiff. The name of the ship was just too far away for him to make it out. Out of the corner of his right eye, a smartly dressed woman came into his view. She was wearing black flared trousers and a bright red, three-quarter-length coat. Her hair was black and curly, and a long black and grey striped scarf was draped around her neck. In front of her was a young girl who looked about six years old and was wearing a blue and grey school uniform. She was walking hand in hand with an older woman in a grey overcoat, who he surmised was probably the child's nanny.

They were on the opposite side of the road to him and were all walking towards the entrance to the pier. As they walked closer, he thought he recognized the woman in the red coat. A cold shiver ran down his spine. 'Oh my God! That's Alexis Polti.'

Alexis Polti was an award-winning celebrity with numerous TV series to her name, such as *The Restorer*. He could only assume that she must be making a TV programme in the area.

Just then, two single-deck, private hire coaches, pulled up right in front of him, blocking his view of the woman. Out of the coaches poured a large contingent of young schoolgirls. There must have been a hundred or more of them. They were all dressed in the same cream and grey uniform, and all about the same age as his own daughter, Becky. Slider had had enough of watching and wanted to see for himself if his mystery woman was who he thought she was. As he got out of his car the two coaches pulled away, leaving a long line of schoolgirls all queuing to go onto the pier. But there was no sign of his mystery woman, in the red coat.

The road was now clear of traffic, so he crossed it and sat on a promenade bench that was close to the entrance of the pier. In the distance, several fishing boats were making their way down the Bristol Channel in the direction of Sully. Slider had always loved his fishing but now it was sea fishing that he was interested in, both on the shore with his good friend Kevin, or on a fishing boat with Steve and Thomas from work. Kevin's stomach never allowed him to venture onto the sea.

As he looked to his left the line of schoolgirls had all but disappeared, so he stood up and walked towards the entrance. There was a gift shop just outside the pier on his right-hand side. The sign said Ye Olde Sweet Shoppe and it sold various colours of sticks of rock with penarth pier written all the way through them. He could remember eating rock when he was a boy and now wondered if his own children would like it. 'I'll think about it,' he said to himself.

There were more important items on his mind, such as a bacon roll and a cup of coffee; rock could wait till later. As he made his way onto the pier, he noticed a new café /restaurant on his left-hand side which was crowded with schoolgirls and a few elderly couples. Further along on the right stood two white-panelled food and drink kiosks. They were identical, and were selling the same food and drinks. The kiosks were surrounded by schoolgirls all vying for attention, so he decided to take a walk towards the far end of the pier.

Penarth Pier was originally two hundred metres long, but in 1947 the Canadian cargo steamship SS *Port Royal Park* collided with the pier in a gale, causing severe structural damage which greatly reduced its length. At the end of the pier he could see someone fishing, so he walked towards the fisherman to see what was being caught that morning. Slider exchanged pleasantries with a few people and observed that large sections of decking had been replaced with teak boards, which his blue sneakers kept slipping on. 'What's the fishing like this morning?'

'I've only caught one small pouting, but I'm hoping for something a bit better.'

'Well, you've got a good day for it, the sea is churning up the bottom nicely. What time is high tide?'

'Oh, in about twenty minutes.'

'Good luck to you then.' He turned and walked towards the other side of the pier, and saw a large grey warship that was heading out towards the open sea. The ship was far too far away to be able to make out its name, but it had two small high-powered craft in front of it, which seemed to be clearing a path for the ship. In the distance, a helicopter was practising take offs and landings on the warship, which looked very impressive to him.

Slider turned and started to walk back towards the kiosks. Not only did he now want something to eat and drink, but he also needed another pee. He was a bit disappointed that he never got to see the woman in the red coat, and come to think of it he hadn't seen the woman in the grey overcoat or the little girl who was with her. The queues at the white kiosks had reduced significantly. He went to the toilet block which was directly opposite, and when he reappeared, only one schoolgirl was waiting to be served at either kiosk. While he waited he noticed several photographs of various species of fish which were being displayed above the counter on his left-hand side. Finally, the little girl moved away, leaving him at the head of the queue. He was just about to say something when from out of nowhere there was an almighty high-pitched, ear-piercing scream. It was the type of scream that stopped everyone in their tracks. Time stood still; even Slider didn't make a move. People on the pier just looked at each other, wondering where the scream had come from.

Suddenly he saw her. It was the woman in the grey overcoat. She had been out of sight at the far side of the opposite kiosk. She was walking backwards very slowly towards the centre of the pier. Her right arm was parallel to the ground and the index finger on her right hand was pointing forward. There was a terrifying look on her face, and again she screamed hysterically. In unison, a large gathering of schoolgirls all rushed to the side of the pier and started pointing downwards towards the sea. Slider rushed to the handrail and saw the little girl in the blue and grey uniform floating on the surface of the water, face down.

He rushed back to the kiosk and stood in front of the young woman who was serving behind the counter. Slider looked directly into her eyes. 'Listen, a young girl has fallen into the sea, call nine nine nine and ask for the coastguard, police, and ambulance!' Without hesitation, he took out of his pockets his car keys and wallet and handed them to her. His own phone had been left on charge in the car. He rushed back towards the handrail, pushing a few schoolgirls out of the way. He had one leg over the handrail when a hand grabbed the back of his collar and pulled him to the ground. His eyes were firmly locked onto the female police officer who had pulled him back, and who was pushing everyone to the far side of the pier. 'What did you do that for?' he shouted.

He got to his feet, and the police officer held her left arm out, shouting, 'Back, get back all of you!'

Slider was angry at this point. The police officer seemed more interested in pushing back the crowd rather than helping the little girl in the water. 'Why aren't you helping the girl in the water?'

'Help is on its way, sir. Now will you all kindly move back to the opposite side of the pier?'

Slider knew that time was of the essence and that desperate times called for desperate measures. So he jumped forward and punched the police officer on the side of her chin, causing her to fall backwards. This gave him the vital seconds that he needed. He vaulted his right leg over the handrail and dragged over his other. He spotted a man in a sheepskin coat standing close to the flare gun that was housed in a glass-covered yellow box. He looked at him and screamed, 'Fire the flare! Fire the flare!' He then slowly turned away from the man and jumped into the sea.

As he descended his stomach dropped away, giving him that awful feeling in his gut. The fall seemed to take forever, then the water came rushing up to meet him. He closed his eyes and braced himself for the impact. He took a large breath of air and disappeared into the cold, brown muddy waters of the Bristol Channel. Under the water something touched his leg, which made him flinch, and the pain in his ears was excruciating. He took a few seconds to relax and quickly used his arms to pull for the surface. He must have pulled four or five times before reaching the surface and the light. Slider's body was freezing cold, and he was starting to shake all over. Although it was early May, the sea was still only a few degrees above freezing. His luck didn't change when, after taking his first breath, a large wave caught him flush in the face and he swallowed a large mouthful of seawater, which went straight to the pit of his stomach. Immediately, he vomited the water back up and the enormity of what he had just done frightened him beyond belief.

He was now breathing hard, trying to get his bearings. The swell on the sea was far larger than it had looked like from the comfort of the pier, and he couldn't see a bloody thing except the walls of water that were hitting him every few seconds. The scale of what needed to be done seemed monumental, but he recovered his composure somewhat and started looking around, trying to see if he could spot the little girl. The saltwater spray was starting to affect his eyes, he was blinking continuously, which made his tear ducts run, and blurred vision was starting to set in.

The current had now moved him further away from the pier. He could hear voices, but it was impossible for him to make out what they were saying. He looked in the direction of the pier, and through bleary eyes could just make out people pointing downwards towards the sea. He wasn't even close to where the people on the pier were pointing. He was in the six o'clock position and the people were pointing towards the three o'clock position, and all he could see was a wall of water coming towards him. Slider's breathing was now under control: instead of breathing through his mouth he breathed through his nose. Even the coldness of the water wasn't affecting him as much as it once had. He turned his head to the right and started to swim in a breaststroke kind of fashion. His clothes were heavy around his body, and he was always struggling to keep his head above the waves.

As he swam in the direction of where the people were pointing, something red in the sky caught his eye. He turned his head slightly further to the right and saw a red flare slowly descend into the sea. Seeing that flare brought out a large grin on his face. 'Thank God,' he murmured. He felt a lot happier now, and a new determination came upon him. After swimming for what seemed an age, a fleck of blue caught his eye. He snapped his head and neck further to the right, but it was gone. Slider stopped swimming and watched. There it was again. He rested the back of his head on the water, looked up at the sky and shouted, 'Thank you, God, thank you!'

He was now swimming arm over arm for all he was worth, and suddenly there she was – three feet away, lying face down in the water. He manoeuvred himself so they were both head to head. He gently put his arms into the armpits of the little girl and pulled his arms towards himself. Slider was now face to face with the little girl. Her face was grey, and she had a large cut over her left eye which was still seeping blood. 'Can you hear me?' he shouted, but there was nothing. He repeated the same words but there was no response, so he delicately put his mouth to hers and blew into her mouth. No response. He tried again and again. Nothing. He tried again for the fourth time and miraculously felt her body move. He waited a few seconds and a thin stream of water seeped out the corner of her mouth. He gently squeezed his arms around the child and a large vomit of water exited her tiny mouth, followed by a gentle cough.

He turned his head, away from the little girl, and real tears flowed down his face and into the cold seawater. 'OK, I've done my bit, now where's the fucking cavalry when you need them?' he muttered under his breath. He lay back on the water and pulled the little girl onto his chest, using his body as a raft. The girl's eyes opened for the first time, and he gave her a wink and babbled, 'Don't worry, you'll be OK now.' But OK they weren't. Throughout the rescue their bodies had been in a current, and now they were heading towards the concrete groynes stretching out from the beach. If they were to hit the groynes they could both be pinned against them and drown, or he might lose his grip on the child and she might drown.

THREE

The British warship HMS *Deacon* was a type 45 Destroyer. It usually carried a crew of 190, although in exceptional circumstances it could accommodate 235 crew members. It could also carry one or two Lynx Wildcat helicopters or one Westland Merlin helicopter. The ship had left Cardiff that morning and was passing Penarth en route to joining the British fleet in the English Channel, before the fleet sailed to the Mediterranean to take part in a NATO exercise.

A lookout using his 7 x 50 binoculars to search for hazards observed a red flare off the starboard side of the ship.

'Lookout to bridge.'

'Bridge, go ahead.'

'Red flare, sir, off our starboard side, seems to have been fired from the pier.'

Six pairs of glasses were immediately trained on the pier.

'Officer of the watch to captain.'

'Captain, go ahead.'

'Sir, there seem to be people in the water, approximately two hundred metres from the pier.'

'Well, it's a job for the RNLI, not us.'

'Apparently not, sir, the Penarth lifeboat is currently in Aberthaw towing back a fishing boat to Cardiff.'

'Well, in that case alert flight crew.'

HMS *Deacon* had a contingent of helicopter flight crew on board and one pair would always be on standby. Today it was Flight Lieutenant Cheryl Daniels' turn to be on standby. She was a twenty-five-year-old pilot who had joined the Royal Navy in 2011 after studying electrical engineering at the University of Brighton. Today she would be flying a Westland Merlin helicopter and would be taking a four-man crew, which consisted of a co-pilot, winchman, doctor, and diver. They lifted off in bright sunshine and would only need a flight time of a few minutes to reach the stricken people. The wind speed today was seventeen knots, which was a moderate breeze kicking up many white horses. The winchman was the first to spot the pair in the water.

'Winchman to pilot.'

'Pilot, go ahead.'

'Sir, we have two people in the water approximately one hundred metres off our starboard side.'

'Roger that.'

The Merlin reduced airspeed and hovered almost directly over the pair. The winchman spoke in a calm voice. 'Ten metres to port … three metres.'

'Pilot to diver.'

'Diver ready, sir.'

The pilot eased the Merlin down to ten metres. The diver adjusted his yellow face mask, crossed his arms, and slipped over the side.

'Diver gone, sir.'

'Roger that, diver gone.'

The winchman gently guided the helicopter directly over the pair and slowly lowered the recovery harness, which was used to extract bodies from the sea.

Slider's worst fears were realized when his left leg was caught on something. The weight of water on his clothes had pulled his legs down, and they were slowly being pulled under the water. His leg was hooked over a groyne, and he was fighting for both of their lives. Centimetre by centimetre they were being sucked under and try as he might he just didn't have the strength to straighten his frozen leg. Suddenly, he felt something pulling at his heel. His leg had straightened, and they were clear over the groyne and back on the surface. Slider looked at the girl's face; she was breathing but only just. From out of nowhere, there was an almighty disturbance in the water. He looked to his right and came face to face with a yellow scuba mask.

'Sir, you're gonna have to let her go!'

Slider's body was numb, he couldn't feel his legs, and his arms were frozen around the child. He was helpless in the water. Hypothermia had set in.

'Sir, you must let her go!'

He looked at the face in the mask. His voice barely audible. 'Take her, please take her ... I'm fucked.'

The diver prised the little girl out of his arms and swam to the lowered harness, which had been set down behind them. Slider lowered his chin and bobbed up and down like a cork. He was all alone in this freezing cold water, but after what seemed like an eternity he heard a calm voice. 'OK, sir, we'll have you out of here in no time!'

'Where did you come from?' he tried to say, but his lips wouldn't move. The diver pointed a finger to the sky. He slowly arched his head backwards and a massive shape filled his bleary eyes. He closed his eyes and let the diver do his work.

Slider and the little girl had been safely lifted out of the sea and were being assessed by the flight doctor who had wrapped them in foil blankets. An intravenous drip had been inserted into both, and both were breathing through face masks.

'Pilot to flight doctor, how are the passengers doing?'

'Not good, both are weak, and both have hypothermia – the man should be OK, but the little girl's pulse is very weak.'

'Pilot to bridge.'

'Bridge, go ahead.'

'We're bringing back two people. One man and one little girl. Both are suffering from hypothermia. Please have medics on standby.'

'Bridge to pilot, will do.'

The Westland Merlin gently touched down on the flight deck, and two trolley beds were rushed to the side of the helicopter. The side panel was pulled back and Slider and the little girl were transferred to the beds and pushed to the lift, which would take them down to the ship's trauma unit. On arrival, they had their clothes removed and were placed into gowns. The medical teams diligently went to work. A group of three medics worked on each patient, checking pupil dilation and monitoring their hearts. Pulse readings indicated both pulses were weak. Hypothermia was present in each body, so they were placed into Bair Huggers which would allow their bodies to slowly regain their normal body temperature. Both Slider and the girl were still unconscious and the next twenty-four hours would be critical.

Commanding HMS *Deacon* was Captain John Nielson, a forty-five-year-old veteran of the Gulf War, where he had worked as a senior officer on a Royal Navy minehunter that was responsible for clearing Iraqi mines near the Kuwait coast. HMS *Deacon* was launched in 2010 and commissioned in 2014. This was his first command of a British warship. The captain entered the trauma unit and spoke to Dr Vandervine, who was in overall charge of all medical staff on board the warship. 'What's the condition of our two patients?'

'Well, Captain, the next twenty-four hours will be crucial. The man will probably pull through, but I'm concerned about the girl. She was in the water for quite some time and her vitals are all very weak.'

'I thought you might like to know that we now have some information on our patients. The man's name is Matthew Slider. He's a forty-two-year-old Carver taxi driver. The little girl is Alice Polti, who is five years old and the daughter of Alexis Polti, who apparently is a TV celebrity. It seems that Mr Slider jumped into the sea to rescue the little girl who had fallen over the handrail at Penarth Pier … Oh, one final point. Mr Slider punched a female police officer who tried to prevent him going in after the girl. That's all for now.' The captain turned and left the trauma unit.

Dr Vandervine addressed his medical team. 'Looks like we have ourselves a real hero on board. Let's try not to lose him.'

A few hours later.

There was a knock on the captain's door. 'Come in.'

Flight Lieutenant Daniels entered the captain's quarters, stood to attention, and saluted. 'You wanted to see me, Captain?'

'Yes, Lieutenant, stand easy. It seems that we have ourselves a problem. We have two civilians in sickbay and we're heading towards a NATO exercise in the Med. What are we going to do with them?'

'Well, sir, we can't take them with us.'

'Very good. Now both are making reasonable progress and should be conscious in the next twenty-four to thirty-six hours, so here's what we are going to do. When they are fit enough to travel, I want you to fly our patients to the heliport in Cardiff where they will be met by an ambulance and taken to the University Hospital of Wales. There they will finish their recovery. Do you understand, Lieutenant?'

There was a long pause before she replied, 'Yes, sir.' Flight Lieutenant Daniels realized that by taking the two recovering patients to Cardiff she and her co-pilot would miss the NATO exercise, as the Royal Navy demands that all warships entering the English Channel must have a full contingent of both personnel and aircraft.

A large grin appeared on Captain Nielson's face. 'Look at it this way, Lieutenant, you might not be going on the NATO exercise but at least you'll have two weeks shore leave, and you might get your picture into the newspapers or on TV.'

She saluted, turned, and left the captain's quarters. 'Great, fucking great,' she hissed through gritted teeth. 'That's all I need: play wet nurse to two patients, then spend two weeks in Portsmouth with those testosterone-fuelled sailors who don't know the difference between shit and dirty water. Why me!'

FOUR

Pamela Turner and her partner Roger Tanner were good neighbours of the Sliders. Roger was fiddling about in the garage when Pam shouted.

'Rog, lunch will be ready in five minutes!'

'OK.'

Pam was a seventy-two-year-old retired freelance fashion photographer. She'd made a name for herself in the seventies and eighties when she worked for *Vogue* and *Cosmopolitan*. She'd also had a regular feature in the *Daily Express* newspaper. That was until a nasty fall in 1988 broke her right hip and an injury to her head forced her into early retirement.

'Rog, how much longer are you going to be?' she shouted from the kitchen.

Roger had been a taxi driver for many years. He'd hated the night shifts and so gave it up to pursue his interest in electrics and basically anything mechanical. If something wasn't working, he was your man to try and fix it, and this is how they met.

'Finally,' she said when he appeared.

'Well, you know what I'm like.'

'Indeed, I do, now hurry up and put the TV on, let's see what's been happening today.'

'You'll never guess what, Pam, there's a Sky TV van outside.'

'Well, you can tell them that we don't want their broadband, it's too expensive.'

'No, they're not selling broadband. It's a Sky broadcasting unit.' He switched on the TV, and they sat down to have their lunch on trays.

'**This is the one o'clock news from the BBC. Reading the lunchtime news: Jane Houseman.**'

'**Our top stories today. The Bank of England has raised interest rates another quarter of one percent, prisons in Scotland are to receive additional funding, England are on the verge of winning the third test against India, and there was a major sea rescue off the South Wales coast this morning.**'

'I wonder what that could be,' commented Pam.

'We'll find out in a few minutes.' They had just finished lunch when the item about the sea rescue was announced.

'And finally, there was a major sea rescue on the South Wales coast this morning. At the scene we have our BBC reporter Adam Evans, who can tell us exactly what's happened.'

'Thank you, Jane. I'm reporting live from the pier at Penarth in South Wales, when at about eleven thirty this morning a young girl who has been named as Alice Polti, the daughter of Alexis Polti, who is better known to us all as The Restorer, met with an accident. Apparently, Alice Polti was visiting the pier with her mother and nanny when somehow she fell over the handrail and into the cold waters of the Bristol Channel. A forty-two-year-old man, who has been named as Mr Matthew Slider and who works as a Carver taxi driver and is from the Llandaff North part of Cardiff, jumped into the sea in a bid to rescue the little girl.'

Roger stared at the TV screen. 'I don't believe it!'

Pam, who had been drinking a glass of Liebfraumilch, dropped her glass on the carpet and fell backwards into her leather armchair. 'Rog, are they talking about Slider from across the road?'

'I think so, that's why the Sky broadcasting unit is here.'

'It is also understood that Mr Slider assaulted a female police officer who had been trying to keep everyone away from the side of the pier from where the little girl had fallen. We shall try and talk to a few people who were on the pier at the time and witnessed what took place.'

Adam Evans turned to a man in a sheepskin coat who was standing near him. 'Hello, I believe that you were on the pier when this incident took place?'

'Yes, that's correct.'

'So, what happened?'

'The pier was crowded with schoolchildren when there was a loud scream, and a child had apparently fallen over the handrail and into the sea. A female police officer tried to hold back a man who was trying to climb over the rail. She pulled him back and he fell to the floor. He got to his feet and shouted at the police officer to do something, then stepped forward and punched her on the chin, knocking her to the ground. He climbed over the handrail and shouted at me to fire the flare gun.'

'Did you?'

'Yes, then the man jumped.'

'Do you think the man did the right thing?'

'Absolutely, because the police officer didn't want to help – in all honesty, they should give him a bloody medal!'

While they were talking a woman in a bright red coat had barged her way through the large crowd of schoolchildren and bystanders until she was standing next to the man in the sheepskin coat who was being interviewed. 'Hello, I'm Alexis Polti. What's been happening here?'

Adam Evans immediately recognized her and interrupted the man who was speaking. 'It seems that a young girl has fallen into the sea.'

Alexis pulled away from the cameras, frantically searching the crowd for her daughter, and came upon her nanny who was sitting on a bench and being comforted by a paramedic. 'Victoria, where's Alice?'

Through sobbing red eyes, she replied, 'S-s-she's gone, Ms Polti. S-s-she's fallen.'

Alexis looked down at her nanny and slapped her hard across her right cheek. 'You fucking idiot!' she screamed. 'I pay you to look after my daughter!'

The paramedic moved his arm quickly to prevent her from slapping the sobbing woman again. 'There's no need for that, miss.'

She glared at him and cursed harshly. 'No fucking need?' Alexis turned and walked quickly back to speak with Adam Evans who was interviewing a young girl. 'Adam, where's my daughter?'

He looked her straight in the eye and pointed. 'Your daughter was airlifted out of the sea, along with a man named Matthew Slider. Both have been taken onto that warship that you can see in the distance.'

'Who's Matthew Slider?'

'Matthew Slider is the man who jumped into the sea to try and rescue your daughter.'

'Right, thank you.' With that, she turned and walked quickly to exit the pier. Raising her hands in the air she shrieked, 'Why me? Why fucking me!'

* * *

Roger looked at Pam and said, 'Have you got Lily's phone number?'

'Yes, why?'

'I think you'd better phone her now and let her know what's happened.'

'I'll get my address book, I think it's upstairs in our bedroom.' Pam came down the stairs, address book in hand. 'Do you want to phone her, or shall I do it?'

'I'll do it.' Roger phoned the number. It seemed to ring for ages.

'Hi Rog, and what can I do for you today?'

He could tell by her voice that Lily had already been drinking today. He came straight to the point. 'Lily, have you been following the TV coverage about the sea rescue that's taken place in Penarth this morning?'

'No, Rose and I went to the garden centre this morning to buy some bedding plants, and we've been in the rear garden planting them.'

'Well, I think you had better sit down and put the TV on. It seems that Slider jumped from Penarth Pier into the sea today, to try and rescue a little girl.'

There was a long pause before Lily said, 'Do you mean my Slider?'

'I'm afraid so. Listen, watch the news and I will phone you back in half an hour.' As Roger put the phone down the doorbell rang.

'I'll get it, Rog.' Pam opened the door and was met by a large group of reporters who were jostling to get close to her. Microphones were pushed towards her, flashing lights lit up the doorway and countless people were speaking all at the same time. 'Roger, come quickly!' she shouted. He rushed to the door, and held it open. Pam ducked underneath his arm and retreated inside.

'Mary Tyler from Sky news. I believe you are a friend of Mr Matthew Slider.'

'Yes, we know Matthew and his family very well.'

'Do you know the whereabouts of his wife?'

'I'm afraid I can't answer that question.'

'Do you know if they have any children?'

Pam was in the hallway listening to what was being said. She took a deep breath. 'Oh my God, Becky and Andy.'

A policeman in uniform barged his way through the throng of reporters and up to the front door. 'Hello, sir, I'm Sergeant Dunscombe from the South Wales Constabulary. I wonder if I could have a word with you.' The sergeant was shown into the lounge and sat on Pam's leather armchair. 'I'm here today to ascertain if Mr Matthew Slider has a wife and family.'

'Yes,' Roger replied. 'He has a wife named Lily, who is currently staying with her sister, Rose, in Hereford. He also has a daughter, Becky, and a son, Andy, who both attend Cardiff Middle School.'

The sergeant phoned through the information to his headquarters.

* * *

Lily's voice was sharp when she looked at her sister and said, 'Put the telly on, Rose, something has happened to Slider.'

She grabbed the remote from under a magazine and switched the TV on. 'What do you mean, something has happened to Slider?'

'That was Roger on the phone, something about him jumping into the sea.' The BBC news was just finishing when Lily said, 'Switch it over to ITV.'

Rose switched it over just in time to hear the report:

'This is the lunchtime news from ITV. The main headlines this afternoon. Scottish prisons are to receive extra funding, England's cricket team are close to winning the third test against India, and on the South Wales coast, a major sea rescue has taken place this morning.'

They both watched the lunchtime news intently. It seemed to be dragging on and on when suddenly the news about her husband appeared.

'Our final story this lunchtime involves a sea rescue that has taken place this morning on the South Wales coast. Our reporter Daniel Pope can tell us exactly what has happened.'

'Thank you. It appears that about eleven thirty this morning a young girl somehow fell over the handrail and into the sea here at Penarth Pier in South Wales. Miraculously, a forty-two-year-old man who has been named as Mr Matthew Slider jumped into the sea to try and rescue the little girl, who we can now name as Alice

Polti, the daughter of Alexis Polti. Both were airlifted out of the sea by a Royal Navy helicopter and taken to the warship HMS *Deacon* that was sailing near Penarth at the time. That, I'm afraid, is all the news that we have at this moment.'

Lily grabbed the remote and switched off the TV. 'OK, Rose, get your coat on, we have to get back to my house.' They wasted no time in closing down the house and getting into the car.

Rose had always loved driving and passed her test on her eighteenth birthday at her first attempt. Her longed-legged body filled her maroon MG Morgan very nicely. It was her pride and joy, a birthday present from an old admirer, of which there had been many. Her long flowing blonde hair caught the breeze as they hurled around the country lanes of Hereford, to try and avoid the main roads and make up some time. Hardly a word passed between them as she pushed the car as fast as she could, although an occasional glance passed between them as the car narrowly avoided the wildlife which inhabited the area.

Lily's head was lost in thought, her mind was elsewhere.

'Sis, phone Roger and tell him we're on the road.'

Lily sat motionless.

'Come on, girl, snap out of it!'

She slowly reached down into her shoulder bag and rummaged around for her phone. 'Hi, Rog, just to let you know that we're on the road and should be with you—'

Rose jumped into the conversation. 'Tell him about forty-five minutes.'

'Did you hear that?'

'Yes, and Lily, the police were just here, and they have gone to pick up Becky and Andy from school.'

'Oh, that's good, I've been worried about them.'

* * *

The siren stopped as the white police car drove through the gates of Cardiff Middle School. Scores of young eyes tracked the vehicle as it avoided the parking spaces and came to a halt outside the main entrance. Out of the car stepped a male and a female officer, both in uniform. As they walked the few steps up to the automatic doors, classrooms of young children looked down on them like hungry vultures. As they made their way into the school, a middle-aged woman dressed in a black suit, white shirt, red shoes, and wearing expensive designer glasses, approached them. 'Good afternoon, I'm Cynthia Dawson, the deputy head. How may I help you?'

The male officer said, 'Hello, I'm Sergeant Faulkner and this is Police Officer Hann. We're here to collect Andy and Becky Slider.'

There was a frown on the face of the deputy head. 'May I be permitted to know why you want to take the Slider children out of school today?'

'It appears that their father Mr Matthew Slider was involved in a sea rescue at Penarth this morning.'

'If you both follow me, I will take you to the head's office.'

She led them quickly along brightly coloured corridors which were adorned with photographs of rugby, football, netball, and cricket teams. There were cabinets full of silver cups and shields and photographs of the schoolteachers and the subjects they taught. At the end of the corridor, they turned right and on their left was a set of double doors. They walked through the doors and immediately in front of them was a staircase that led to the upper floors. Opposite the staircase on the left was the head's office. They all stood outside the oak-panelled door which had a brass nameplate: Headteacher. John Jefferies CBE.

The deputy head knocked on the door and entered. The head was sat behind his oak-panelled desk, talking to two boys. 'I'm very sorry to interrupt you, Mr Jefferies—'

He raised a hand and stopped her in her tracks. 'Alright, you two boys can go.'

After they'd left, the deputy head said, 'These two police officers have come to collect Andy and Becky Slider.'

The head stood up and walked around his desk to shake hands with the two police officers. 'Hello I'm—'

'Yes, sir, I know who you are,' said Sergeant Faulkner.

John Jefferies CBE was born in Swansea and had been a gifted winger for Aberavon. Many believed that he could have gone on and played for Wales, but persistent knee injuries cut short his rugby career. So he turned his attention to teaching and coaching young rugby players, and in 2004 was awarded the CBE for services to youth rugby coaching.

'We saw your photograph in the corridor, but we're in a desperate hurry,' added Officer Hann.

The sergeant gave the headteacher a full account of what had happened that morning. On hearing the news, he swiftly left the room, and raced up the staircase to the first floor. He entered the art class without knocking and looked around for Becky Slider. On spotting her face behind an easel, he walked quickly up to her and said quietly in her ear, 'Becky, you have to come with me.' The head helped her to take off her apron and gather up her blazer and pink backpack. Just before leaving the room, he looked at Ms Crandon, the newly appointed art teacher, saying, 'I'll explain later.' He spoke again quietly to Becky and ran up another flight of stairs, walked halfway along the corridor to the computer room. Again, he entered without knocking and was met head-on by Mr Sedgebeer, the teacher. In a loud and exhausted voice he shouted, 'Where's Andy Slider?'

Someone answered, 'He's gone to the toilet.'

'When he gets back, tell him my office straight away!' There were loud groans from the pupils on hearing what the head had just said. As he left the room, he saw Andy approaching. He rushed up to the boy. 'Follow me quickly, your father's had an accident.' They both flew down the stairs to where Becky was still waiting. Andy dragged his sister down the stairs and the three of them walked quickly to the head's room, where the police officers and the deputy head were waiting. They then escorted the police officers and the Slider children to the automatic doors that exited the building. The head shook hands with the officers, and said gently to Becky, 'I hope your father gets better soon.'

The young girl nodded her head and left the building, holding her brother's hand. As they approached the police car, a gang of boys' who were playing football in the tennis courts suddenly stopped and stared at the Sliders through the chain-link fencing. One of them shouted, 'Andy, you're going to jail!'

The other boys laughed out aloud.

This, however, didn't go unseen by the head who in a loud voice called out, 'You boys, my office now!' As Andy walked around the side of the car to get in, he gave the gang a two-fingered gesture which was also seen by the head, who yelled, 'And that's enough of that!'

The police car moved forward slightly and performed a 180-degree turn to leave the school premises. On passing the group of boys Becky poked out her tongue and calmly raised her middle finger, which Officer Hann spotted straight away. 'You shouldn't be doing that, young lady.' She said with temper in her voice.

Becky, quick as lightning, responded with a voice sounding like an angel, 'My daddy's a taxi driver and whenever people upset him, he always does it.'

The two police officers looked at each other and shook their heads gently from side to side. As the police car moved onto the main road the siren was turned back on, and the car headed towards the children's home. Officer Hann finished speaking to her superiors back at headquarters, then turned to look over her shoulder at the children. 'When we get to your house, keep your heads down and don't say a word.' Both nodded at the same time.

They drove swiftly past the lake towards Llandaff, the journey being uneventful, apart from the pedal cyclist who entered the roundabout without looking and almost collided with the police car. 'Bastard!' shouted Sergeant Faulkner.

Andy and Becky looked at each other and giggled. It was a fifteen-minute drive to their house, but temporary traffic lights near their house made the journey longer. As the police car approached their road, none of the occupants could have envisaged what they were about to see.

The section of road around College Road had been requisitioned by TV networks. Scaffolding platforms had been erected either side of the Sliders' house and were occupied by the BBC and ITV. Across the road, Sky news had erected a platform in the front garden of Pam and Roger's house, with cameras and lights that looked directly across the road. Channel 5 were sited next to Sky.

Further along the road, a toilet block and a mobile canteen facility had been set up, which the children of the street were taking full advantage of, but unknowingly they were being pumped for information about the Slider family.

With all the cameras, lights, stepladders, and people talking, anyone passing by would have imagined that they were on a film set of a major Hollywood film. As the police car slowly made its way to the front of the children's house, all hell suddenly broke loose. Reporters surrounded the car, digital flashlights were everywhere, pictures were being taken from every conceivable angle. Calmly Sergeant Faulkner said, 'When we get out of the car, remember, keep your heads down and don't say a word.'

The police officers got out first and opened the rear doors for both Andy and Becky. The boy got out first on the offside of the car and looked admiringly at all the cameras. Slowly his sister got out. Once out of the car, Becky started smiling and waving at the cameras. She walked hand in hand with Officer Hann around the back of the car to the pavement. Andy took his sister's hand, and both walked up their driveway, waving and smiling as if they were royalty.

Once inside the house, Sergeant Faulkner looked at the two children. 'What did I tell you two about keeping your heads down?'

Becky looked at the sergeant, and in a gentle voice said, 'Mummy says that we should always try and make a good impression on people.'

Andy chipped in, 'Yeah, we might not be on the telly again!'

The sergeant looked at Officer Hann. 'That's kids for you.'

No sooner had they entered their house than the doorbell rang. The children looked out of the bay window and saw Roger and Pam waving at them, alongside another policeman. The young man let them all in and Sergeant Faulkner conversed with the other sergeant and then addressed them all. 'Officer Hann and I are now leaving, but we shall leave Sergeant Dunscombe here until everything is sorted out.' Sergeant Faulkner looked at the two children, bent down slightly, and whispered, 'You two look after yourselves.' Andy and Becky both nodded. The sergeant had a last word with Sergeant Dunscombe then he and Officer Hann left the house and drove away.

As soon as the front door was closed, Sooty came halfway down the stairs, put her head between the spindles, and gave a meow. Becky looked at her. 'Didn't Andy feed you today?'

'Yes, I did!' came the response from her brother's room.

She picked up the cat, carried her into the kitchen, and plonked her down in front of her food bowl, which was empty. 'Don't worry I'll look after you,' Becky said as the cat munched away on the food she had just been given.

Andy was busy on his computer when he caught sight of a maroon MG Morgan pulling into their driveway. There was a honk-honk from its old-fashioned horn. He rushed out of his room and shouted down the stairs, 'Mum and Aunty Rose are here!' He carried on down the stairs and opened the front door. 'Mum, what's happened to Dad?'

'Son, I'm not really sure.'

'Hello, Aunty Rose.'

'Hello, Andy. Be a good boy and get our bags from the car, will you?'

He stepped out into the spotlights again and there were calls of 'Andy, Andy, over here!'

Sergeant Dunscombe, who was standing outside the front door, raised his arms and in a stern voice said, 'No questions, no questions.' Andy gathered the bags from the car, gave a cheeky grin and a wave, and went back inside the house.

Lily and Rose walked into the lounge, and both sat down on the black leather sofa that was adjacent to the fireplace. 'Fix me a drink will you, Rose, I need something large at this moment.'

'Sorry, but you're off that stuff for the time being.'

'I wish someone could tell me what's been going on,' Lily said in an exasperated voice.

Becky walked into the room clutching the cat in her arms. 'Mum, what's happened to Dad?' Slowly she started to cry.

Rose put her arms around her and looked her in the eye. 'Don't worry, your father will be alright. Here, blow your nose in this.'

With tears rolling down her cheeks the young girl said, 'But where is our dad?'

Roger, who was sitting in a black leather armchair to the side of the fireplace, said, 'I know where your father is.'

The children looked at him and together said, 'Where?'

'Your father jumped into the sea this morning to try and save a little girl who fell over the handrail at Penarth Pier.'

Pam entered the lounge carrying a tray containing a pot of tea, milk, and some cups and saucers. 'Anyone want a cup of tea?'

In unison they all answered, 'No, thank you, Pam.'

Andy was pressing Roger for more details. 'So where is my dad now?'

'Your father is aboard HMS *Deacon,* which is a Royal Navy Destroyer and it's somewhere in the Bristol Channel. Oh, and before I forget.' He put his hand into the pocket of his leather jacket. 'The police officer gave me your father's wallet and car keys.' He placed them down on the glass coffee table in front of everyone.

Lily sounded tired when she muttered, 'Thank you for everything Rog.' She paused for a moment before saying, 'So, what do we do now?'

Everyone just looked at each other, with vague expressions on their faces.

FIVE

Slider was still unconscious, but he was breathing on his own.

Dr Vandervine, however, was being pressed by the first officer as to when he would regain consciousness. 'Let's say eight to twelve hours, but it could be sooner.'

'And what's the status on the little girl?'

'Her condition is slightly worse, but again she's breathing on her own, so technically she could wake up at the same time as Mr Slider. She's got a bad cut on her forehead, but it shouldn't be a problem for her.'

Three hours later a young female nurse was putting drops into Matthew Slider's eyes when she saw his head flinch. She stopped what she was doing and spoke quietly into his ear. 'Can you hear me, Mr Slider?' There was a small movement from his head. The nurse immediately went to fetch Dr Vandervine.

The doctor rushed in and spoke quietly to him. 'Can you hear me, Mr Slider?' Out of his mouth came a small groan. 'Glad to have you back with us.' He walked over to the wall-mounted phone. 'Sickbay to bridge.'

'Bridge, go ahead.'

'Could you please inform Captain Neilson that Mr Slider has regained consciousness.'

The captain looked at his first officer. 'One down, one to go – all we need now is for the little girl to wake up.'

Forty-five minutes later, Nurse Watts was changing the dressings covering Matthew Slider's eyes when she saw his arm move and he spoke for the first time. 'Where am I?' he murmured.

'You're aboard HMS *Deacon* and please don't touch the dressings over your eyes.'

'I wondered what that rumbling sound was. How long have I been here?'

At that moment Dr Vandervine re-entered the room. 'Mr Slider—'

He interrupted him and in a whispered voice said, 'Please, Doc, just call me Slider.'

'Well, Slider, you've been here with us for almost eighteen hours. The ship has remained here in the channel until we can ascertain what's best for you and the little girl.'

'How's she doing?'

'Sorry to say she's not regained consciousness yet, but hopefully it shouldn't be too long now. So, how are you feeling?'

He took a few seconds before saying, 'Salty ... I can smell salt, and my tongue tastes of salt.'

'Well, that's hardly surprising considering what you've swallowed.' Slider slowly inched his body up the pillow and peeled back the dressings covering his eyes. 'Careful now, don't go overdoing it.'

'I'm OK, but I could murder a cup of coffee.'

The doctors and nurses all gave out a small laugh. 'Well, perhaps later, but firstly try and drink some water.'

'Water!' he bawled. 'I think I've drunk enough bloody water to last me a lifetime.'

'OK, tell the nurse what you would like then.'

He took a few seconds to answer before replying. 'I would like a hot mug of coffee with milk, and with one spoonful of demerara sugar, please.'

'Anything else?' the nurse asked.

'Could you please turn down the lights as they are making my headache worse.' The doctors and nurses all left the room, leaving Slider to doze, alone with his thoughts. Shortly after, a young nurse entered his room with a tray containing his coffee. His salty tongue gave the coffee a unique taste and reminded him of the time when his daughter once used salt instead of sugar; at the time she swore that she didn't do it on purpose and that it was a complete accident. And with the voice of an angel, how could he ever doubt her word. But even now she still giggled when he reminded her of this incident. Even though it tasted strange, the aroma of his coffee seemed to awaken his senses somewhat. He pulled back the bedsheets and eased his legs out of the bed, then sat on the side of the bed and drained his coffee cup. As he did so, a new face entered the cubicle.

'Hello, I'm Doctor Rathkey, and you must be the famous Slider that everyone is talking about.'

'Yes, that's me, guilty as charged.'

'Oh, I wouldn't plead guilty just yet, your trial hasn't even started.' With that, he collected some papers and left the room.

Slider pulled himself up onto his feet and, being slightly bemused, inched his feet slowly towards the door. Sticking his head into the passageway he observed the doctor reading his notes. He was breathing quite hard when he called out, 'Doctor Rathkey, what did you mean when you used the word trial?'

He walked back to speak to Slider, who was leaning against the door. 'Well, according to the TV reports, you assaulted a young police officer on Penarth Pier, causing her ABH (actual bodily harm) which carries a prison sentence of six months.'

Slider looked mortified. After all that he had done and everything he'd been through, he could still end up going to jail. He took a couple of deep breaths and grunted, 'Just my luck!' Turning slowly around, he passed the cubicle on the opposite side of the bulkhead, and was shocked to see the little girl sitting up in bed. 'Good God! When did sleeping beauty wake up?'

Nurse Watts was plumping up her pillow when she observed him leaning against the door. 'Why don't you come in and sit down before you fall down.' The nurse pulled a chair over from the far bulkhead and placed it by the side of the bed. He gently lowered himself into it and exhaled slowly. When he looked comfortable the nurse said, 'Well, Slider, I would like you to meet Alice Polti.'

He took a few seconds to compose himself and then smiled at her. 'Hello, Alice, how are you feeling now?'

The little girl looked tired. Her black curly hair was matted, and her dark eyes were glazed and drawn. She mumbled, 'I'm afraid, where's my mummy?' and tears started rolling down her cheeks.

The nurse put a comforting arm around her. 'There's nothing to be afraid of.' Turning her head towards Slider she said, 'This is Mr Slider, the man who jumped into the sea to rescue you.'

Seconds passed and nobody spoke.

The tears began to flow more quickly down the child's face. She pulled her tiny arm from underneath the bedding and reached out to him. 'Thank you, Mr Slider.'

He looked at her, then stood up. 'Don't worry, we'll soon have you back with your mother.' Before leaving the room, he looked down at the little girl. 'Alice, was your mother wearing a red coat when you were walking towards the pier?'

She lifted her dark brown eyes. 'Yes.'

He smiled to himself. 'I thought so. So, is your mother The Restorer?'

'Yes, and Mummy's not going to be very happy.'

Slider roared with laughter. 'I bet she's not, Alice, I really bet she's not.' He slowly left the room, laughing out loud, and returned to his own cubicle.

Slider's clothes had been washed and ironed and put into a vacuum bag which had been placed at the foot of his bed. His blue sneakers had been dried and were on the floor next to his bedside locker. 'About bloody time!' he said as he entered his room. He took his watch out of the bag: the time read 7:20 p.m. – too late in the day to get dressed now, he thought. Observing Nurse Watts leaving Alice's cubicle he called out to her. 'Nurse, would it be possible to use your phone so that I can call the family and let them know I'm OK?'

She entered his cubicle. 'I'm sorry, but the crew of this ship aren't allowed to use their mobile phones while we are at sea. When the crew comes aboard they have to take the SIM card out of their phone and place it in a plastic bag along with the phone and hand it to the purser, who puts it in the strong room safe.'

'Why do they have to give up their phones in the first place?'

'Because this is a warship and using a phone would give our position away to the enemy.'

'Yes, I suppose that makes sense. So, Nurse … sorry, I've forgotten your name.'

'It's Nurse Watts.'

'Well, Nurse Watts, how do you send a message to your family?'

'I don't have any way of contacting my family while we're at sea. Does that satisfy you?'

'Yes.'

'Look, why don't you get some rest, and we can talk again later.' As the nurse turned and left the room, she said to herself out loud, 'And they say women talk too much!'

The next morning at eight o'clock Slider was violently awoken by a booming sound that seemed to last forever and reverberated around the whole ship. He caught sight of a nurse passing his cubicle and waved a hand to attract his attention. 'Can you tell me, mate, what's happening?'

'The gunners are having a live firing exercise this morning.'

'Do they do that every morning?'

'Oh no, it's only when we go on an exercise.'

'What kind of exercise are you going on?'

'Well, I'm not really supposed to tell you because you're a civilian, but there's a large NATO exercise in the Med, and we're going to be part of it.'

He laughed and said, 'I can't go on any exercise with you … I've got to go home!' Slider sat on the side of his bed in his newly washed and pressed clothes. Today he was having a bad headache. He sat with his head in his hands, closed his eyes, and just wished the live firing exercise would stop. Eventually, it did; he looked at his watch, it was 9:37 a.m.

Nurse Watts, who had been assigned to look after both patients, stuck her head around the door. 'How are we today, Slider?'

'I'm sorry, Nurse, but today is a bad day for me.'

'And why is that?'

'I've been diagnosed with a tension headache. Some days are good, some days are bad. And with all that firing going on, it's made the pain in my head a lot worse.'

'Have you been prescribed any medication?'

'I've been taking Nortriptyline for several months, not that it does me any good though.'

'I'll tell you what, I'll have a word with the pharmacist and see if he's got something for you.'

'Thank you, that would be a great help. I'm also famished, and at this moment I could quite easily eat a scabby dog.'

The nurse laughed. 'I'll let the kitchen staff know.'

Slider closed his eyes. When he opened them again, a tall muscular man wearing a toque blanche, a white breasted jacket, and white houndstooth patterned trousers, stood quietly in front of him. He was startled to see the man. 'Sorry, mate, I didn't hear you come in.'

'That's OK. I'm John Reardon. I'm the head chef on this warship, and I believe from what Nurse Watts told me that you're the famous Slider who would like a scabby dog for breakfast.'

He smiled. 'At this moment, mate, I could eat anything.'

'So, what would you like for breakfast?'

'A full English breakfast would be perfect, thank you.'

'And what would you like to drink?'

'A large pot of coffee, with milk and demerara sugar please. Oh, and a newspaper if you have one.'

'I'm sorry, but we don't have any current newspapers on this ship, and the ones we do have are months out of date.'

'You don't seem to have much in the way of entertainment on this ship.'

'Well, this is after all a warship and not a cruise liner. We do have TVs in the restroom.'

'Would it be possible for me to watch the TV?'

'Unfortunately, most of this ship is out of bounds to you.'

'Fine, I'll just have to grin and bear it then.'

'Don't worry, from what I hear you won't be with us for much longer.'

'Really?'

The head chef then touched the right-hand side of his nose twice. 'Breakfast will be in fifteen minutes.'

'Great, thank you,' he called out as the chef walked away.

His breakfast was brought in on a tray, along with a packet of twelve Nortriptyline tablets.

'That was bloody gorgeous,' he remarked as a member of the catering staff came to collect his tray. 'Please tell Chef Reardon that it went down a treat.' Slider stood up with a cup of coffee in hand and walked into Alice's room. 'Oh, I see that you've had breakfast as well this morning.' The young girl was sitting up in bed with a tray across her lap and was spooning down her cereal. There was also a glass of milk half-drunk on the tray. Her clothes were in a vacuum bag which had been placed on a chair next to her bed, along with her black shoes.

One hour earlier.

'Captain, we've just received a communication from the Admiralty.'

'Go ahead and read it out.'

'To Commander John Nielson. It is of the utmost importance that Mr Matthew Slider and the young girl Alice Polti are transferred off HMS *Deacon* with the utmost speed.

Ms. Alexis Polti has requested permission from the Admiralty to land an airbus H145 helicopter on the flight deck of HMS *Deacon*. Permission for this had been denied by the Admiralty.

Therefore, it has been agreed that Ms. Alexis Polti will land the airbus H145 helicopter at the National Coastwatch Lookout Station at Gwennap Head. Grid reference SW 365 217 at 12:00 hrs GMT today.

There the transfer will take place. You are thus ordered to comply with this arrangement, and then proceed with all possible speed to re-join the British fleet.

First Sea Lord,

Admiral Sir Alan Davison KCB'

'Well sir, she certainly knows some people in high places.'

'I believe Ms Polti was responsible for redesigning the interior of the former Sea Lord's home in Belgravia. I was there last Christmas and he happened to mention it to me. Apparently, she's a good-looking woman, but has a temper and a foul mouth to match.'

'Not the sort of woman to take the Henley Regatta then?' The men looked at each other and laughed out loud.

It was eleven o'clock and time for the captain to have one last word with his guests before their imminent departure. Slider was talking to Alice when he entered the room. 'Good morning to you all. I'm Captain Nielson and it gives me great pleasure to inform you that you will be departing this ship at eleven forty this morning. It seems the young girl's mother has friends in high places. Earlier today this ship received a communication from the Admiralty instructing us to fly you both to Gwennap Head.'

Slider interrupted him. 'Where's that to, Captain?'

'It's close to Land's End. There's nothing much there except for some sea birds and a national Coastwatch lookout station which monitors the sea and shipping around that area. It's quite a remote place.'

'So, who will be collecting us?'

'Well, it seems that the young girl's mother, Ms Alexis Polti, travelled to the oil refinery at Milford Haven and subsequently got hold of a pilot along with an airbus H145 helicopter, which is generally used to transfer oil workers to and from the oil platforms. This ship has been instructed to land you both at Gwennap Head at midday today.' The captain turned and looked directly at Slider. 'Mr Slider, do you think that I could have a quiet word with you outside, please?'

'Certainly, sir.'

Both men walked out into the passageway.

'Firstly, I would like to shake your hand and congratulate you on that amazing rescue that you performed – it must have taken some guts to jump into a rough sea like that?'

'Well, someone had to do something. I think I was the person who was in the right place at the right time, and I wasn't prepared to watch a young child drown in front of me, especially as I have a young daughter of a similar age.'

'Quite so. One other point. I've been following your story on the news, and I want you to prepare yourself for what's about to happen to you once you reach the mainland. You will be arrested and charged with the assault on the female police officer. This offence currently carries a jail term of six months. Now, I'm a reasonably good judge of character, and you don't get to be a captain of a warship if you're not, and you, Mr Slider, strike me as an honest and decent man, even though you have only been with us for a short while. So I wish you the best of luck at your trial and the next time this warship is in Cardiff, I do hope that you will come and visit this ship and bring with you your family.'

'Thank you, Captain Nielson, for that appraisal; it really does mean a great deal to me.' The men smiled at each other and firmly shook hands.

'OK, it's time to get ready to leave, so if there is anyone you would like to say goodbye to, then now is the time.' The captain left and returned to the bridge.

'Did you hear that, Alice? It's time for us to go home.'

The young girl looked immaculate in her cleaned school uniform, and for the first time had a large smile on her face. Word had spread throughout the ship that Slider and the youngster were leaving. As they walked along the ship's narrow passageways, several crew members who were standing in the doorways wished them well. As they approached the pharmacy, both double doors had been opened inwards and Doctor Vandervine and Nurse Watts were waiting their turn to shake hands with them. Slider stopped at the pharmacy and shook hands with the doctor.

'Thanks for everything, Doc.'

'That's OK, it's what we're here for.'

'Again, thank you, Nurse Watts.' He held out his hand to shake hers, but she evaded it and planted a kiss firmly on his lips, which didn't go unnoticed by other crew members who cheered and whistled.

As they turned a corner, a large crew member with a bushy beard was standing half in and half out of a doorway that had the sign "Quartermaster's Stores" just visible on it. As he moved closer, the crewman held out his right hand and said, in a strong Scottish accent, 'Great work, Slider.' Slider shook his hand and noticed from his blue naval shirt that he was the quartermaster. 'Before you both leave this ship we would like to present you with some mementoes of your stay with us.' He reached inside his store and brought out two Royal Navy sweaters. 'It's going to be a bit chilly up on deck, and we wouldn't want you both to catch a wee cold now.'

Slider tried on the sweater, and it fitted like a glove. Alice's sweater had been tailored to fit her small body. They were also given a navy-blue baseball cap with the words "Royal Navy" stitched to the front in white cotton. Slider was not often lost for words, but these gifts brought out his emotional side. 'Thank you all very much for your help and kindness. We will never ever forget your generosity and what you have all done for us.'

Further along the passageway were the kitchens. Again, the doors were opened inwards, and Slider could see Chef Reardon stirring a large circular pot. 'Goodbye, lads, and thanks for looking after us.' The chef stopped what he was doing and briskly walked over to him, shook his hand, and wished them the best.

Just past the kitchens was the first flight of ladders (stairs). Slider took the hand of Alice and helped her to the top, where they were met by Doctor Rathkey and a group of officers and naval Wrens. 'We all wish you the very best of luck, and we hope that you have a safe journey home,' the senior officer said.

As the pair climbed the second flight of ladders, the temperature suddenly dropped, and they could hear the wind blowing. Just before they walked onto the flight deck a young deck officer stopped them. 'Sir, I'm Deck Officer Butt and the deck crew would like to present you both with these all-weather anoraks.' They were navy blue and had the words "Royal Navy" printed on the back in white lettering.

Slider slipped his on, and the fleecy lining instantly made a difference. 'Alice, do you feel warmer?'

The young girl, who had been given the tailored version to wear, nodded and murmured, 'Warmer now, thank you.'

They stepped onto the ship's deck and into the bright sunshine for the first time, which made Slider pull down the peak on his naval cap. This was their first view of HMS *Deacon,* and its size was far larger than he had imagined it to be. While they stood still awaiting instructions, crew members were busying themselves in readiness for the imminent departure of their guests.

An officer slowly approached them. 'Mr Slider, Ms Alice, I'm Deck Officer Mullins and we would like you both to wear these life jackets during your flight.' They slipped them over their heads and Officer Mullins attached the cords at their backs. They were instructed to follow him. As they walked towards the helicopter pad, the deck officer informed them that they would be given a guard of honour to see them safely onto the helicopter. When the Merlin came into view, two lines of twelve crewmen in their best dress uniforms made a path for them. Officer Mullins took a position next to the crewman in the guard of honour and spoke very softly to Slider. 'Goodbye, and good luck.'

They walked slowly through the guard of honour and towards the Merlin helicopter. High above them, he could see Captain Neilson and his officers on the bridge, and it brought a lump to his throat when he saw them saluting him. He stopped for a moment, stood up straight, and slowly touched his temple with the fingertips of his right hand in recognition of this rare honour. When they were next to the helicopter, a crewman jumped out and placed aluminium steps for them to enter. Slider helped Alice into the Merlin and then went inside himself. The crewman placed the steps inside, jumped into the helicopter, and slid the door panel closed. Slider attached their safety harnesses and the Merlin's engines roared into life. He smiled as he looked at the little girl. 'Well, Alice, this is it. Don't forget to wave now.' The Westland Merlin helicopter slowly lifted off the flight deck, and they could be seen smiling and waving as it ascended into the sky.

SIX

They had only been in the air for a short time when a crewman pointed out Land's End in the distance. The sun was high in the sky, and the view in all directions was spectacular. As the Merlin flew closer a white building was pointed out which was Gwennap Head. A white helicopter with red markings could be seen on the grass, and around it people could be seen waving at them.

Slider tapped Alice's shoulder to get her attention. 'Your mother's down there.' A tear could be seen rolling down the little girl's cheek. The Merlin's speed slowed dramatically as it hovered and came to rest a short distance from the other helicopter. Slider undid his seat harness and helped Alice out of hers, and both waited for the rotor blades to come to a stop. He could clearly see three people, but not one of them looked like the girl's mother. A crewman moved past him, slid the door panel open, jumped out and placed the aluminium steps by the side of the aircraft. 'Let's go and find your mother, shall we?' Slider said as they stood up. He helped the little girl to the top of the steps and the co-pilot carefully helped Alice down the three steps and onto the grass. He followed close behind.

A voice called out, 'Mr Slider!' He stopped and turned his head to the right. Coming towards him was the pilot of the Westland Merlin helicopter which had just brought them here to Gwennap Head. The pilot took off her white flying helmet and extended her right hand. 'Hello, I'm Flight Lieutenant Daniels and I would like to congratulate you on your heroic rescue.' They shook hands, and she said, 'It wasn't easy pulling you two out of the sea.'

It took a few seconds before he was able to speak. 'So it's you I've got to thank for saving our lives.' They laughed, before he moved in closer, put his arms around the pilot, and gave her a big kiss on each cheek. 'Thank you, thank you very much for saving our lives.'

'That's OK, it's my job.' They turned and walked towards the other helicopter, chatting about the finer points of the rescue on the way.

As they moved in closer everyone just stopped walking and looked at the opposite crew, as if this were a shootout in a western film. Only a few steps separated them when the person in the orange BP flying suit removed their flying helmet and black curly hair caught the breeze. 'Mummy! Mummy!' screamed Alice. The little girl ran towards her mother who knelt on the grass. She threw her arms around her daughter and kissed her passionately.

Slider just stood there with his mouth wide open. He had finally found his mystery woman, and she was kneeling just a few feet in front of him. Emotions were high, and tears were rolling down everyone's cheeks. He walked towards the woman, extended his right hand and said, 'Hello, I'm Matthew Slider and I'm pleased to meet you at last. I believe I'm in your debt for bringing us this helicopter and taking us back home.'

The woman stood up, with Alice by her side. 'Hello, Mr Slider, my name is Alexis Polti and if anyone is in debt then it's me. From the bottom of my heart, I want to ...'

He could see that she was starting to emotionally fall apart. Her eyes glazed over, and floods of tears cascaded down her beautiful, chiselled face. Her words became warped and garbled, so he stepped forward, put his arms around her and she nestled her head on his left shoulder. He stroked the back of her curly black hair with his right hand and gently whispered, 'Come on, come on, it's OK.' After a few seconds she regained her composure.

Flight Lieutenant Daniels stepped forward and offered Alexis Polti a tissue, which she gratefully accepted. 'I'm sorry about that, Mr Slider. It's not very often that happens.'

'It's perfectly understandable, Ms Polti.'

'Please, Mr Slider, just call me Alexis. Now, where was I? Oh yes. Words cannot express what you have done for me and my family by saving the life of my daughter, Alice, and I will always, always be in your debt.' And with that, she planted her red lips firmly on his.

Her daughter then pulled at her mother's side. 'Mummy, Mummy, what will Daddy say?' She pulled her head away from his, and they all started to laugh.

Flight Lieutenant Daniels tapped Slider on his shoulder. 'It's time for me to get going.'

'OK, I'll walk back to the helicopter with you.'

'No, no, you stay.'

'Well, thank you again for everything.'

Alexis stepped forward, put her arms around the pilot, and thanked her for everything that she had done. She wiped her eyes again and stepped back. They all watched as the Westland Merlin lifted off from Gwennap Head. Everyone waved as it rose into the blue sky. When it disappeared, they turned and walked back to their helicopter.

Slider, who was slightly anxious, said, 'Alexis, where are you taking us now?'

'I'm taking us all to a private nursing home situated to the east of Cardiff.'

'Do you mean Sparta?'

'Yes, that's the one. I've also brought Nurse Angela Walsh with us, and she will look after you and my daughter on the flight.'

He looked at her and smiled. 'Hello, Nurse Walsh.'

'Please, Mr Slider, I'm a private nurse so please call me Angela.' The nurse was tall, curvaceous, with long black hair, and wore black designer glasses, which appealed greatly to him.

Slider looked at Alexis and she looked at him and raised her eyebrows. He gave a gentle nod of approval.

A white Land Rover with spotlights on the roof rack and the word Coastwatch written on the side pulled up alongside their helicopter, and a middle-aged man wearing a black anorak and black cap got out. 'Hello, I'm Officer Willis and I'm in charge at this Coastwatch station. We were told to expect you by the Admiralty, but no time was mentioned.' He turned and smiled at Slider. 'Well, you must be the famous Mr Matthew Slider that the whole world is talking about. Please, let me shake you by the hand.'

'Please, will everyone just call me Slider.'

'Well, how would you and your party fancy a nice cup of tea or coffee before you depart?'

The thought of the taste and smell of coffee was very appealing to Slider, who looked at Alexis, who looked at her watch and grimaced. 'Well, we really do need to get going.'

But a lifeline was thrown to him when Alice said, 'Mummy, I want to go to the toilet.'

Slider struggled to keep a straight face.

'Very well, but we're leaving in twenty minutes.' The pilot though decided to stay with the helicopter. Slider immediately jumped into the front seat of the Land Rover and rode shotgun, while the three women sat in the back. A place that Alexis was not used to, judging by the huffing and her sarcastic comment of 'This is not a place I'm used to' as she closed the rear door. The vehicle drove along a well-used track and came to a stop on the gravel parking space, just a few metres away from the entrance of the national Coastwatch lookout station.

Mr Willis bolted from the car and called out, 'Why don't you all have a walk around while I'll go and put the kettle on!' Alexis and Alice followed Mr Willis into the building.

Nurse Walsh looked at Slider. 'How are you feeling now?'

'To be perfectly honest I'm really tired and knackered, and this strong sunshine has also brought on my headache again.'

'Did the medics on the ship give you anything?'

'Yes, they gave me a strip of twelve Nortriptyline tablets, but I've nearly used them all.'

'I'll see what I've got in my bag when we get back to the helicopter.'

'Thank you,' he replied, and slowly began massaging his forehead with the tips of his fingers.

Alexis and her daughter walked back out and onto the grass and were followed by Mr Willis who was carrying a tray of cups and saucers and pots of tea and coffee. He put the tray down on the garden bench which was situated underneath the window by the front entrance. 'If there is anything else you need, please don't hesitate to let me know.'

'Thank you,' they all replied. Alexis took charge of pouring the teas and coffees, spooning in the sugar, and passing around the cups.

'Is there any brown sugar?' Slider casually asked.

She turned her head sharply to look at him as she was handing Angela her cup. 'Are you trying to be funny?'

'No, not at all, but I do like demerara sugar in my coffee.'

'Well, I'm sorry to say that this is Gwennap Head, and not your usual café.' Then Alexis started to laugh, and soon the laughter spread to all four of them.

Slider finished his second cup of coffee and announced that he was going to the loo. Once inside he could see someone speaking on the phone, while two other men were using a computer and studying a chart. Mr Willis saw him enter and pointed with his finger in the direction of the toilet. There was also a cat sleeping in a cardboard box next to the fireplace. As he re-entered the main room, the thought of using a phone came rushing back to him. 'Mr Willis – what's your first name?'

'Wayne, please call me Wayne.'

'Well, Wayne, would it be possible for me to use your phone to call my wife?'

'For you, anything. I must point out to you that this is not a secure line – CB wireless users and other radio hams may be listening in.' Slider sat down in Wayne's swivel chair and just thought for a moment before dialling home. Wayne could see that he was full of emotion and said quietly as he left the room, 'I'll be outside.'

Slider took a deep breath and tapped the keys slowly and gently.

* * *

Lily Slider called out. 'For God's sake, not again, this is getting a bit much! Slider must know every driver in the city, and if it's not the phone ringing it's the doorbell. Will someone please answer that phone? Andy, answer the phone.'

'But Mum, I answered the last two.'

Becky put her head around the door and gave her mother some white envelopes which had just come through their letterbox.

Lily said, 'More Get Well cards for Slider by the look— Darling, would you go and answer the phone for Mummy please?'

'OK.' The young girl gave her mother a kiss on the cheek and walked to the phone which was on a small table between the armchair and fireplace. 'Hello, this is Becky Slider, how may I help you?'

There was a slight pause for a second or two, then a voice said, 'Hi, darling, it's your dad.'

The high-pitched scream brought Rose running in from the rear garden, where she had been watering the plants. She ran into the lounge to hear Becky shouting, 'Daddy, Daddy, where are you?' The whole room lit up like a Roman candle, with everyone shouting and screaming. So much so that Sergeant Dunscombe, who was standing outside the front door to keep the press and TV cameras at bay, suddenly found himself peering in through the front bay window. Becky's face was a mass of joyous tears as she handed the phone to her mother. The two children were jumping up and down like lunatics. Rose found herself sitting next to her sister with her face in her hands, and tears dripped from between her fingers.

Lily had one finger in her ear and seemed to be shaking uncontrollably. 'Darling, where the hell are you?'

'Well, it's a long story, but I'm at Gwennap Head with Alexis Polti, her daughter, and a nurse.' He could hear the screaming and shouting in the background. 'Put the speakerphone on, darling.'

'What did you say?'

Slider repeated himself. 'Put the speakerphone on.'

'OK. Andy, press the speaker button.' Andy did what his mother told him, and they all had their first chance to hear Slider's voice. He seemed rejuvenated after finally hearing the voices of his family. Immediately the questions started to come thick and fast.

'Daddy, when will you be home?' asked his daughter.

'Dad, I really miss you,' babbled the young boy, who seemed genuinely upset.

'Did those Wrens take good care of you?' asked Rose, who was laughing.

Lily, sounding concerned, said, 'When do you think you'll be home, darling?'

He felt a tapping on his left shoulder. It was Alexis. 'Time to go.'

Slider stopped talking and looked at Wayne who was pouring himself a cup of tea. 'Wayne, how long will it take us to fly to Cardiff?'

He looked at a chart of Great Britain which was pinned to a wall beside the kettle. 'Well, as the crow flies, we are about two hundred and forty miles from Cardiff, and with a crew of six of board, say an hour and a half to two hours.'

Slider looked at his watch. The time was 12:33 p.m. 'Lily, are you still there?'

'Yes, go ahead.'

'We're going to be leaving in the next few minutes and will be flying by helicopter to the Sparta nursing home in Cardiff. We should be there between two and two thirty.' Slider put the phone down and thanked Wayne for the use of it.

Alexis was half in and half out of the door, looking at him. 'When you're ready!'

'I won't be a minute, I just need the toilet.'

She threw another huff. 'We'll be waiting in the car.'

Slider left the Coastwatch station and walked gingerly towards the Land Rover. He noticed that Alexis was already sitting in the front seat. He used the knuckle on his index finger and tapped on the side window. When she lowered the glass, he said, 'I want to walk to the heli.'

'Why?' asked Alexis, who noticed that he seemed despondent.

'Captain Nielson spoke to me before we left, and I'm starting to think about what's going to happen to me once we reach the mainland. I also need to stretch my legs.'

She got out of the Land Rover, linked arms with him, and they both began a slow walk back to the helicopter which was sited about thirty metres away. 'Look, Slider, I want you to know that everything is being taken care of. I've made the necessary arrangements for my legal team to meet with you in a few days' time, so don't worry about a thing. You're one of the family now, and we Italian women always look after our family members.'

He looked at her and said quietly, 'I'm lost for words.'

'Well, that must be a first for you. Now, if you don't mind let's get going. And by the way, when was the last time you had a shower and a shave?'

'I really don't know.'

'Well, if you're not able to shower yourself, perhaps Angela can give you a bed bath and a shave when we get to the nursing home.'

'What's a bed bath?'

She raised her eyebrows and smiled. 'You'll love a bed bath, Slider, you really will.'

He was breathing quite hard when they reached the side of the helicopter and took a moment to compose himself. The co-pilot was standing next to the steps and helped Alexis aboard. Once on board she took off her orange BP flying suit and threw it onto a spare seat, put on her black Barbour jacket and sat down. The co-pilot offered his hand to Slider, but he struggled aboard unaided.

Inside the Airbus H145, there were two wheeled stretchers. Alice was already lying in hers. Slowly and gently he lowered his six foot one inch frame carefully into his. Angela attached the belt around the stretcher to prevent him from falling out. 'How's the head now?'

He took a few seconds, then said, 'The same as usual. It's always there; it never goes away.'

The nurse slipped a pair of ear defenders over the young girl's ears and handed Slider a pair. 'Put these around your ears, they will help to deaden the noise.' As the helicopter lifted off, they all waved to Wayne and his staff through the side window. Slider lay back on his stretcher, closed his eyes, and went to sleep.

90 minutes later.

Slider's shoulder was being tugged, and in the far-off distance he could hear a faint voice and the sound of the ear defenders being pulled off his head. 'Wake up, for God's sake, wake up!' He slowly opened his eyes and was confronted by a pair of large bosoms staring down at him from inside a white shirt which had the top three buttons undone. He took a few seconds to fully awaken and heard the unmistakable voice of Alexis. 'Stop staring at my tits and listen! From what I gather there's going to be a large contingent of TV cameras and reporters all waiting for us at the nursing home. It seems highly likely that someone overheard your telephone call back at the Coastwatch station and has alerted the media. Now, we can't have you just walk into the nursing home otherwise you will be arrested on the spot. So, when we are close to landing Angela will sedate you and you will be put into a wheelchair and wheeled in along with my daughter. Any questions?'

'I could murder a cup of coffee.'

'If you think I'm going to watch you urinate out the side of this helicopter, then you are very much mistaken.'

'Is there a bucket on board?' he asked with a smile.

She looked at him, had a small giggle, and returned to her seat. Slider was now wide awake and the sight of the Second Severn Crossing loomed large in front of them. Alexis spoke to Angela who was sat opposite her. A short time later the nurse stood up, stepped across Alice, and knelt next to Slider. She opened her black medical bag and prepared an injection for him. 'Roll up your left sleeve, please.'

'I hate injections.'

'Then don't look.'

He looked to his right and felt the sting of the needle as it entered his arm. His eyes flickered briefly as he fell into unconsciousness.

* * *

Inside the Slider household, the phone rang for the umpteenth time. On hearing it, Rose, who had been in the kitchen, darted into the lounge, picked up the phone just before Becky, and gave her a 'ha ha ha.' The young girl was not amused and poked out her tongue. Rose did likewise and put her thumb on her nose and wiggled her fingers. Becky put her thumbs on her temples, wiggled her fingers, and poked out her tongue again. They laughed and finally Rose answered the call. 'Hello, this is Rose Harper, how can I help you?'

'Hi Rose, this is Alexis Polti and we're on board the helicopter. Is Lily Slider there, please?'

She was standing right behind her sister, along with Becky and Andy, and was handed the phone. 'It's Alexis Polti for you.'

'Hi, Alexis, it's nice to speak to you at last.'

'Same here. I just thought that I would bring you up to speed about what's happening at our end. Now, we can't have your husband just walk into the Sparta nursing home otherwise the police will have him arrested on the spot, so we've sedated him, and he will be put into a wheelchair and pushed inside. I have also booked a private wing at the nursing home which you and your family can use.'

With emotion in her voice, Lily said, 'Thank you, Alexis, that's very thoughtful of you.'

'Think nothing of it, it's the least I can do after what your husband had done for me and my family. Now, what's happening at your end?'

She looked out of her bay window. 'Well, there's an awful lot of activity going on outside my house. The TV cameras and reporters seem to be packing up and getting ready to move on, and not before time. All in all, we've all had a few chaotic days – the phone hasn't stopped ringing so we're all on a rota to answer it. Drivers are turning up at all times of the day and night, and schoolchildren have been arriving to see Andy and Becky, and bringing them homework, which they're not thrilled about.'

'What time are you leaving for the nursing home?'

'Well, I'm not sure. What time will you be landing?'

Alexis leaned over the co-pilot's shoulder and spoke to him for a few seconds. 'Lily, we were a bit late leaving, but the pilot reckons about twenty minutes.' She looked at her wristwatch. 'So, we should land at the nursing home around two forty. How are you getting there?'

'Carver taxis have given us two cars and drivers for us to use whenever we want, and we can be on the road in a few minutes.'

'Well, I suggest that you and your family leave right away.'

'OK, will do.' Lily put the phone down, opened the front door and spoke to Sergeant Dunscombe, who was standing outside the house. She went back inside and closed the front door. The sergeant walked across the road and along the pavement to where the Carver taxis were parked and spoke to the drivers. He then walked back and took up his position outside the house. Roger and Pam crossed over the road to the Sliders' house and rang the bell. On entering the lounge, they were amazed at the vast quantity of Get Well cards that occupied every flat surface in the room. Lily looked at them and said, 'One hundred and sixty-three, and that's just in this room alone. I've had the children putting up string lines across the walls to hang them all on.' She pushed back the sliding doors that separated the lounge from the dining room. 'And in this room, we have two hundred and four cards.'

They both stood motionless. Quietly, Pam said, 'Where have they all come from?'

'From everywhere. Taxi drivers from all the major companies in Cardiff have been arriving at the house with Get Well cards and bunches of flowers, along with boxes of chocolates – we've even had a few cards from Carver drivers in America. Anyway, Pam, we have to go so please look after the house until we get back and don't forget to feed the cat.'

A few moments later the Slider family and Rose emerged onto the driveway. A couple of photographers started to take pictures of the family group and shouted questions at them. Nobody though said a word. Sergeant Dunscombe spoke to Lily and instructed her and her family not to move until the Carver vehicle had stopped outside the house. Seconds later the black BMW pulled up and the driver got out and opened the doors.

'Mum, can I sit in front with the driver?' Andy always liked sitting in the front of any vehicle he was in.

'Of course you can.'

He walked around to the front of the car, waved to a few bystanders, opened the door and got in. The others got into the back of the car. As the car moved off they waved at Pam and Roger, who were looking out through the downstairs bay window. They had only travelled a few hundred metres when the Carver driver noticed flashing headlights behind him. He immediately pulled over and stopped. A white police car pulled up alongside them. Andy lowered his window and a familiar face smiled at him. 'Do you remember us, son?'

'Yes, you're the two police officers who came to my school to collect me and my sister.'

'That's right, I'm Sergeant Faulkner and this is Police Officer Hann. We're your police escort to the nursing home. Andy, isn't it?'

'Yes, that's me.'

'And where's your sister?'

'She's sat in the back with my aunty and my mother.'

Becky leaned over and pressed the button which lowered the glass. She leaned towards the window waved and muttered, 'Hello.' She was about to say something else when Rose closed the window and pushed her back into the middle.

Lily, whose mind was elsewhere suddenly snapped and in a raised voice said, 'Just remember, you two, we're going to the nursing home to meet your father! Now, Andy, close the window, and driver, let's get going.'

Sergeant Faulkner closed his window and the police car started to move rapidly forward, with its blue light flashing. The taxi followed close behind with its headlights on. Once out of the suburb of Llandaff North the two cars approached the Eastern Avenue bypass. The police car accelerated rapidly, which took the Carver driver by surprise. Within seconds they were hitting eighty miles per hour, which the women found alarmingly too fast for comfort. Lily spoke to the driver and the car slowed down. As they passed the University Hospital of Wales, Becky could see a red helicopter landing at the hospital's heliport and pointed at it.

'Mum, is that Dad over there?'

'Sorry, darling, no, that's the helicopter for the Heath hospital. The nursing home where we're going is further down the road.' A few minutes later they left the bypass and approached the roundabout at the junction with the A48. The Sparta nursing home would only be a short distance away. Taking the first exit off it they approached the nursing home.

Andy could see a helicopter coming towards them in the distance. 'Mum, is that Dad's helicopter?'

'Well, Alexis told me that it's a white helicopter with red markings. What colour is that one?'

There was a pause of a few seconds then he shouted, 'It's white, Mum! It's white!' As it flew closer they could all clearly see that it was white. In the front of the car the young man was glued to the glass, saying 'Dad, Dad!' And in the back of the car rivers of happy tears were flowing everywhere. The helicopter was almost overhead when Andy lowered the window, put his arm out, and started waving. The Carver driver, who was also caught up in the moment, started beeping his horn.

Sergeant Faulkner, who was slightly in front of them, turned to Officer Hann and said, 'Looks like our boy's come home.'

As the cars approached the Sparta nursing home there was a truly wondrous sight to behold. A hundred or more taxis were parked half on the road and half on the grass verge. The sound of beeping car horns was everywhere. Drivers had formed into groups, talking amongst themselves, and all were waiting for the moment when they would see their man home again. Some drivers were even standing on the roofs of their vehicles, waving and shouting.

This was a major welcoming home, a welcome fit for a hero. And in the eyes of the people of Cardiff, the country, and around the world, Matthew Slider was a true hero. The crowd of people was so large that the police car and the Carver taxi could only creep very slowly towards the entrance of the nursing home. The taxi was directed to a parking space just inside the grounds, and as soon as it stopped Andy was out like a shot. He opened the rear door and pulled his Aunty Rose out, then Becky, and finally his mum. They all stood behind a blue and white police tape and waited for the arrival of Slider. As the helicopter came into view it loomed over Sparta nursing home, and the sound from the hundreds of friends, drivers, and well-wishers reached an ear-piercing crescendo. It was so loud that the two children had to put their hands over their ears. Rose put her arms around her sister and shouted, 'He's home, Lily, he's home!'

Inside the helicopter, Alexis was for once quiet. The sight of so many people waving at them was beyond even her expectations. She looked down at Slider, who was awake, but only just, and muttered, 'It could only happen to you.'

The helicopter hovered slowly over a giant white letter H which had been taped down onto the largest car park. Blue and white police tape cordoned off three sides of the car park and police officers kept the large crowd from encroaching too close. The time was a quarter to three when the wheels finally touched down to rapturous applause. The two engines were turned off and the large crowd waited anxiously for the rotor blades to come to a halt. When the blades finally stopped turning, the large crowd fell silent, all waiting for the panelled doors to open.

SEVEN

The co-pilot slid open the side panel and placed the aluminium steps in front of the open hatch. Nurse Angela Walsh was the first to exit and waited by the bottom of the steps. She turned and waved for the two nurses who were standing by the nursing home's entrance to bring forward the wheelchairs for Alice and Slider. Both were placed at a right angle to the helicopter. Alexis came down the three steps, turned, and waited for her daughter. The moment the little girl was spotted by the vast crowd the cheering started again. She picked her up from the top of the steps and carried her to the wheelchair. A nurse put a tartan blanket around her, and she sat still with her head bowed.

Next came the moment that everyone had been waiting hours for: the appearance of Matthew Slider. He poked his head out through the hatch and the waiting crowd caught its first glimpse of their hero. The eruption of cheering and shouting was truly deafening. He stood motionless for a few seconds, just taking in the sight and sounds of the cheering people. Calmly, he raised both his arms and started waving to them.

'Mum, is that Dad?' Becky asked.

Rose looked down at her and said, 'Of course it's your dad. What made you say that?'

'He looks different, that's all.'

Lily jumped in and said, 'Your dad's got a beard and moustache, darling, that's why he looks so different.'

Andy quietly quipped, 'I think it makes him look old.'

'Look, you two! Your father's been through a lot in the last couple of days, so let us all be thankful that he's been returned to us alive and well.'

'I'm sorry, Mum, if I upset you.'

'I'm sorry as well,' said her son.

'Well, let's not have any more talk like that.' Rose put her arm around her sister and gave her a hug.

Slider stepped down onto the tarmac and a wheelchair was pushed alongside him. The nurse motioned for him to sit in it. He raised his right hand and shook his head in rejection of the chair. Alexis moved quickly to his side and spoke quietly in his ear. 'For Christ's sake sit in the chair; you're supposed to look tired and frail. If you walk into that nursing home the police could arrest you on the spot and cuff you!' He stood still for a moment, bowed his head, and fell into the wheelchair. The nurse put a blanket over his legs and both wheelchairs were pushed along the footpath towards the main entrance.

Sergeant Faulkner and Police Officer Hann were standing either side of the Slider family. Slider and Alice had almost reached the main entrance when Andy took his sister's hand and ran down the grassy embankment and onto the footpath. Standing in front of their father they both cried out, 'Dad, Dad!'

Slider lifted his head, opened his eyes, smiled, and murmured, 'Hi, guys.' He opened his arms wide for his children to run into and kissed them. On seeing this act of affection, the vast crowd cheered frantically.

The two police officers escorted the remaining Slider family towards the assembled entourage at the entrance to the Sparta nursing home. Lily Slider stood in front of her husband and looking down at his dishevelled state said, 'What on earth have you been up to?'

He looked up and smiled. 'You know me, luv – could never keep myself out of trouble.'

'Don't I know it! It's your trouble that drove me to drink.'

Alexis tried to defuse the situation by saying, 'Shall we all make our way inside?'

Andy turned to his mother. 'Can I push Dad inside?'

'Of course you can. If I push him I might crash.' This sarcastic remark raised a laugh throughout the group and appeared to put everyone at their ease.

Slider spoke softly. 'Wait a minute, son, I want to have one last look.' He turned his wheelchair around and looked at the vast crowd. With his right hand raised he made a clenched fist. In the crowd, he was able to recognize a few drivers and pointed to them with his finger. The sight of so many people clapping and cheering seemed to moisten his eyes. Once inside the nursing home, the party was met by the receptionist, Rachel Rees, who would escort them all to their rooms.

Sergeant Faulkner stood in front of Slider and sharply said, 'Not sure what to make of you. On one hand, I want to shake your hand, but on the other, you assaulted one of my young police officers and right now I feel like giving you a slap.'

'Sergeant!' yelled Alexis.

He looked at Alexis, then turned back to look at Slider. 'I'll be seeing you again.' He ruffled his dark hair with his meaty right hand and spoke quietly in his ear. 'Seventy-two hours, Slider, seventy-two hours, and you're mine.' The two police officers turned and left the building.

Alexis Polti led the way, pushing her daughter's wheelchair along a corridor which had a black tiled floor and eggshell painted walls. On both sides of the corridor the walls were covered in abstract art pictures which looked meaningless. As Slider's wheelchair reached the men's toilet, he told his son to stop and apply the brakes. Alexis stopped and turned around to see what was happening. She walked back towards Slider who was being helped to his feet by Nurse Walsh and his son. 'What now?'

'I need to use the toilet.'

Alexis looked at Lily and Rose, who were walking arm in arm, and huffed. 'Is he always like this?'

The two sisters smiled and nodded, and in unison said, 'Yes.'

Becky, who had been quiet up to this point, hit the nail on the head when she announced, 'Daddy peed in bed once.' This drew howls of laughter and a sideways glance from her father.

He looked at them and said, 'I've never wet a bed. That accident was caused by a leaking hot water bottle, as you very well know.' Andy pushed open the toilet door for his father, who used his hands on the walls to keep himself from falling over. The facilities inside the men's toilets were vastly superior to anything that Slider had ever seen before. The walls and floors were covered in beautiful black tiles, with a gold pattern running through them. The toilet cubicles were of a copper colour and the urinals had gold plated handles and fittings. After relieving himself he walked slowly over to the wash-hand basins, which were a sparkling white with gold plated taps, and above them circular mirrors which had lights running around the circumference.

He washed and dried his hands, stood in front of the mirror with a hand on either side of the basin and stared at himself in the lighted mirror. Slider was shocked at his appearance. This was the first time that he had seen himself in a mirror since leaving his own house. Now, not only did he possess a moustache and a partial beard, but he also looked old. The skin covering his muscular body looked very white and blotchy. He turned his head to the right and shouted, 'Andy, Andy!'

The boy pushed open the door and asked, 'Did you call me, Dad?'

'Go and find Alexis and tell her to come in here please.'

A few seconds later she pushed open the toilet door slightly and called out, 'What's wrong?'

'Would you please come in here for a moment.' She pushed the toilet door wide open, and gingerly looked around the side of the cubicle and found him stripped to the waist and staring into the mirror. He caught sight of Alexis and seethed. 'I want you to clean me up … I can't believe what I am seeing in this mirror … I look old and decrepit!'

Alexis stood by his side and put her arm around his waist. She could see that he was visibly upset, and a tear rolled down the side of his face. She planted a kiss on the side of his face and stated firmly, 'Considering everything that you have been through in the past couple of days, the stresses and strains on your body, and your near-death experience, I'm surprised that your body is not in worse shape than it is. And just remember this, Mr Slider – I told you when we first met that I was going to look after you and your family, and that's exactly what I and my team are going to do. Now, if you don't mind, let's get out of here before people start talking!' Alexis exited the toilet and in the corridor spoke to Lily, who was still arm in arm with her sister. 'It's nothing to worry about; your husband's worried about his appearance.'

Both women burst into fits of laughter. 'Slider, worried about his looks? That's a first.'

Andy and Becky looked at their mother, thinking she was in distress. 'Mum, Mum, what's wrong?' asked her daughter.

'Nothing, darling, nothing at all. Your father seems to have discovered his feminine side, that's all.'

The toilet door opened, and Slider slowly emerged. 'I'm going to need a long hot bath and a shave,' he announced in a tired voice. His son turned the wheelchair around and his father slumped into it. Andy and Alexis finally reached the junction at the end of the corridor. Rachel Rees turned around and using her arms indicated that the Slider family would be using the rooms to her right and the Polti family would be using the rooms to her left.

Once inside his room Slider found it to be more spacious than he could have imagined. The beds headboard was positioned against the wall in the centre of the room, with a large Samsung television attached to the opposite wall giving the patient a clear view of the screen. A black wardrobe and a large black leather corner sofa were positioned against the wall on his left-hand side, and to his right, a large picture window gave him a clear view of the nursing home's modest garden. Two black leather armchairs were neatly positioned at the right side of his bed. He sat on the side of the bed and tried to untie his shoelaces, but his aching back made it difficult. 'Andy!'

'Yes, Dad.'

'Help me take my sneakers off … I can't reach the laces.' His son untied the white laces and took off his father's blue sneakers and placed them beside the bed. Slider moved his legs onto the bed and lay lengthways on it. He closed his eyes and took several deep breaths.

Becky climbed onto the bed and laid her head next to her father's, gazing into his face. 'Dad, Dad.'

His eyes were still closed when he answered, 'Yes, darling.'

'I love you, Dad.'

Still with his eyes closed he turned his head and kissed his daughter somewhere on her head. He felt more movement on the bed and could feel the presence of someone else lying next to him. 'You'll never guess what, Dad.'

'What's that, son?'

'The goldfish have had babies.'

Still with his eyes closed he smiled and said, 'How many?'

'Not sure exactly … the water's a bit murky, but I've seen five so far.'

'That's great, son.'

Becky started to twist the hairs in her father's beard and spoke quietly to him. 'Dad, can women have beards?'

'No, darling, only men.'

'Good, I don't like beards. Are you going to shave your beard off?'

He opened his eyes and in a tired voice said, 'Yes, as soon as I've had a cup of coffee and a hot bath. Son, go and get your father a cup of coffee, please.'

'OK.'

Alexis had been standing in the doorway listening. 'Stay with your father, Andy, I'll make the coffee.' A few minutes later she returned with a cup of coffee in a white floral cup and saucer. She smiled at his children and introduced herself to them. 'Hello, you two, I haven't met you before, have I? I'm Alexis Polti, but please call me Alexis. Your brave father saved my daughter Alice from drowning. You should be extremely proud of him.'

'We are,' said Andy. 'We just don't like to see him like this.'

Looking at them both she quietly said, 'Don't worry about your father. Once he's had a bath and a shave he'll be as good as new. Now, would you both like something to eat?'

'Yes, please, I'm starving,' said Becky.

Andy just nodded. Alexis phoned the kitchen department. Within a few minutes, a trolley was wheeled into the bedroom, with cakes, milk, bottles of fizzy drinks, and another pot of coffee for their father. While eating his cream cake and walking around the room Andy said, 'Dad, what's through that other door?'

Yawning, Slider lifted his head slightly off the pillow. 'Open it, son, and have a look.'

Through the adjoining door was another bedroom. He gazed into the room and was shocked at its size. 'Wow!' He turned to look at his father. 'Is this for us, Dad?'

'I imagine so, son.'

The children went into the bedroom and jumped onto the double beds. Both were looking up at the ceiling when Becky said, 'This is the biggest bedroom that I have ever seen.'

'I love it,' beamed Andy. 'Let's go and find Mum and Aunty Rose.' They ran into the corridor and found their mother talking with Rose, Angela, and Alexis. 'Mum, Mum!' shouted her excited son. 'Come and look at our bedroom!' The two children pulled their mother into the bedroom and were followed in by the other women.

'Oh, yes, this is very nice,' said Lily, who'd been feeling rather melancholy for the past few days.

'Are you alright?' asked Alexis.

'To be honest with you, I haven't come to terms with this at all ... it's all been rather a blur to me.'

'Well, don't you worry yourself, leave everything to me.'

She walked into her husband's bedroom and gazed down at his bruised and tired body. 'I'm afraid I'm not coping with this very well.'

He lifted his arm and pulled his wife's head towards him and kissed her gently on the lips. 'You're doing fine, and if it's any consolation I'm having trouble as well. Everything is happening too quickly for me, and my head's spinning like a top.'

Alexis put her head around the door, smiled, and said, 'Angela has run a bath for you.'

Slider smiled. 'That's exactly what I need.' He sat up slowly on the bed and eased his legs to the side. 'Give us a hand, luv.' Lily helped her husband onto his feet and put her arm around his waist. Slowly the pair walked towards the bathroom which was on the opposite side of the corridor from their bedroom. The smell of perfume and other fragrances hung heavy in the air. On entering the bathroom, a strong laugh emanated from him. The bathwater was a deep colour of pink, and bubbles covered most of the surface. 'This is a first, I must say. I haven't had a pink bath since I was a child.' The nurse appeared with his loungewear and placed it on a red leather chair by the side of the bath. 'Where did you get those from?'

'Your wife brought them. I'll get you a cup of coffee when you're ready.'

'Thank you, Angela, you're a star. If it's no trouble, could I have my cup of coffee now please?'

'Certainly, you can; milk with one spoonful of demerara sugar, I've been told.'

'Spot on.'

'Right, I'll be back in five minutes.'

Slider sat on the red chaise longue which was next to the chair and surveyed the bathroom. Just like the toilets the bathroom oozed class and sophistication. It had the same black tiled floor and walls as the toilets. The bath was much longer than a usual bath, and at the end of the bathroom was an ornate white basin which had gold plated taps and a circular mirror with lights positioned all around it. In front of the basin was a red swivel chair which had a foot lever to raise and lower it. And just above the basin, a gold shower head with a gold hose which was connected to the taps. In the corner of the bathroom was a beautiful red plant, which occupied a copper-coloured pot.

Just as he finished looking around, a gentle tap on the door and a voice called out, 'I've brought you your pot of coffee.' He stood up and opened the door for the nurse, who placed the tray of coffee on the copper-coloured table which stood next to the chaise longue. He cast his eye over the tray, and everything was there, plus a few chocolate biscuits. 'I'll leave you to it, and when you've had your bath I'll cut and wash your hair for you, and give you a shave if you're not up to it.'

'Thank you, Angela, I would appreciate that very much. The nurse left the bathroom, closing the door behind her. Slider poured himself a cup of coffee and placed the cup on the side of the bath. 'Bloody perfect, a hot bath and a cup of hot coffee; what man could ever wish for more.' He undressed, put his leg over the side of the bath, and gently touched the bathwater with his toes. 'Ooh, lovely,' he said quietly to himself. He lowered himself slowly and carefully into the pink bathwater, which was just a fraction too hot for his body.

For a few seconds he remained motionless with his eyes closed, trying to get used to the hot water covering him. A minute or so elapsed then he leaned forward, picked up his cup of coffee, and leaned back against the bath, sipping the coffee slowly while pondering what to do next. Just when he thought he was in heaven, a vicious knocking on the door brought him back to his senses. 'Are you in the bath, Slider?' came a booming voice.

'Can't I have a bath in peace?'

'Listen, we don't have much time. My legal team will be here in two days' time, and we have to get you suited and booted.'

'What time is it, Alexis?'

'It's ten past four.'

'I'll be out of here by five.' He could hear her muttering to herself but was just unable to distinguish what she was saying. The sound of her high heels disappearing into the distance brought a smile to his face. Having finished his bath and coffee, he put his hands on the side of the bath and eased himself up and onto his feet. Slowly, he put his right leg over the side of the bath and onto the white bathmat. Turning, he brought his left leg out of the bath and onto the mat. He reached for the gold chain and pulled the bath plug out. The tide mark left by his body was a dirty brown colour, so he used the white cotton flannel which was hanging off a tap and meticulously removed it. He looked for the towels and found them on a heated towel radiator which somehow he had overlooked. The white bath towels were crisp and new, and on the label it said "100% Egyptian Cotton". He pushed his face into the towel, and it smelled beautiful. After drying himself, he put on his loungewear and his black and white striped bathrobe that his wife had brought from their house and poured himself another cup of coffee. He was halfway through drinking it when there was a gentle tapping on the door.

'Mr Slider, it's Nurse Angela. Are you out of the bath yet?' He gently eased himself off the chaise longue and walked slowly to the bathroom door, opened it, then returned to his seat. She sat beside him and asked, 'So how are you feeling now?'

'Well, my body doesn't smell as salty as it did, but I feel so tired and lethargic, and my head's not so good either.'

'Look, I don't want you worrying about your tiredness. You've been through a very traumatic ordeal, so your body will naturally take time to heal itself. I'll give you some sleeping tablets, so tonight you can have a long undisturbed sleep, and I'll see if we can find something else for your head.' Slider smiled and thanked her. He finished his coffee and replaced the cup in the floral saucer. 'Are you ready to have your hair cut and washed?'

'Yes, but I've just got to go to the—'

Angela interrupted him. 'Don't be too long.' He returned a few minutes later, and plonked himself down into the swivel chair and stared at himself in the mirror. 'Just give me twenty minutes and I'll have you looking like a new man.'

'Carry on then.' He leaned back into the chair, closed his eyes, and listened as she pumped up the chair and started snipping away at his hair.

'Where do you usually go to have your hair cut?'

'There's a barbershop called Jacks in the Cathays part of Cardiff. It's owned by an Italian man and I've been going there for years.'

'Has he told you that you've got quite a few grey hairs hidden away in this dark hair of yours?'

'Well, Angela, if you were a taxi driver and had people running out in front of your car every day, you'd have grey hairs as well.'

'Yes, I suppose you're right. Now, turn around please and lay your head back, and I'll wash your hair.' Having his hair washed as well as having his scalp massaged almost sent Slider to sleep, but a gentle tapping on the door and the sound of his daughter's voice opened his eyes and disturbed his slumber.

'Dad, can I come in?'

'Of course you can, darling, the door's open.'

Becky pushed opened the door and moved slowly along the damp bathroom floor and stood next to her father. 'Dad, your hair is awfully dirty.'

'Well, that's the Bristol Channel for you.'

'Can I stay and watch your beard being shaved off?'

'Certainly you can. If you ask Angela nicely, she might even let you shave a little bit off my face.'

A large grin appeared, and Becky was transfixed on her father's beard and moustache. Slider's hair was washed several times and a white creamy conditioner was applied. A white towel was quickly wrapped around his head. 'Dad, why have you got a towel around your head?' Angela looked at Becky and told her that the towel was to keep the conditioner in the hair, and it would be washed out after her father had had his shave. The dirt in his hair had left a brown tide line around the basin. This was quickly washed away, and a white flannel was soaked in hot water, wrung out and placed over her father's face. 'What's the flannel for, Dad?'

Her father was unable to speak so Angela told her it was to open the pores in the skin. 'You certainly ask a lot of questions, young lady.'

'Yes, my mum says that I should always ask if I don't understand something.'

'Quite right too.'

The basin was filled half full of hot water, and the razor was left to soak. The flannel was removed from Slider's face and the nurse applied some shaving gel to the palms of her hands and mixed it into a lather. Carefully she applied it to his face. Becky turned her head towards the door and saw her brother watching from the doorway. 'Dad's having a shave.'

Andy ambled in and stood next to his sister. His father moved his eyes to look at his son, and through pinched lips mumbled, 'You'll have to do this one day.'

'Can I have a go now, Dad?'

'Join the queue!' Angela joked. 'Your sister also wants a go. Right, you two, let me show you how to use a razor.' The nurse took the razor out of the basin, looked at the children and told them to watch carefully. 'You start at the top and very slowly and gently pull the razor down the side of the face to the jaw, then slowly over the jawbone and down to the bottom of the neck. Lift the razor off the face and place it in the hot water, swish it around to remove the hair and gel, and start again.'

Both children stood motionless and watched as the nurse finished one side of their father's face. Becky looked up at the nurse. 'Nurse Angela, can I have a little go, please?'

'What do you think, shall we let your children have a turn?'

Slider rolled his eyes over to his children and wiped the foam off his lips with his finger. 'A little go each, but be very, very careful.'

The nurse washed the plastic disposable razor and handed it to Becky, who gripped it between her thumb and index finger. Angela placed her finger on the side of her father's face between his eye and his ear. 'Right, young lady, gently place the razor by my finger.' Becky placed the razor on her father's face. 'Now pull the razor down, very gently and slowly.' She did this and everyone held their breath. The nurse placed a finger on Slider's jawbone. 'When you reach my finger please stop.' Becky did this and stopped. The nurse removed the razor away from his face and washed it in the basin. They all clapped hands and Becky gave a large grin. The razor was then handed to Andy.

Slider looked at his son and calmly said, 'Be very careful now.'

Andy placed the razor on his father's face, just to the left of Becky's track, and moved the razor slowly down. The nurse watched very closely and said, 'Stop.' She took the razor from Andy and washed it in the warm water. 'All over.'

'Thank God for that!' said Slider. 'Can I breathe now?'

Becky looked at Andy and giggled. 'Let's tell Mum what we did.' The two children left the bathroom, laughing, and went to find their mother. Nurse Angela resumed shaving Slider's face and when she'd finished, she wiped the excess foam off his face with a damp flannel. A white hand towel was placed over his face. The nurse carefully patted his face dry, lowered the chair and swivelled it around.

Slider looked intently at his new face in the mirror, and after moving his face from side to side announced, 'Perfect, bloody perfect.'

'Good, I'm glad you're happy. Turn around and I'll wash the conditioner out of your hair and blow dry it.'

Alexis strode into the bathroom and looked down at Slider's face. 'Well, you've scrubbed up a lot better than I thought you would.'

'Oh, thanks a lot!'

Alexis was struggling to keep a straight face as she said, 'By the way, the dental hygienist will be seeing you tomorrow morning at ten o'clock to clean your teeth and, if possible, try and remove those coffee stains from them ... some hope though.'

He rolled his eyes over and let out a sigh.

'Tonight, we eat at six thirty so don't take all day in here.' With that, she walked towards the door, but looked back at him just before disappearing into the corridor. It was a look that Slider didn't miss.

The nurse finished drying his hair and applied some moisturising cream to his face. 'There, we are all finished. So, what do you think?'

He lifted himself out of the chair and looked closely at himself in the mirror. 'Great job, Angela.' He slowly leaned forward and kissed her cheek.

'Here, keep the jar, you might want to put some moisturiser on other parts of your body,' she added with a wink. She turned and walked slowly out of the bathroom. He tossed the jar in the air, caught it one-handed and gave out a small laugh and left. In the corridor, he saw Alexis and Rose talking together. They walked towards him, and Rose commented on his smart appearance.

'You certainly look much better, so how are you feeling now?'

'Well, I don't smell as salty as I did and Angela has cleaned me up, but my lack of energy still worries me.'

Alexis took over the conversation. 'I've spoken to Angela, and she tells me that she's given you some sleeping pills, so they should help with that. Tomorrow is going to be a busy day for both of us. I'm taking Rose into town to buy you a suit for your trial. My solicitor is also arriving in the morning, and she will want to talk to you about that assault on the pier.'

Slider said, 'What time is it?'

Alexis looked at her gold wristwatch. 'It's five twenty-five, why?'

'I want to watch the BBC news at six. I haven't seen the news for a few days and I want to catch up on what's been happening in the world. There might even be something about myself on the news.'

Alexis and Rose looked at each other, smiled, and both gave out an 'Oooh.'

Slider turned and ambled along the corridor towards the rooms used by the Polti family. He saw his daughter talking to Alice on her bed. He tapped on the open door. 'Can I come in?'

'Yes, Mr Slider,' said Alice, who appeared a lot happier and brighter.

'I'm very pleased to see that you've recovered well from your ordeal, but please, just call me Slider like everyone else.'

'Dad, I don't call you Slider.'

'I know; that's because you're my daughter.' And with that, he picked her up and gave her a big kiss. She brushed her fingers along her father's face and commented on how soft his skin was, and how nice he smelled.

'Dad, what's this sticky stuff on your face?'

'It's moisturiser, and it's used to make my skin soft.' He hadn't seen much of the wing that his family was sharing with the Polti family, so he left Alice and his daughter and ambled out into the corridor. Across the floor from the Polti suite was a door labelled Dining Room. He entered the room, where an elderly woman in a black dress and white apron was laying out cutlery on the glass-topped table. Around the table were black metal chairs upholstered in red. There were place settings for twelve people. On suddenly seeing Slider the woman gasped.

'Oh, sir, you startled me.'

'I'm sorry.'

The woman suddenly stopped what she was doing and walked over to him. 'Excuse me, sir, are you the Mr Slider who saved the life of that little girl?'

'Yes, that's me.'

'Well, sir, I would just like to say how wonderful it is to meet you. My name is Barbara and if there is anything you need then please let me know. Dinner tonight will be at six thirty.'

'So, Barbara, what's on the menu for tonight?'

'Well, Mr Slider, I am also one of the chefs at this nursing home, and we've prepared turkey with all the trimmings or cod with chips or potatoes. To follow it's either apple pie or trifle, which I thought the children would like.'

'Sounds wonderful, Barbara, but please, just call me Slider.'

'OK, and you can call me Babs, everyone else does.'

'Thank you, I will.' His eye then caught sight of a grey folding screen at the far end of the table. 'What's the screen for, Babs?'

'I was going to open it after laying the table, but you can push it back now if you want.' He turned the key and unlocked the screen which went from floor to ceiling and across the room from wall to wall. As he pushed back the screen it concertinaed like bellows and revealed a large lounge area with black leather reclining sofas and armchairs. A large coffee table stood in front of each sofa, smaller tables had been placed next to the armchairs and on the pine wall was a large Samsung television. His heart nearly missed a beat when he spotted it — partly hidden by a leather armchair and a curtain was an upright piano. He walked over to it and ran his hand over the curved lid. His eyes gazed at the beautiful colours and patterns in the walnut veneer. Gently, he lowered himself onto the red upholstered piano seat and lifted the lid. 'Do you play?' came an enquiring question from Barbara.

'No, not really. Becky is the piano player in the family, I merely dabble.' He placed his right thumb on Middle C and proceeded to play the C Major scale.

He knew it wouldn't take long and he was right. He had only played half the scale when Becky came running into the dining room and shouted, 'Dad, Dad, where did you find it?' Her father finished the scale and proceeded to play it again. 'Dad, can I play?'

Slider leaned forward and kissed his daughter on her cheek. 'Of course you can.' He got up off the piano seat and sat in the armchair next to the piano, raising the recliner.

Becky altered the height of the seat and moved it in closer. 'What shall I play, Dad?'

'Anything, darling, you choose.' He sat and watched as his daughter prepared herself before playing. After playing a few scales she rolled up her sleeves and started to play. Becky's playing soon attracted the attention of others. Andy and Alice entered the room and were quickly followed by Lily and Rose, who sat together on one of the three-seater sofas. Slider got up from the armchair and squeezed himself in between his wife and sister-in-law and put his arms around them both. He kissed his wife gently on the side of her cheek.

Lily squeezed her husband's hand while watching her daughter play, and tearfully said, 'God knows where she gets it from, cause it's not from my side of the family.'

He looked at his daughter, who played with such precision and confidence that it moistened his eyes. 'Becky's a gifted one, that's for sure.' Slider caught sight of Alexis just inside the doorway and saw her tapping her watch with her index finger. Frantically he turned to his wife and looked at her wristwatch: it was 5:56 p.m. He jumped up and started to look for the TV remote.

Becky suddenly stopped playing and asked, 'What are you looking for, Dad?'

'The TV remote. The news will be on in four minutes.'

'Here it is.'

'Thanks, Alice.'

Slider switched on the TV and sat back down. Becky then sat on her father's lap. Andy decided to sit on the floor in front of his mother, and Rose beckoned Alice to join them. Alexis was standing at the back of the sofa and leaned over. 'Does anyone want anything?'

'A pot of coffee would be nice.'

'I might have known that's what you'd say.'

Rose looked at Alexis. 'Yes, a cup of tea please.'

'I'll have one as well,' said Lily, who was starting to yawn.

Alexis looked at the children. 'What about you lot?' She looked at each one in turn and each one nodded.

'BBC News on BBC 1 now, with Stephanie Howard and Nigel Sandler at six o'clock.'

'Please nobody speak,' said Slider, whose eyes were fixed on the screen.

'The Bank of England has again raised interest rates by one-quarter of one percent. Prisons in Scotland are to receive three million pounds in extra funding. The England cricket team have won the final test against India to win the series. And yes, he's finally home. Matthew Slider, the Carver taxi driver who jumped into the sea to save the life of a little girl, has flown back to a hero's welcome in Cardiff.'

Slider sat back on the sofa with his fingers locked together across his stomach and soaked in everything he was hearing and seeing. He was so engrossed in what he was watching that he was lost to everything happening in the room around him. A stabbing finger in the neck by Alexis soon brought him back to reality.

'Coffee?'

He reached over the back of the sofa and was handed his cup. 'Thanks.' Cups of tea were handed to Lily and Rose. Alexis wheeled the trolley around to the front of the sofa and was handing bottles of soft drinks to the children when Slider suddenly jumped down her throat. 'You're blocking the telly!'

She looked at Becky, who was giggling along with Andy and Alice, and asked her quietly, 'Is your father always like this?' The young girl looked at her dad, then looked back at Alexis and gently nodded.

Andy chipped in, 'He's worse than this sometimes.'

Lily and Rose laughed out aloud.

Alexis turned her head slightly to look at Slider. 'Are you going to get dressed today, or are you going to sit around in your loungewear all night?'

He had a deep sigh and said, 'After dinner, I'm going to take a sleeping tablet and have an early night, so no, I'm not getting dressed.' With that he rose to his feet, walked to the trolley, and poured himself another cup of coffee. He had his back to the TV and was spooning in the demerara sugar when he heard.

'It's on, Dad!'

Slider stood motionless as he watched the news item about his arrival at the Sparta nursing home. 'God, look at all those people.' He slowly walked back to the sofa, placing his coffee cup on the table, and sat on the arm of the sofa. A large grin appeared across his face when he recognized some of his mates in the crowd. 'Look,' he said, pointing with his finger. 'There's Phil, Alan, Chris, Paul, Liam, Huw, Frosty, and Gary. There's Ian from Dragoon, with Guy. There's Thomas and Jama the hackney drivers, and that's Les the Capita driver. Gosh, I'm staggered that so many of the boys have turned out.' The sight of so many drivers and well-wishers started to emotionally affect him. Rose caught sight of a tear slowly trickling down his cheek and gave her sister a gentle nudge with her elbow.

Lily turned to her husband and rubbed her hand down his back. 'Are you OK, darling?'

'I'm overwhelmed, there must be two hundred drivers or more.' He put his index finger to his mouth and watched intently. 'I don't remember seeing so many people when we landed.'

'You were still under sedation, that's why it looks different,' Alexis told him.

'This goes to show how we taxi drivers can come together and help each other.' Slider scrutinized as much of the report as he could and then a thought came to him. 'Darling, where's my car?'

'Oh, Roger was given the car keys and your wallet by the police, and he's brought them over to our house.'

'Lend me your phone, please. I should have thought of this earlier.'

EIGHT

Roger and Pam were having dinner on a tray while watching the evening news, when the phone rang. 'Rog, the phone,' said Pam, who was busy pouring the wine.

'Why does it always ring when we're eating?' Roger put his tray down onto the small hexagonal table, which was next to his armchair, walked to the fireplace and picked up the phone, which was on the mantelpiece next to a photograph of himself and Pam. 'Hello.'

'Hi, Rog, how are you?'

'Slider!' He turned sharply and looked at Pam. His face suddenly changed to a bright red colour and his hands started to shake.

Pam, who was sitting on the sofa, took off her glasses, put both hands over her eyes and wept.

A few seconds passed and Roger had regained his composure. 'Slider, oh Slider, it's so good to hear your voice, how are you, mate?'

'Well, I'm getting there slowly. I'm still very tired and I've got Alexis Polti shouting and balling at me.'

'I'm what!'

'That was her by the way.' Slider turned his head slightly in the direction of Alexis and caught her eye. 'I said you're looking after me.'

'That's better. Who's that on the phone?'

'It's Roger, my neighbour from across the road. He's looking after the house for us.'

'Let me speak to him. Roger, this is Alexis Polti and I just want you to know that Slider is a real pain in the ass!'

Roger could be heard laughing loudly.

Alexis then handed the phone back to Slider. 'See what I mean, Rog? Anyway, I'm phoning you to find out what's happened to my car.'

'You won't believe this, mate, but your car was caught in the background when the BBC did their report from the pier, and it became a bit of a tourist attraction. People were even taking selfies next to it. Anyway, the police got a bit tired of it and took your car to the police station down at Cardiff Bay, where it stayed overnight.

Carver got to hear what happened and their management team put it on a trailer and returned it to your house yesterday, and it's now parked in front of the house underneath the sycamore tree. I've put a cover over the car to keep it clean, and when Rose moves her car I'll move yours back onto the driveway.'

'Thanks, Rog.'

'So, when can Pam and I visit you?'

'Well, I'm seeing the dental hygienist tomorrow at ten o'clock so come up about midday. Also, could you please bring me my phone which is in the car, along with my wallet and car keys. Oh, and the phone charger.'

'Dad, ask Roger about Sooty.'

'Rog, Becky wants to know if the cat is OK.'

'Tell her not to worry. Pam is looking after her very well.'

'OK, see you tomorrow then. Bye.'

'Dad, Sooty's got a name, you know.'

'Sorry, darling, I'll try to remember that.'

Barbara entered the room and announced that dinner would be ready in five minutes. Alexis grabbed the remote and switched off the TV. 'Come on, you lot, let's go and have dinner.'

As they all walked into the dining room, Becky asked, 'Dad, can I play the piano afterwards?'

'Of course you can, but only for a short while.'

Place names were on every plate, with the group wandering around the table to find their seats. Alexis was seated at the head of the table with her daughter to her right. Opposite Alice sat Becky, and next to Becky sat her father. Opposite Slider sat his son Andy, who had his mother sat next to him. Opposite Lily sat Rose, who was next to Angela Walsh the private nurse.

The evening meal was a great success, with laughter all around the table. Andy announced that this was the best meal that he'd eaten since Christmas day, which brought a stare from his mother and a comment of, 'Thank you, son, you know where our kitchen is if you need it.' Howls of laughter and raised eyebrows by his Aunty Rose turned his cheeks bright red.

Slider was unusually quiet, which didn't go unnoticed by Alexis. 'You're quiet tonight.'

'I was just thinking. This is the first time we've all been together, and with your permission, I'd like to ask your daughter about that day on Penarth Pier.' The room suddenly fell silent.

Alexis leaned towards her daughter. 'Do you want to talk about it, darling?'

'I just wanted to see the big ship, but I couldn't see.'

'Where was your nanny, Victoria?'

'She was buying me some ice cream.'

'What happened next, darling?'

'I saw some schoolgirls who put their shoes inside the railings, and stood on the lumpy bits to look higher, so I did the same. When I was looking at the big ship, some girls barged into me and I fell into the sea.' Tears cascaded down the little girl's cheeks. 'I'm so sorry, Mummy.'

Alexis got up out of her seat, picked up her daughter and gave her a big hug, and placed a kiss on her cheek. 'You won't be doing a silly thing like that again, will you?'

'No, Mummy.'

Looking at Slider she said, 'Mr Slider might not be there next time.' The room burst into laughter and applause. Alexis asked, 'Who would like champagne?'

'Yes, please,' was the response from everyone.

Barbara brought in a bottle of Moët & Chandon Imp☐rial Ros☐, which was Alexis's favourite champagne, and began pouring it into the champagne glasses. The children, however, had to settle for fizzy lemonade. With the glasses filled Alexis stood up and announced a toast. 'Ladies and gentlemen boys and girls, the last couple of days have been truly extraordinary. I don't think anyone of us will ever forget the heroic feat performed by Slider which has brought us all together this evening. So, I would like you all to stand up and drink a toast to our hero Mr Matthew Slider.'

Everyone stood up, raised their glasses, and replied, 'Matthew Slider.' This was accompanied by a large round of clapping.

He had a large grin on his face and was just about to take a sip from his glass when Alexis said, 'Not you, Slider.'

'What do you mean, not me?'

'You have some sleeping tablets to take later. So I'm afraid you're on the lemonade with the children.'

He didn't say a word for a few seconds. When he looked at the three children, Becky had her hand over her mouth to control her laughter, Andy was looking down at the floor with his hand covering his eyes and sniggering, while Alice was staring at him and giggling loudly. Turning his gaze on Alexis he said, 'Thanks very much, it's nice to know that you still have my interests at heart.'

'Look, it's going to be a big day for you tomorrow, so I need you sober and alert. You've got the dentist at ten o'clock, Roger and Pam at midday, and in the afternoon my solicitor Irene Asher and her assistant Lynn Williams will be arriving.'

Becky, with her lemonade finished, interrupted them. 'Dad, you said I could play the piano.'

'Yes, I did. Let's go into the other room and we can all listen to you play.'

Everyone stood up from the table and took their glasses with them into the lounge area. Except for Slider who had his usual cup of coffee in hand. He sat in the middle of the sofa with Rose on one side and his wife on the other. The children felt happier just sitting on the floor. Alexis and Angela occupied the armchairs. Becky sat at the piano and played a few scales to warm up. 'What do you want me to play, Dad?'

'Well, you're here to entertain us, so why don't you start with 'The Entertainer.'

'OK.'

The young girl proceeded to play, and the room fell silent. The quality of her playing took the room by storm, heads were turned in disbelief at her ease of playing. When she finished a large round of applause caused Barbara to enter the room. Becky moved on to playing 'The Maple Leaf Rag,' which was roundly applauded at the end.

Slider got up and walked over to his daughter and spoke quietly in her ear. 'We've got time for one more, so why don't you play our favourite piece?'

'You mean Fred?'

'Yes.'

Alexis looked at Slider. 'Your daughter's very good, a natural.'

'Well, wait till you hear her play our favourite piece.' Everyone sat down and were still as Becky began to play Fryderek Chopin's Prelude no 4 in E Minor. Heads were bowed as the beauty of the piece took over the room. Tissues started to appear and eyes were moistened. Alexis also shed a tear, which was very unusual for her. At the end, Becky's piano playing received a rapturous round of applause. Slider walked to the piano, picked up his daughter, embraced her, and kissed her on both cheeks. 'That was absolutely beautiful. I'm so proud of you.'

Alexis walked over to them and said to Becky, 'You have a real talent, young lady, and it's a talent that shouldn't be wasted. If you get the right qualifications at school, then I'll find you a place at a top London college of music and drama.'

'Hold on a minute, that's going to cost a lot of money!'

'Listen, Slider, you're family now so let me worry about that.'

He put his arms around her and softly said, 'Thank you.'

'Well, you can thank me by getting an early night. I need you and your head clear for tomorrow.' With that, he turned and said good night to everyone, and slowly walked to his bedroom.

The next morning Slider was up early. He had showered, shaved, and was dressed all before eight o'clock. He walked into the dining room and greeted his wife. 'Good morning, darling, and how are you today?'

'You're a chirpy one this morning.'

'I'm OK today – the head's not too bad and I'm feeling more energetic. Are the kids awake yet?'

'I think Becky's awake, but you know what Andy's like in the morning.'

'I'll go and get him up.' Slider walked purposely along the corridor to his son's room and knocked on the door. 'Andy, are you awake yet?' After a pause of a few seconds, he pushed the door open to discover his son still asleep in bed. 'Come on, it's time to get up.'

'What time is it, Dad?'

'It's quarter past eight and breakfast will be at half past, so I need you up straight away. It's going to be a long day for both of us. I've got to see the dentist and the solicitor, and you've got a pile of homework to do and so has your sister.' He threw back the duvet and was up straight away and walked into the en suite bathroom to shower. 'My God in heaven, it's a miracle,' muttered his father with a smile. Back in the corridor he tapped on Becky's door and got an answer straight away. 'Breakfast at eight thirty, darling.'

'OK.'

In the dining room Slider was talking to his wife and Rose when Alexis entered with a dressmaker's tape hanging around her neck. 'Come here, Slider, I need to measure you.'

'Anything for you, Alexis.'

'You're in a good mood this morning, all showered and shaved, and you've combed your hair. Things are looking up. Now, let me measure your collar.'

He stepped in front of her, and she placed the tape around his neck. 'You're not going to strangle me, are you?'

'That thought has crossed my mind several times since we've met, but no, not today,' and started to laugh.

Lily and Rose who were standing close by also laughed.

'Right then. Neck … sixteen and a half. Waist … thirty-six inches. Chest … put your arms out, forty-three-ish. What's your leg measurement?'

'You're not going to measure my inside leg, are you?' he asked, smirking.

'Not bloody likely!'

'It's thirty-three,' said Lily, adding that her husband had never bought himself any clothes since they'd been married.

The children entered the dining room. Andy asked, 'What's happening, Dad?'

'Well, son, Alexis has been measuring me up for a new suit.'

'I think you'll look very smart in a new suit – better than those clothes you wear to work.'

'Why, thank you, Becky, it's very nice of you to say that.'

'Dad, what colour will it be?'

'Black, son, I only ever wear black suits. Black is more distinguished looking.'

Barbara wheeled in the hostess trolley and took the lids of the various oval dishes which had been keeping everything hot for a traditional English breakfast. There were also different types of cereals, with milk and orange juice in tall clear jugs. Tea and coffee were also readily available in tall stainless-steel flasks. During breakfast, the day's schedules were talked over. Slider had his own appointments. Becky and Andy would be going back to their house along with Alice to collect their homework. Alexis and Rose would also go back to the house and then go into town to buy Slider a suit. Lily, though, would remain at the nursing home with her husband.

At nine thirty the six-seater black Mercedes Carver taxi pulled up to the nursing homes entrance. There was still a large contingent of people outside. TV cameras were also noticeable as the five of them walked through the automatic doors and to the opened doors of the waiting car.

'How's Slider today?' came a call from a man holding a microphone.

'He's very well, thank you.'

'When can we speak to him?'

Alexis knew that was a pivotal question, and it would only be a matter of time before Matthew Slider would have to stand in front of a battery of cameras and reporters and talk about the past couple of days to the whole world. After a brief pause, Alexis announced that Slider, with his friends and family, would be holding a press conference at the Sparta nursing home at five o'clock the following day. On entering the seven-seater taxi, Rose sat in the back with Alexis, her daughter, and Becky. Andy was happy sitting in the front next to the driver.

Rose looked at Alexis. 'He's not going to like it.'

'Well, it has to happen sooner or later, so it might as well be tomorrow.'

As the car made its way into College Road, the large assembly of reporters and TV crews was still present. 'Look at this,' said Andy, who was waving to the bystanders.

Alexis said, 'Is this where you live?'

'Yes, that's our house by the large sycamore tree, and that's my Aunt Rose's car on our driveway.'

'Thank you, Andy. It will be moved when I take Alexis into town.'

'Stop laughing, you lot. Now, when we get out don't say a word, wave and smile but no talking, and Andy...'

'Yes, Alexis.'

'...help your sister and my daughter out of the car, please, and hold their hands until we get to the front door.'

'OK.'

Once the car had stopped Sergeant Dunscombe walked quickly to hold back the reporters and camera crews that surrounded it. Questions were coming thick and fast, but nobody uttered a word. The taxi driver got out and opened the rear door. Alexis got out first, followed by Rose. The sergeant briskly walked around the car and opened the front passenger door for Andy to get out. 'Nice to see you again, young man.'

'Thank you.'

He put his arm around the boy and guided him through the vast throng of reporters who were all eager for information about the condition of his father. He seemed overawed by all this attention and kept his head down, taking hold of his sister's and Alice's hands once he reached the pavement. The five of them walked up the driveway to the front door, turned and waved to the crowd. Roger and Pam had seen the taxi arrive and had opened the front door so they could enter the house quickly. Rose walked in first followed by Becky, Andy, and lastly Alexis with her daughter. Introductions were made, with Roger inquiring about Slider's health.

Alexis was looking at Becky who had Sooty in her arms and said, 'I think just about now Slider's getting his comeuppance from the dental hygienist Miss Gregory.' A wave of laughter filled the hallway. Pam opened the door and led the way into the lounge.

* * *

Slider was stretched out on a leather recliner watching an old episode of *Ground Force*. He loved his garden, and only last year had planted Queen Elizabeth roses in the front borders, and recently he'd built a pond in the rear garden and stocked it with goldfish. A voice interrupted his viewing.

'Mr Matthew Slider?'

'Yes, that's me.'

'Hello, I'm Miss Gregory. I'm your dental hygienist and have been asked to clean your teeth and give them a scale and polish.' He had a morbid hatred of dentists and would put off seeing one for as long as possible. He had deliberately missed his last appointment, which was six months ago, but there was no way out of this one. 'Would you follow me, please?' Miss Gregory was a tall black woman dressed in a light blue smock and black trousers. She looked to be in her early thirties and had a figure that was charming.

Once inside the dental unit he sat in the black reclining chair and felt his body temperature start to rise almost immediately. Slightly behind him and to his left was the hygienist's assistant, who had a pleasant smile and radiant white teeth. A pair of glasses were placed over his eyes to shield him from the bright light that shone down on him. The recliner was slowly tilted back, and he was given a saliva ejector to hold which would remove saliva and tooth debris.

'If you want me to stop just raise your hand' she instructed through her blue face mask. He pushed his head hard into the headrest and gripped one armrest firmly as the hygienist started to scrape away at his teeth to remove the plaque and tartar. Slider had his eyes closed and could feel every tooth being violated by the action of the scalar. And it just seemed to go on and on. 'Your teeth are in a terrible state, Mr Slider; you really should visit your dentist more often.' He could feel the beads of perspiration gathering on his forehead, and was immensely relieved when the hygienist stopped. The recliner was moved to a more upright position and he was given a cup of blue liquid to swill around his mouth and spit out. 'How are you feeling?'

He wiped his mouth with a tissue. 'Well, you're not as heavy-handed as my own dentist, that's for sure.'

'Why, thank you, I do try to be as careful as I can. Are you ready for me to carry on?'

'You mean there's more to come?' She looked at her assistant and raised her eyebrows. The chair was reclined again. He closed his eyes and firmly gripped the armrest. This time he could feel the slow rotary tool grinding away over his teeth. It wasn't as painful as the scraping but the sound reverberating throughout his head reached a painful moment. He opened his eyes and raised his arm. 'I need to spit.' After rinsing his mouth, he asked, 'How much more do you have to do?'

'Your teeth are heavily stained with caffeine so it's going to take a bit longer than usual; say another ten minutes.'

That was the longest ten minutes of his life, and he was mightily relieved when it all finally stopped, and his recliner was upright. Slider left the dental unit and was met by his wife who had been sat outside reading a magazine. 'My poor husband, how are you feeling now?' she asked with a smirk on her face.

'I'll never get used to going to the dentist even if I live to be a hundred,' he confessed, wiping his mouth.

'Show me what they've done then.' He reluctantly opened his mouth for his wife to look at his teeth. 'Very nice, very nice indeed,' she said as he moved his head and tongue for her to see more closely. 'So what would you like to do now?'

'A cup of coffee and a lie-down would be perfect.'

'Alright, but don't let Alexis see you drinking coffee, or she'll have you back in that dentist's chair. Now go and have a lie-down and I'll bring you a cup.' He was lying on his bed mulling over the day's events when his wife walked in. She placed the cup down on the bedside cabinet and lay next to him. Stroking his hair, she said, 'It's been a while since the two of us have been alone with no one to bother us.' He turned his head to face her and kissed her gently on her right cheek, then moved in even closer, kissing her passionately. His right hand inched slowly over her ample left breast. 'Oh darling, I've missed you so much.'

'I've missed you too. It's only the thought of you and our kids that's kept me going these past few days.' Slider started to unbutton his wife's blouse, when there was a knock on his bedroom door.

'Would you believe it!' said an exasperated Lily.

He slowly got up off the bed and opened the door a few inches. Rachel Rees, the receptionist, was standing there and seemed slightly embarrassed. 'I'm so sorry to disturb you, but there are some gentlemen in reception who've come to visit you.'

He turned to face his wife who was doing up the buttons on her blouse and easing herself off the bed. 'I won't be a minute darling. I'll just go and see who it is.' He put on his black and white dressing gown and followed Rachel Rees. As he turned the corner into reception, he was met by several drivers with whom he worked.

'Slider, you old bastard, how are you?' A large grin appeared across his face and laughter emanated around the five of them. Handshakes, backslapping, and, unusually for Slider, hugging greeted him from Alan, Hugh, Frosty, and Gary.

'Well, who let you four in?'

'We went to your house and saw the taxi pull up with your kids and a few others. We also spoke to a smart bit of stuff, Alexis I think her name was, and she said it would be OK for us to visit you,' said Frosty.

'We've all been very worried about you, mate,' said Alan, whose eyes were noticeably red.

'Tell you what, boys, why don't we all go into the lounge where we can have a proper chat.' As Slider led the way, Barbara suddenly appeared from the kitchen area. 'Babs, could we have a pot of tea and coffee please?'

'Of course you can. Anything else?'

'A couple of bacon sandwiches would be nice.'

'I'll see what I can find.'

Slider and his good friends had a detailed discussion about the incident on the pier and the subsequent rescue he performed. Nothing was left out. 'Well, mate, you've done well here, it's like a five-star hotel. I never imagined this nursing home would be so lavish.'

'Well, Hugh, that's the difference between us working class and the rich. I'm just sorry that this is our last night here.'

Barbara was wheeling in her trolley when she overheard the group talking. 'Oh Slider, you're not leaving us, are you?'

'I'm afraid so, Babs, this will be our last night, then it's back home.'

'Oh dear, we'll be so sorry to see you leave.'

'Well, if it's any consolation, I'll miss this place and the staff who've looked after us.'

Barbara continued pouring the teas and coffees and handed around the plates with the bacon sandwiches. 'What would you like for dinner tonight?'

'A steak dinner would be very nice.'

'A steak dinner? Can we stay as well, Babs?' asked Gary, who had a large grin on his face.

'Sorry, gentlemen, but Slider needs his strength building up.'

Lily entered the lounge and plonked herself down on her husband's lap. 'Have you met the boys before?'

'I think I met them when you had trouble with the car battery earlier in the year.'

'Yes, that's right. Well, that's Gary, Frosty, and Hugh on the sofa, and that's Alan in the armchair.' With the greetings over she reminded her husband that Roger and Pam were arriving at midday and returned to her bedroom.

Hugh said, 'So how's your wife and kids coping with being on the TV and in the papers?'

'Well, it was a major shock for them to begin with, but now the wife has come to terms with it and the kids love seeing themselves on the TV, and I think they'll be sad when it's all over.'

Alan looked at his watch; it was eleven thirty. 'Look, mate, we'd better be going if you've got other visitors.' He took a brown envelope from his inside jacket pocket and handed it to Slider. 'All the drivers have been very worried about what might happen to you, so we've had a whip-round for you.'

He accepted their gift and could tell by the weight and feel that it contained a considerable amount of money. 'Lads, I don't know what to say.'

'Look, you don't have to say anything, just get this trial over and get back to work as soon as you can.' Slider shook hands with them and watched as they walked towards the exit doors. Just before they left, Alan came trotting back along the corridor. 'I knew there was something else to tell you. Janey O'Mara from Carver's head office in Ireland is flying over today to pay you a visit.'

'Do you know when she'll be arriving?'

'Later today we've been told.'

'Thanks for letting me know, now go back to work.' They both laughed, then he watched as his good friend left the building. Slider walked back to his bedroom and lay down beside his wife. 'That was nice of the boys to come and visit me.'

'Did they bring you anything?'

'Yes, a brown envelope. They had a whip-round for me in case I go to jail.' He gently placed the envelope on his wife's stomach.

Lily took hold of it and peered inside. 'My God, there must be hundreds in here, all in twenties!'

He was looking up at the ceiling when he said, 'Darling, do you think I did the right thing by jumping into the sea to save Alice?'

She rolled on top of him and stared down at him. 'Of course you did the right thing, who else was going to save that young girl?'

'There was no one else.'

'Well, there you are. If it hadn't been for you Alice would have drowned, so don't beat yourself up about it. You were in the right place at the right time, and no matter what happens at your trial I will always love you and be at your side.'

Slider got off the bed and placed the *Do Not Disturb* sign on the outside of his bedroom door and climbed back onto the bed. He and his wife continued passionately from where they had left off.

NINE

The two women were putting on their coats when Alice asked, 'Mum, where are you going?'

'Rose and I are going into town to buy Mr Slider a suit. You three will go with Pam and Roger back to the nursing home in the Carver taxi, and we'll all have lunch together at about one thirty.' She kissed her daughter then spoke to Pam and Roger. Rose kissed Becky and patted Andy's head. As the front door opened, Alexis spoke briefly to the police officer, and the hardstand was cleared. The MG Morgan fired into life straight away, the sound sending Sooty scuttling back into the house. The car slowly rolled back onto the main road, and as it accelerated away, Rose gave a honk-honk on its old-fashioned horn, and both waved as they passed the house.

Once they'd left the suburb of Llandaff North, Alexis said, 'This is a beautiful car, Rose, wherever did you get if from?'

'I had it two years ago as a birthday present from one of my gentleman friends.'

Alexis gave her a sideways glance. 'Did you indeed?'

'Yes, I did. I'm not ashamed to say this, and I hope we can keep this between ourselves, but I work as an escort, and I meet gentlemen from all walks of life. And one client of mine, Jonathan Weeks, who's an importer and exporter of classic cars, gave this to me as a birthday present. I drive to Bristol once a month to visit him, and we spend the weekend together, and very occasionally we travel to France for a few days.'

'Good on you, girl,' said Alexis, giggling. 'Does your sister or Slider know about this?'

'I haven't told them, but I think they have their suspicions – whenever the three of us go into Cardiff for a drink or a meal, I always seem to draw glances from other men.'

'Well, you're a very beautiful woman, Rose, and with your figure you could easily be a fashion model.'

'Perhaps.'

'No perhaps about it. I know a few fashion photographers in London; why don't you leave it to me and I'll see what I can do. What do you say?'

'Why, thank you, Alexis, that's very sweet of you – yes, I would appreciate that very much.'

'Think nothing of it. You're family, just like the Sliders.'

The morning rush-hour traffic had abated significantly by the time they entered the city centre. Rose parked her car in Windsor Place, drawing admiring glances as it pulled up neatly into a parking space. 'Alexis, do you think two hours will be enough?' she asked as she fed the parking meter.

'Yes, that should be more than enough.'

The women strolled arm in arm along Queen Street, looking at all the various suits in the shop windows. And then into Castle Street, and giggled like schoolgirls when they imagined what Slider would look like in a suit. 'Tell you what, we'll take the next turning on the left into High Street and walk down to St Mary Street and have a coffee.'

'Please Rose, don't mention that word coffee, it gives me a vision of you know who. I've never known anyone drink so much coffee as he does, and as for his peeing, well, it's no wonder he wet the bed.' The sound of their hysterical laughter drew glances from passers-by.

'Let's go in here and have a cup of tea before I faint.' They entered a small family-run café. Alexis ordered two cups of tea and two toasted tea cakes. Out of the side window, she could just see the clock tower of Cardiff Castle. 'That's a beautiful castle, Rose. When was it built?'

'Well, there's always been a fortress on that site, even going back to the times of the Romans. But I believe it was Lord Bute who paid to have it built. I think he also built several of the university buildings, and in recognition they named a park after him, Bute Park, which is behind the castle.' The teas and toasted tea cakes duly arrived, piping hot, with butter seeping through the sides. With butter covering her lips Rose inquired, 'So tell me, Alexis, have you a family back in London?'

'Yes, I've got a husband, Roberto. We live in a three-storey townhouse in Kensington. And apart from my TV work, I also help my husband to make wedding cakes, which we make together in the large basement of our house. And that reminds me, I'm going to have to go back to London for a while; my husband's been frantic with worry about Alice, and he needs to see her.'

'Yes, I can understand that. When will you have to leave?'

'Tomorrow, although I'll be back in time for Slider's trial.' Alexis looked at her watch just as the clock tower was striking twelve. 'We'd better get going if we're to join the rest for lunch at one thirty.' Having left the café, they crossed the road to look at suits in several different outlets. Alexis commented on how beautiful the city centre was, with its arcades running off the main streets. They ventured down one and entered a family-run tailor's which had several suits that caught Alexis's eyes.

'He's not going to wear something like that,' said Rose.

'You leave Slider to me. I'll make him wear a bloody kilt if I have to.' Alexis carefully examined the label on a two-piece suit that had caught her eye. It had a charcoal-grey lining with three internal pockets. And on the outside it had two buttons to fasten the jacket, with two pockets on the right side and one on the left, including a top pocket.

'That's a very nice suit, but don't you think you're being a bit extravagant?'

'No, after what he did for me nothing's too much for Slider. But don't tell him I said that.' After handing the suit to the sales assistant, Alexis looked at the shirts and picked out two, and chose a few ties which she thought would go nicely with the suit.

Rose said, 'To be perfectly honest with you, I've never seen Slider wear a tie.'

'Well, he's going to have to wear one at his trial, and there's going to be a lot of people who he needs to impress.'

As they left, Rose carried the plastic bag containing the shirts and ties, while Alexis carried the suit. They walked back up St Mary Street and turned into the High Street Arcade and worked their way back onto Queen Street. The walk back to the car was uneventful and they made it back with just six minutes remaining on their parking ticket.

* * *

Once Rose's car was out of sight they trooped back into the house. They were careful not to say a word to the throng of reporters, who were still continually asking questions about Slider. Roger talked with Sergeant Dunscombe for a few minutes and went inside, closing the front door. Becky adopted her usual position, which was on the piano seat, and started to play a few scales. On hearing the piano being played, Alice came into the front room with a cold drink in hand and stood beside her. 'Would you like me to teach you a few scales?' Draining her glass of Cola Alice nodded, took her empty glass back to the kitchen and handed it to Pam, who was washing a few cups and saucers, then ran back and sat on the piano seat next to Becky.

Meanwhile, in the rear garden, Andy was feeding the goldfish. He was joined by Roger, and together they tried

151

to count the number of baby goldfish. The water was green and cloudy which made it difficult. 'How often does your father clean the pond filter?' he asked, as he stared into the water.

'Not very often. He says he's going to do it but something else always gets in his way.'

'Well, I'll come over tomorrow morning, and if it's not raining I'll do it. You'll also have to watch out for frogs who will eat the smaller goldfish.'

'I didn't know that!'

'Yes, and the cats and birds. It's always best to put some netting over the pond to protect the fish.'

Pam joined them in the garden. 'Rog, you haven't forgotten that we are meeting Slider at midday, have you?'

'No, I've spoken to the sergeant and the taxi will be here at a quarter to twelve.'

Pam looked at Andy and told him that a letter was on the mantelpiece addressed to him, from his school. The young man went inside and read it. Andy couldn't contain his excitement. So much so that he hugged his sister and Alice. The shouting and cheering brought Roger and Pam scurrying in from the garden.

'Whatever is it?' asked Pam, who was panting for breath.

'You're never going to believe this.'

'Go on, read it out,' said Roger, who was laughing.

'Dear Andy and Becky,

The board of school governors met last week, and it has been decided that it would be unfair to ask you both to sit your exams while your father is awaiting his trial.

Therefore, your exams will be put back to the autumn of this year. And to give you time to revise, you and your sister will not have to return to school until Monday, September 3rd, 2018 when the new term starts.

Yours sincerely,

Mr John Jeffries CBE (Head of Cardiff Middle School.)'

After he'd read it, Andy handed the letter to Roger who handed it to Pam, saying, 'You lucky pair of buggers, you.' Becky was also jumping up and down, and Andy had to grab hold of his sister to prevent her from falling over. Alice remained on the piano seat, laughing. The doorbell rang. Roger opened the front door and Sergeant Dunscombe informed them that the Carver taxi had arrived. It only took a few minutes to lock the shed door, feed Sooty, and put their coats on 'You'd better take the letter with you to show to your parents.'

They walked down the driveway to the awaiting car. Roger and Pam sat together as did Alice and Becky. Andy took up his usual position, which was next to the driver. The number of TV crews and reporters had diminished considerably, prompting Pam to ask Roger. 'Where do you think they've all gone?'

'I don't care where they've all gone; at least we'll have a bit of peace and quiet for a while.' The roads around the suburb of Llandaff North were quiet, apart from the roadworks which seemed to spring up every few weeks and take forever to complete. Once they were on the dual carriageway the journey to the Sparta nursing home was a relatively short journey. When they arrived at the nursing home, they realized why there were hardly any reporters around the house. The car park and entrance were surrounded with camera crews, all contesting for the best positions. 'Andy, you and your sister had better come with me; Pam will help Alice out of the car.'

'OK.'

The staff at the private nursing home were on hand to help the passengers to exit the car and get through the hordes of camera crews and reporters. Once they were inside they were greeted by Rachel Rees.

'You made it through the melee of reporters?'

'Only just. That's not something we would want to do every day though,' said Pam, exhaling hard.

'Mr Slider is expecting you. If you follow me, I will take you through to the lounge.' The children already knew where to go and ran on ahead. As they walked past the dining room and into the lounge, they were greeted by Slider and his wife Lily who were waiting for them.

'Oh, Slider, it's so good to see you again.' Roger hugged him and looked visibly moved.

Pam stepped in and placed the palms of her hands on either side of his face and kissed him on the lips, quietly murmuring, 'It's nice to see you looking so well.' Lily led them to the sofas and Slider took a seat in the middle of the three-seater, with his wife on one side and Pam on the other. Roger sat in the armchair. The sound of talking brought Barbara out of the kitchen. Pots of tea and coffee were ordered and Barbara was informed that Roger and Pam would be staying for lunch.

'So, how are you feeling now, mate?' Roger asked.

'I'm feeling a lot better now, though it was touch and go for a while. Jumping into that sea was the most frightening experience of my life.' Taking hold of his wife's hand he continued, 'While I was in that freezing water my whole life seemed to flash in front of me. I thought only of Lily and my children and wondered if I would ever see them again. This experience has changed me forever, Rog, and it's reminded me that life is precious and that my wife and children will always come before anything else.'

Barbara trundled into the lounge and placed the pots containing the tea and coffee, as well as a tray with the cups, saucers, jug of milk, and sugar, on the coffee table in front of the large sofa. 'Is there anything else I can get you?'

'No, thank you, Babs, we're fine,' replied Lily, who was looking quite tired. Pam began pouring the teas and coffees and remarked how posh the nursing home was.

'Pam,' said Slider, 'it's like a five-star hotel here. I've never seen anything like this before.'

Roger smiled at him. 'It's a good job you have Alexis looking after you.'

Slider picked up his coffee cup, took a sip, and placed it back down. 'I owe Alexis everything; without her ... well, I don't know where I would be.'

'Well, you can start by being a bit nicer towards her. She's done an awful lot for this family and you could try to be less snappy towards her,' said his wife sharply as she stirred her tea.

'When am I ever snappy?'

'All the time, Dad,' said Becky, who had run in from the bedroom.

'Not you as well. You know I don't mean anything by it.'

'Well, that's the point, darling; we know you don't mean anything by it but Alexis doesn't. So please try a bit harder to be nice ... Yes?'

'Oh, for pity's sake … Pam, am I ever hard work?'

Pam had her teacup glued to her mouth and wasn't saying anything.

'Dad, can Alice and I play the piano for a bit?'

'Of course you can, darling. There, see how nice I can be,' he said as he looked at each one in turn. They exchanged knowing glances and started to giggle. 'What?'

'Oh, darling, why don't you show Roger and Pam around, while Alice and I listen to Becky play? And find out what that son of yours is up to.' Slider gave them a tour of their rooms and en suite facilities, which they found jaw-dropping. He spoke of his upcoming meetings with the solicitors and the press conference which was scheduled for five o'clock the following day, and then slowly guided them back to the lounge. 'Did you see Andy?'

'Yes, he's playing games on his laptop. I also told him that lunch was at one thirty and not to be late.'

* * *

Rose decided to take the scenic route back to the Sparta nursing home and drove along Roath Park Lake, which Alexis thought was stunning, especially as today the sun was out and several rowing boats could be seen on the water, along with a vast array of waterfowl that inhabit the lake. This made it a magical moment for both. It was twenty-five past one when they finally reached the nursing home, and a honk-honk on the horn soon brought out the three excited children.

'Hi, Aunty Rose, is that my Dad's new suit?' asked Andy.

'No, this is his shirts and ties which you can carry, and please put them on his bed carefully.'

'I've been teaching Alice a few scales on the piano,' said Becky, who in the eyes of Rose always seemed very mature for her age.

Alexis put her arm around her daughter. 'Hello, darling, and what have you been doing?'

'Becky's been teaching me the piano.'

'Has she indeed? I suppose that will be on your list to Father Christmas this year.' Alice took her mother's hand and they all walked inside, where Slider and his wife were chatting with Pam and Roger, and plonked themselves down on the sofas. Barbara appeared and announced that lunch would be ready in a few minutes and would be soup, battered haddock with chips and peas or pasta.

'Sounds wonderful, Babs,' said Slider, who had moved to stand behind Alexis. He slowly leaned over the sofa and whispered in her ear, 'Have you bought me something nice?'

'You know I have, but what you'll make of it God only knows.'

'Can I try it on now?'

'No, we're having lunch shortly and it would be just like you to get something down the front of it.'

'Come on, I'm not that bad!'

'Oh, Dad.'

'That's right, Becky, take the women's side. Rog, back me up!'

'Sorry, mate, I'm staying out of this one.'

It started just as a little giggle at first, but the laughter grew and grew, and even Slider got caught up in the laughter.

'Yes, I suppose you're right.'

During lunch, Alexis tapped the side of a wine glass with a knife to get everyone's attention. When the room fell silent she said, 'I've got two important announcements to make. Firstly, I'm travelling back to London tomorrow evening with my daughter. Her father hasn't seen her since the accident and has been fraught with worry. Also, and I'm sorry to drop it on you like this, Slider, there's going to be a press conference in this room at five o'clock tomorrow afternoon when the various TV networks will gather, along with the newspaper reporters, to talk about the incident on the pier and the subsequent rescue. It had to happen sooner or later so I've chosen tomorrow.'

Slider looked dumbstruck and after a few seconds said, 'So who will you want at this conference?'

'Well, obviously yourself and your wife. I'll be there with Alice and my solicitor Irene Asher and her assistant Lynn Williams. They'll be taking control of the conference and will deal with any awkward questions.'

The remainder of the lunch was eaten in relative silence, with everyone engrossed in their own thoughts. Once the plates had been removed, Barbara started passing the teas and coffees around, and to break the stillness and to spark some life and conversation back into their lunch, Alexis looked at Slider and said, 'Why don't you try on your new suit?'

'I'm not sure; I feel a bit deflated.'

'Go on, Dad, let's see it on you!' said his son, smiling.

'Alright, anything for a quiet life.'

'Go on, you know you want to,' said Rose, who was sitting with her arm around her sister. Slider picked up the plastic suit bag from the armchair and carried it into his bedroom. Rose looked at Alexis and raised her eyebrows. Alexis knew what was coming. She sat nonchalantly staring at the walls and started counting in her head. She had reached seven when the expletives started.

From a distance, it was difficult for everyone to make out exactly what he was saying. But the adults in the room certainly knew. He strode out of his bedroom and into the dining room, threw both arms out to the side and stated in a loud voice.

'It's blue!'

Alexis got up out of her chair, walked over to Slider and asked him to turn around, which he did grudgingly.

'It's a very good fit.'

'I thought you were buying me a black suit!'

'No, it was never my intention to buy you a black suit and I'll tell you why. When I graduated from the London School of Economics, my father bought me a blue suit and his words to me were, "The importance of a good blue suit can never be overstated. A blue suit is the most versatile of accoutrements." So, I hope you'll look after this suit and come to cherish it. One final point, you should always wear brown shoes with a blue suit, never black. Do you understand?'

'Yes.'

'I bought him a pair of brown shoes last Christmas, but he never wears them,' said Lily, who was chatting to Pam. 'It looks very good on you, darling. Now go and take it off before you spill something on it.'

'Dad, I think it looks better than a black suit,' said Andy, who was spooning down his ice cream.

Out of her office window, Rachel Rees caught sight of a grey Carver taxi pulling up outside the main entrance. The driver got out and opened the rear door and out stepped a woman who looked to be in her early thirties. She had shoulder-length fair hair and was wearing black trousers with a short black jacket. The driver lifted her silver-coloured suitcase from out of the car. The receptionist was waiting to greet her as she entered the foyer.

'Good afternoon, I'm Rachel Rees, how may I help you?'

'Hello, I'm Janey O'Mara, and I'm a Carver executive at our main office in Ireland, and I've come to visit Mr Matthew Slider who is a driver for our company and is recovering at this nursing home.'

'If you just wait here for a moment I'll go and find Alexis for you.'

'Excuse me, is Alexis the mother of the little girl who fell into the sea?'

'Yes, she is.' The receptionist found Alexis in the lounge and spoke quietly in her ear. 'There's a Janey O'Mara in reception who's here to visit Mr Slider.'

'Did she say where she's from?'

'She says that she's a Carver executive from Ireland and has just flown over today to visit him.' Alexis followed Rachel Rees to reception and introduced herself to Ms O'Mara.

'Hello, I'm Alexis Polti and I'm so happy to meet you. I wondered if anyone from Carver's management was going to pay Mr Slider a visit.' The two women shook hands.

'I'm Janey O'Mara, and it's nice to meet you. I've been on holiday on a yacht in the Indian Ocean and I only found out about the terrible accident two days ago. I've been travelling non-stop to get here. How are your daughter and Mr Slider?'

'Both are recovering very well, thank you. If you would like to follow me I'll introduce you to them.'

As they walked along the corridor towards the lounge, Ms O'Mara glanced at Alexis and asked, 'Has either your daughter or Mr Slider sustained any injuries?'

'Thankfully not, and considering what they've been through they're in remarkably good condition. A bit tired but overall both are in surprisingly good health. By the way, please call me Alexis.'

'Thank you, Alexis, and please call me Janey.'

The two women smiled at each other and entered the lounge. Slider had changed out of his new suit and was lazing, eyes closed, on the leather recliner in his black jeans, white T-shirt, and dressing gown when Alexis's voice and a tap on his shoulder awakened him.

'Alexis, can't I have just a few moments of peace without you disturbing me?'

She looked at Janey and said, 'I'm afraid you'll have to get used to Slider and his ways. Come on, wake up, there's somebody here to see you.'

He opened his eyes, yawned, and was startled to see another woman standing next to Alexis. He roused himself and stood up, held out his right hand, and introduced himself. 'Hello, I'm Matthew Slider and I'm pleased to meet you.'

'Hello, I'm Janey O'Mara and I'm a Carver executive from Ireland, and I'm so pleased to meet you at last. I couldn't believe it when I read the transcript of what you had done, and I would like you to know that everyone at the Carver corporation is very, very proud of you, and the actions that you took.' She turned to Alexis. 'So, where is your daughter?'

'She's about somewhere, probably playing with Slider's children. You'll see her before you leave, but if you'll excuse me, I have a phone call to make.'

'While we're on our own, Mr Slider, I would like you to know that Carver will be taking care of the bill for this nursing home and your legal expenses, plus you'll be receiving a generous bonus. I spoke with our CEO earlier today and he would like to invite you and your family to holiday in New York, plus a guided tour of our head office.'

'Thank you, Janey, that's kind of you, but you'd better talk to Alexis about the bill for my stay here. She's been exceptionally good to me, and I wouldn't want you to upset her. And please, call me Slider.'

'Don't worry yourself, Slider, I run the Carver network in Ireland and wouldn't dream of upsetting anyone.'

'Well, that's good to know. Why don't you join us all for a cup of coffee and you can meet the family?'

'Thank you, I would like that.'

He led Janey to the far side of the lounge where Lily, Rose, Roger, and Pam were sat talking about tomorrow's press conference. 'Everyone, I would like you to meet Janey O'Mara who's from the Carver office in Ireland, and she's flown over today especially to visit me.'

Introductions were made and Lily asked, 'Will you be staying for the press conference tomorrow?'

'Well, I didn't know there was one until you just mentioned it, but yes, I will be here for that. What time is it due to start?'

'The TV cameras and the press will be allowed inside from three thirty, and it will start at five o'clock.'

'Have you had lunch today, Janey?' asked Pam.

'I had something to eat on the plane, but a cup of tea would be nice.' Pam headed off to the kitchen to find Janey a cup and saucer, and duly poured her a cup of Earl Grey tea.

'So how long will you be staying with us in Cardiff?' asked Lily.

'I'll be staying here for as long as it takes.' She looked at Slider and said, 'Mr Slider is now a VIP and I want to make sure that everything is being done to help with his recovery and his impending court case. I also want to make it clear that I'm not here to interfere with the work that Alexis is doing. I know that she has worked tirelessly for him, and I want to work with her and not step on her toes.'

'Did I hear my name mentioned?' asked Alexis who was edging towards the group.

'Yes, you did. I was just saying that Carver and I would like to help you in any way that we can, but we don't want to interfere with or alter any plans that you might already have made for Mr Slider.'

'Thank you, Janey, I think you've come just in the nick of time because after tomorrow's conference, I'll have to travel back to London with my daughter, Alice. Her father has been at his wits end with worry as he hasn't seen her since the accident and it will also give me a break.'

'So, Alexis, what's next on the agenda?'

'I had a phone call from my solicitor Irene Asher not so long ago, and she will be here within the hour, accompanied by her assistant Lynn Williams.'

Pam spoke to Lily and told her that she and Roger would be leaving shortly and going back to the house. 'You don't have to rush off just yet, Pam,' said a tired-looking Lily.

'Well, we can see how busy you're both going to be, so we'll get out of your hair and go back to the house. Oh, and before I forget, Andy's had a letter from his school.'

'OK, thanks for letting me know.'

Roger and Pam put their coats on and walked with Lily and Rose towards the main entrance. Slider found the children and told them to come and see them off. Then the customary round of kisses began. They entered the taxi and were waved off by everyone.

'Now, what's this letter from the school about?' asked his mother.

'Oh, that.'

'Yes, that. Let me have a look at it, please?'

Lily read the letter and handed it to her husband. 'You're a lucky pair of so-and-sos.'

Becky was giggling as Andy said, 'This is like our best Christmas and birthday presents all rolled into one.'

'Well, just remember, you two, you still have to do some studying if you're going to pass your exams at   the end of the year.'

'Yes, we both know that, Dad!'

'Right, let's all go back inside, and I for one could do with a cup of coffee.'

'So, Alexis, which room will you be using for tomorrow's press conference?'

'Well, Janey, everyone needs to be comfortable and relaxed so I would personally use the lounge area. What do you think?'

'How about if we turn all the sofas and armchairs so they are all facing towards the dining room, which will give seating for eight people?'

'Well, I make it ten people in our group, so the kids will either have to sit on the floor or on someone's lap. Yes, that will work nicely.'

Slider, who was sat drinking coffee, noticed through the lounge window another taxi pulling up in front of the entrance. 'Alexis!'

'Yes.'

'We've got more visitors.'

'It's Irene Asher and Lynn Williams, my solicitors.'

'Oh, for pity's sake, please tell me you're joking!' said Slider, who was shaking his head.

'No, but what were you expecting? A younger woman wearing a red Giorgio Armani jacket with matching skirt, back-seam stockings, red stilettos, and perhaps designer glasses?'

'No, not exactly, though that would have been nice, but the one on the left is wearing a green tweed jacket and skirt, a brown hat with brown shoes, and she could have her knitting in that bag that she's carrying. And as for the other one, she looks like she's just stepped out of the nineteen thirties. They're like Miss bloody Marple and Miss Lemon!'

Alexis and Janey were reduced to fits of hysterical laughter, and when it ceased Alexis wiped her eyes, looked at Janey and blurted, 'Can you see what I've had to put up with?'

'Mr Slider, I do like a man with a sense of humour, but please remember these two women are all that stand between your freedom and jail, so please treat them with the utmost respect. But in the unfortunate event that you should go to jail, I can assure you that Carver will keep you well supplied with porridge oats.'

'Alexis knows that I was only joking.'

'Slider, I'll be glad when I can get back to London and have some peace and quiet.' With that, she started to walk towards the main entrance to greet her solicitors.

'You'll miss me though?'

Alexis softly murmured something that he couldn't quite hear.

TEN

The ladies entered Sparta nursing home and were warmly greeted by Alexis. 'Irene, Lynn, it's so very good to see you both.'

With the formality of hugs and kisses duly taken care of, Irene asked, 'So, what's this Mr Matthew Slider like?'

Alexis escorted Irene and Lynn towards the lounge and on the way said, 'You're going to love Slider, he's incorrigible. He drinks coffee by the gallon which results in him paying a visit to the loo every five minutes and his sense of humour and off-the-cuff remarks will have you laughing and screaming at the same time. When he saw you exit the taxi, he commented that the two of you look like Miss Marple and Miss Lemon.'

'I rather like Miss Lemon,' said Lynn, chuckling.

'Well, we'll soon put Mr Slider in his place,' said Irene, who was glaring at Alexis, and not finding it funny.

'Please, don't be too hard on him, it's just his manner. I found him a difficult man when I first met him but I've grown used to his ways, and he and his family mean a lot to me.'

'Soppy girl. Lead the way, let's see what he looks like.'

On seeing the arrival of Alexis's solicitors, Slider had quickly changed out of his jeans and T-shirt and was looking smart in a pair of black trousers and white shirt. He had also shaved and combed his hair. He was sat on a sofa chatting to his wife when Alexis and her solicitor appeared.

'Slider, I would like you to meet my solicitor Irene Asher and her assistant Lynn Williams.'

He stood up and walked around the side of the sofa, held out his right hand and shook hands with them. 'Hello, I'm Mr Matthew Slider, and I'm pleased to meet you both. Please call me Slider.'

'Well, Slider, it's finally nice to meet you at last. I've read a lot about you in the newspapers and that was a truly heroic rescue that you performed. It's such a pity that a female police officer was injured in the process. Now, you can call me Irene and this is my assistant Lynn, and you'll find us much more accommodating than Miss Marple or Miss Lemon.'

He looked Alexis in the eye. 'Oh great, thank you very much!'

'Sorry, I couldn't resist it.'

'Don't you worry yourself; my assistant and I have heard it all before and we're not easily offended. All we ask of you is that you're honest with us at all times. But what we don't want, and what will offend us, is some fact that you have failed to mention coming to light. Do we understand each other?'

'Yes, perfectly.'

Janey O'Mara emerged from the kitchen and joined the group.

'Irene, Lynn, I would like you to meet Janey O'Mara who is a Carver executive and will be standing in for me when I leave for London.'

'Hello, I'm very pleased to meet you both. I saw you arrive and I've ordered us a pot of tea.'

'Thank you, Janey, that will be most welcome. Why don't we make ourselves comfortable and talk about tomorrow's press conference, but I'll need to speak with Slider privately.'

Barbara entered the dining room and wheeled her trolley into the lounge. 'Thanks, Babs, we can help ourselves from here,' said Alexis.

'Are there any others here?'

'No, I've told them all to make themselves scarce for an hour or so, I think they've all disappeared into one of the bedrooms.'

The conversation between the five of them was difficult for Slider, who was more used to talking with a group of men rather than women. He felt as if he was being examined by Irene, who hadn't spoken a word. Her eyes though were fully focused on him, as if she were trying to get the measure of the man she would be defending. He interrupted the women and said, 'If you don't mind me saying so, you're being rather quiet, Irene.'

'Well, sometimes it's better to listen than to talk.'

'So, do you think I could go to jail?'

'Yes, I do, but it's up to me to make sure that doesn't happen, which is why I need you to be truthful with me at all times. If you can't remember something just say so.'

Slider got up and poured himself a second cup of coffee and held the cup to his mouth when Alexis cheekily said, 'And you'd better cut down on your coffee drinking, we can't have you running back and forth from the witness box when you're in the courtroom.' He looked pensive as he stared at the abstract art pictures hanging around the room.

'Don't worry yourself, there's a long way to go and we'll be meeting the police after tomorrow's conference and a better understanding of your position will emerge.'

'Thank you, Irene.'

'Now, if you've finished your coffee I think we should go and have a quiet talk somewhere, and you can give me an account of exactly what happened on Penarth Pier.' The group broke up with Slider, Irene, and her assistant Lynn all leaving the comfort of the lounge and slowly they sauntered along the corridor to a small meeting room that had been reserved for them. The three entered the room which had a wooden table in the middle and two chairs on either side of it, and no windows. 'Right, Slider, I'm going to ask you some questions about that incident on the pier, and I want you to answer truthfully. Lynn will be taking notes. Is that understood?'

'Yes'

'So, your full name is Matthew Slider, you're forty-two years old, you're married to Lily Slider and you have a daughter Becky who is nine years old and a son Andy who is eleven. Is that correct?'

'Yes, it is.'

'So, what is your occupation?'

'I work for Carver, who are a private hire taxi company, and I've been working for them for eighteen months, although I have been a private hire driver for sixteen years.'

'Now let's talk about Monday, May the seventh, two thousand and eighteen, the day of the accident. Explain to me what brought you to Penarth Pier.'

'I collected a fare, an ambulance woman from the University Hospital of Wales in Cardiff. I drove her to the University Hospital Llandough, which is on the outskirts of Penarth. There I decided to drive to Penarth Pier, which is about a ten-minute drive away, for a bacon roll and a cup of coffee.'

'Why didn't you drive back to Cardiff and have something to eat and drink there?'

'I've been diagnosed with a tension headache for more than ten years, and the sun that morning was very bright, and it had brought on my headache. Sea air seems to alleviate my headache somewhat.'

'Are you currently on any medication?'

'I've been taking tablets on and off for the past ten years. I've taken Amitriptyline, Duloxetine and now I'm taking Nortriptyline, but none of these tablets have helped my condition.'

'Do you have your tablets with you?' He took from his pocket the white plastic container with his tablets in, and placed it on the table in front of her. She looked closely at the label and handed it back to him. 'Right, we've established how you arrived at Penarth, now talk to me about parking the car and walking onto the pier.'

'After driving through Penarth town centre, I drove down the hill towards the pier and spotted two parking places close to the pier and reversed into one of them.'

'What happened next?'

'The sun was very bright and shining directly right into my face so, I slid my seat back, closed my eyes, and took several deep breaths.'

'What happened when you opened your eyes?'

'I saw a large container ship heading towards the docks in Cardiff. As I looked to my right I saw Alexis Polti walking along the pavement towards the entrance of the pier, and in front of her was Alice, who was hand in hand with her nanny, Victoria.'

'Carry on.'

'My view was suddenly blocked by two single-deck coaches which pulled up and stopped right in front of me. A large party of schoolgirls then exited the coaches.'

'Go on.'

'I was intrigued to find out if it was Alexis Polti who I'd seen. I locked the car and walked across the road but my view was blocked by the schoolgirls. The next time I saw Alexis was on Gwennap Head.'

'So, tell me what happened when you entered the pier?'

'When I eventually got onto the pier I headed towards the two white kiosks which sold food and drinks. But the large number of schoolgirls surrounding the kiosks made it impossible for me to be served. So I decided to take a walk to the end of the pier. I noticed a man fishing, so I went and had a chat with him.'

'Continue.'

'After five minutes or so, I walked back to the kiosks and eventually found myself at the head of the queue. I was about to give the girl my order when there was a very loud scream from Victoria.'

'Now, Slider, take it nice and slow.'

'Time stood still for a few seconds as nobody knew where the scream had come from. I saw Victoria walking backwards, towards the centre of the pier. There was a terrible look of anguish about her. She had her right arm parallel to the ground and was pointing with her index finger. A large group of schoolgirls all rushed to the side of the pier and were screaming and pointing down at the sea below us.'

'So, at this point Alice Polti had fallen into the sea?'

'Yes, that's correct.'

'So, what did you do?'

'I ran to the handrail and saw Alice lying face down in the water. I ran back to the kiosk and told the girl what had happened and told her to phone the police and coastguard. I handed over my wallet and car keys; my own phone had been left on charge in the car.'

'Now we have arrived at a pivotal moment. What did you do after handing over your keys and wallet?'

'I ran through a crowd of schoolgirls to get to the handrail. I had one leg over the rail when somebody grabbed me by the collar and pulled me to the floor. When I got to my feet, I realized it was a female police officer who had pulled me back. I shouted at her and asked her why she had stopped me.'

'What did she say?'

'She told us all to get to the far side of the pier and that help was on its way.'

'So, what did you do when told to move?'

'Well, Alice was drowning and there was no sign of any help forthcoming, so I took it upon myself to do something.'

'And that was?'

'Well, time was of the essence and the police officer was blocking my way, so I stepped forward and knocked her to the ground, which gave me the time to get over the handrail and jump into the sea.'

'How did you knock the female police officer to the ground?'

'I punched her on the jaw.'

His solicitor shook her head. 'Why didn't you just push her out of your way, why punch her?'

'I had to make sure that I could get past her; pushing her might not have been enough.'

'I see. I'm sorry to have to ask you this, but have you ever hit your wife?'

'You what?' he yelled. 'You of all people ask me a question like that!'

'Mr Slider, this is the type of questioning that you will be faced with at your trial, and your prosecutors will be trying to ascertain if you're a violent man who hits women. So, what is your answer?'

'No! I've never hit my wife or any other woman.'

'Good, I'm glad to hear it. Would you like a cup of coffee now?'

'Yes, I would … I'm sorry for that outburst.'

'Don't worry, you're doing just fine.'

Slider got up and left the room. Irene was chatting to her assistant when Alexis put her head around the door. 'How's my boy doing?'

'Well, he's got a bit of a temper, but he'll be fine.'

Slider was drinking coffee and looked lost in thought when Alexis approached him. 'How did it go?'

'Not too bad.' He took a mouthful of coffee and said, 'There's something that's been bothering me about you.'

She sat down next to him. 'Go on.'

'On the day of the accident you were wearing a red coat, but I didn't see you on the pier. So where did you disappear to?'

'You didn't see me on the pier because I didn't go onto the pier. I said goodbye to my daughter and Victoria at the entrance to the pier, and went into the sweet shop to buy a stick of rock. Then I got into a waiting taxi which took me up to Penarth town centre, where we were filming a TV programme for Channel 5.'

'I knew I couldn't have missed seeing you on the pier.'

'Stalking me, were you?' she said with a laugh.

'No, not exactly. But I was sat in my car and I saw Victoria walking hand in hand with Alice and you were just behind them, and I just wasn't sure if it was you that I saw, so I went onto the pier to have a closer look.'

'So you wanted to check me out'?'

'If you want to put it like that, then yes.'

'Do you like the TV programmes that I make?'

'I like them a lot. I can't believe, though, that people can be so stupid when they go into business for themselves. They seem to think that all they have to do is to get a manager in and a few others, and they can just sit back, count the profit, and the business will run itself.'

'That's why I have to return to London, to make sure that my husband and staff are OK.'

'I'd like to meet the rest of your family one day.'

'When your trial is over and you're fully fit, and if you're not in jail, I'd like nothing more for you and your family, as well as Rose, to come and spend some time with my family at our home in London.'

Slider planted a kiss on her cheek. 'Thank you, and if you ever need a driver, well, you've got my number.'

Barbara appeared from the kitchen and approached Alexis and Slider who were still sitting together.

'Excuse me for asking, but what time would you like to have dinner tonight?'

'Well, Babs, shall we say dinner for six thirty.'

'And will your guests be staying?'

'Yes, there will be three more for dinner tonight.'

Slider stood up, looked at Alexis and muttered, 'My headache's come back, so I'm going to lie down.'

The following afternoon at three o'clock, Rachel Rees saw the first of the white Sky TV vans pulling into the car park, closely followed by two Sky saloon cars. She had barely stepped outside to greet them before camera crews and other personnel were busying themselves unloading cameras, uncoiling cables, and carrying various other pieces of paraphernalia into the dining room. There they were met head-on by Alexis who had seen it all before with her own TV film unit and wasted no time in outlining the area that they could use. Dining room tables and chairs were quickly moved to the far walls, and a boundary tape was placed down on the floor over which no one would be allowed to cross. Alexis approached a woman from Sky who seemed to be in charge. 'Hello, I'm Alexis Polti, and I'm looking after the Slider family and their friends. So, if there is anything you need or want then please come to me first.'

The women shook hands.

'Thank you, Alexis. I'm Lin Lee, and I'm pleased to meet you. I'm in charge of Sky's outside broadcasting unit. In fact, I worked with you many years ago when you were making a series for Channel 5. I had just graduated and was working as a coffee runner, and general dogsbody for the crew.'

Alexis laughed. 'Please, Lin, don't mention the coffee word around here; you'll understand why later.'

A group of men wearing jeans and T-shirts entered the dining room and started to position their tripods and cameras. Alexis spotted them and chatted with them briefly. Suddenly a deluge of men and women entered the dining room, all carrying pieces of recording equipment. The sound of people all talking at the same time and the sound of microphones being tested was quite overwhelming. Alexis clapped her hands firmly to try and regain some order in the room.

'Can I have your attention please.' The room fell quiet. 'Hello and welcome to you all, and thank you for coming. I'm Alexis Polti and I'm sure that some of you might have worked with me in the past and know of my reputation for getting the job done, so if you need anything then please come to me first. Tea and coffee urns have been set up for you by the double doors that you've just walked through, and toilets are by the exit doors.' Alexis spotted a familiar face in the crowd and walked over to him. 'Well, well, Paul Lumis, so how are you keeping these days? Channel 5 still got you running around after me?'

The man stopped what he was doing, and on seeing her smiling face hugged and kissed her. 'Alexis, it's so good to see you again. I've been so worried about you and your daughter. Is Alice OK?'

'Alice is doing very well, thank you, Paul. I'm so fortunate to have her back alive and well, and it's all down to Slider. Without him she would surely have drowned.'

'I'd love to meet him. What's he like?'

'Wait here and I'll go and fetch him.' A few moments later she returned to the dining room with Slider on her arm. On seeing him, the camera crews from the various TV networks and others from their entourage surrounded him and gave him a round of applause. Everyone was eager to shake his hand. Eventually, Alexis dragged him away and introduced him to Paul Lumis. 'Paul, I would like you to meet Slider. Slider, I would like you to meet Paul, who was my cameraman many years ago.'

'I must say this is a privilege for me to meet you. So how are you feeling now?'

'I'll feel a lot better once I've had a cup of coffee.'

'Leave it to me, I'll get it for you.'

'Thanks, Paul, milk with one spoonful of demerara sugar, please … So, who was that, an old boyfriend?'

'Don't be silly, he was someone who I worked with many years ago. How's the head now?'

'So, so.'

Paul returned with Slider's coffee, while Alexis drifted away to speak with an ITV reporter. 'Alexis was telling me that you used to work together in the past?'

'Yes, that's right, Alexis had a programme called *The Restorer* and I was her cameraman. It ran for about two years. So how long have you been a taxi driver?'

'Sixteen years now. In fact, you and I have similar jobs in a way, always meeting different people and travelling to obscure places.'

'Yes, I suppose you're right, except you have a nice warm car and I'm usually getting rained on.' The two men began laughing together. 'Can I ask you about the heroic act of bravery that you pulled off on the pier?'

'Not now, if you don't mind, my head is not too good, and you'll hear about it all very shortly.'

Alexis interrupted the men and dragged Slider away. 'It's quarter to five, so I suggest you go and check on everyone, and I'll be along in a few minutes.'

'OK.'

He went back to his bedroom and was confronted by his whole family who was all busying themselves.

'Dad, why is Aunty Rose always looking in the mirror? She's been there for ages.'

'Son, that is one of the great mysteries in life. As you get older you'll find that women are always looking in the mirror and take forever to get ready.'

'Well, it's not fair. I've got Mum, Aunty Rose, and Becky all pushing me out of the way, and I've not even combed my hair yet, and we're going to be on TV.'

'Oh, come here, Andy,' sighed Rose. 'Sit on the bed and I'll comb your hair. Do you want me to put some hair gel on you?'

'What's hair gel?' She showed him the plastic pot with the hair gel. He touched it with his finger. 'It's like jelly and sticky. No, thank you, Aunty Rose.'

'I've got gel on my hair, and it makes it all shiny and nice,' said Becky, who was helping her mother with the zip on her dress.

There was a knock on the door and the sound of Alexis's voice. 'How are we doing in there, are you nearly ready?'

Slider opened the door and was stunned to see Alexis wearing a short, figure-hugging red dress. 'Wow, you look great!'

'Thank you, now kindly avert your eyes. If you and your family are ready, then we can start.'

The Slider family entered the lounge and sat on one of the three-seater sofas. Slider sat in the middle with

Rose on one side and his wife on the other. Their two children were quite happy to sit on the arms of the sofa. Irene Asher and Lynn Williams occupied the other sofa, along with Janey O'Mara. Alexis sat in an armchair with her daughter, Alice. For a few moments, there was a stillness in the room.

Alexis stood up and walked to the centre of the lounge and addressed the gathering of reporters, journalists, and various TV networks. She introduced in turn the Slider family members and other important invited contributors and guests. And then said, 'When you're ready we'll begin.'

'Mr Slider, Clive Middleton from BBC. This is the first time that millions of people from Britain and around the world will hear your account of what happened on that terrible day, so how are you feeling today?'

'For the past ten years, I've been diagnosed with a tension headache and today is not a good day for my head. But apart from that I'm feeling quite well. My body is recovering well, and I'm hoping to return home within the next few days.'

'Do you think of yourself as some kind of hero?'

'I do,' said Alexis.

Slider laughed. 'Hero is just a word, a label if you like, and I think that my actions were justified.'

'Mr Slider.'

'Please, just call me Slider.'

'Do you think, Slider, that your actions of assaulting a young female police officer were justified?'

'You don't have to answer that question,' said his solicitor.

He looked at his solicitor. 'It's OK, it's a fair question to ask.' He turned back to the reporter. 'Did I badly hurt that female officer? No. Does she have life-changing injuries? No. Will she be able to return to work? Yes. In my estimation, all that's been damaged is that officer's pride, and if she'd had the guts to do what I did, she would now be a police sergeant and not the coward some people think she is.'

With that statement, applause went around the room.

Slider slowly walked over to Alice, picked her up in his arms, and held her aloft for all the cameras to see.

'If it wasn't for me, this young girl would surely have drowned. And I'm sure you wouldn't want that to have happened.'

'It's Daniel Pope from ITV. I was there to report the accident from the pier, and I was wondering if you thought you would drown on that day?'

'Let me tell you, Dan, jumping into the sea was the most frightening experience of my life. I had Alice in my arms, I was freezing to death in that seawater, and it was only the thought of my wife and children that kept me going. I was so fortunate to have HMS *Deacon* passing the pier. They saved our lives and I owe my life and the life of Alice Polti to the Royal Navy.'

'Linda Carter from Sky TV. When do you think you'll return to work?'

'I'm sorry, but that's the furthest thing from my mind.'

'Did you suffer any injuries at all?'

'Just a few scrapes and bruises, nothing major. Alice had a bad cut on her forehead, but you can see it's healed nicely.'

'Sian Wallmer reporting for Channel 5. Are you worried at all about your impending trial?'

'Well, I haven't been charged with anything yet, so no.'

'If you are charged with assault and are found guilty, does the prospect of going to jail worry you?'

'Well, Carver, my employer, has informed me that they will keep me well stocked with porridge oats in the event of that happening.' That remark sent a ripple of laughter around the room.

'If I may say so, you seem to be taking it all quite casually.'

'Well, at this moment I am an innocent man, so why worry about what might happen. I'll only start worrying when something does happen.'

'Do you think you should be awarded a medal for your heroic actions?'

'I think there are more deserving men and women who should be recognized for a medal rather than myself. I might have been a hero for one day, but some people put their lives on the line every day.'

'Sian Wallmer again. I would just like to say how refreshing it is to have someone who answers a question directly like you do. Usually when we interview people we never seem to get a direct answer to a question.'

'Well, Sian, that's the difference between the working class and the snobs. We working class always tell it like it is, whether you like it or not.'

Alexis looked at her watch; it was 5:55 p.m. She stood up. 'Thank you all very much, but we have run out of time and that I'm afraid was the last question, so unfortunately we'll have to bring this meeting to a close.' There was a round of applause and Slider stood up and hugged his wife.

'Well, darling, how did I do?'

'You were yourself, and I thought you handled the questions very well.'

Andy and Becky stood beside their father and put their arms around him. 'Dad,' said Becky, 'I thought you were great.'

'Why thank you, darling. What do you think, son?'

'I think you put them in their place.'

'Well, that was the general idea – always speak your mind and never worry what people may think about you.'

Alexis said, 'Well, Slider, that was an impressive show that you put on for us.'

'I'm glad you thought so. I tried to stay relaxed, and I remembered what Irene told me about not losing control of myself. So, yes, I was pleased with my performance.'

'What would you like to do now, darling?'

He looked at his wife. 'A cup of coffee, a shower, and then a lie-down until dinner.' With that, he and his family retired to their bedrooms for a well-earned rest.

It was a quarter to seven, and everyone was seated around the dining table, except for Slider.

'Becky, darling, go and find out what's taking your father so long.'

'Yes, Mum.' She knocked on her father's door. 'Dad, we're all waiting for you.'

'I'll be right there.' He walked slowly into the dining room, looking weary, and sat down next to his wife.

She looked at him. 'Is everything alright, darling, we were all wondering where you were.'

He looked around the table. 'I'm so sorry to have kept you all waiting, but I'm feeling rather run down tonight.'

'Don't you worry yourself. Being cross-examined by the media can take its effect on you. I've been a solicitor for over thirty years, and I'm still exhausted at the end of the day. And by the way, you did very well this afternoon. One criticism though: you do go blabbing on about things which are irrelevant to the question, so please try and stick to simple answers.'

He grinned. 'Yes, message understood.'

'I've ordered your steak well done as you were late, is that alright?' asked his wife, who was topping up various glasses with wine.

'Yes, that's how I like it, thank you.'

'I also think you deserve a glass of champagne tonight, after your wonderful performance,' said Alexis, who was tying a bow in her daughter's hair ribbon.

'Thank you, but I'll stick to the soft drinks if you don't mind. My head is not so good, and an early night might be called for.'

'Can I play the piano after dinner?' asked Becky, who was reaching for a drinking straw.

'Not tonight, darling, you can play tomorrow morning after breakfast. Tonight, I need a peaceful night's sleep.'

'OK, Dad.'

The conversation criss-crossed around the table, but Slider hardly said a word. Everyone around the table could see that he wasn't his usual self. Beads of perspiration could be seen on his forehead and his dinner was hardly touched.

His wife whispered in his ear, 'If you're not feeling very well, why don't you have an early night?'

'You won't mind if I leave the table?'

'Of course not.'

He stood up, announced that he wasn't feeling very well and left the table. Irene looked at Lily. 'Does your husband often have these headaches?'

'No, not very often, but he's been under such a lot of pressure and he's not the sort of man who often complains about his head so it must be pretty bad tonight. But tomorrow, he'll probably be back to his usual self, so don't worry, I've seen this happen many times.'

'Mum, I've just realized, I'm the only man around this table now that Dad's left, and you're all talking girlie things.'

'I'm sorry, son, if we've been neglecting you. So tell us what you've been doing then.'

'Well, I've been playing an on-line computer game called Castles and Wizards against Liwei. He's an eleven-year-old schoolboy in Singapore, and we've been playing the game for seven weeks and last night I finally beat him, and now I've got the fourth best score in the world,' he announced rather smugly.

'Well, son, that is very impressive, and I'm very proud of you.'

'Thanks, Mum.'

'So, Andy,' said Alexis, 'what do you want to do when you leave school?'

'I'd like to go to university and study computer science, and go on and make computer games or robots.'

'You know your way around a computer then?'

His mother laughed. 'Alexis, you wouldn't believe the trouble Slider gets himself into when he's on the computer. His favourite line is "Thank God for Andy."'

A ripple of laughter went around the table.

'If it's any consolation to your father, I also had the same problem,' said Irene. 'An awful lot of older people have problems involving computers, which is why schoolchildren such as Andy here are taught at such an early age. Right, Andy?'

'Yes, sometimes I have to tell my teacher, Mr Sedgebeer, what to do.'

'Becky, darling, will you go and have a look to see if your father's OK?'

'Yes, Mum.' Becky returned a few minutes later. 'Dad's asleep on the bed.'

'Thank you, darling.' The evening dinner continued, but without Slider's input it didn't really sizzle as it usually did. His jokes and one-liners were sadly missed by all.

ELEVEN

The following morning, the weather was bright and breezy in Cardiff. Lily had got up early to check on her husband, but found he was still sound asleep at seven thirty, which was unusual for him. The sound of plates and cutlery rattling led her to the kitchen, where Barbara was starting to prepare the morning breakfasts.

'Good morning, Babs, and how are you today?'

'The car wouldn't start this morning, so I was a bit late getting here.'

'I know that problem only too well. You wouldn't believe the times when we all had to push Slider's car to get it going.'

'I've just made a pot of tea, would you like a cup?'

'Yes, please, and I'll take a cup for Rose as well.'

'This is your last day with us then?'

'Yes, but it will be nice to go back home; there's nothing like your own bed to sleep in.'

Lily put two cups of tea on a tray and took them back to the bedroom that she shared with her sister and her children. She gently pushed the door wide open with her red slipper and put the tray down on the bedside table. 'Wake up, Rose, I've brought you a cup of tea.'

'What time is it?'

'It's twenty to eight and it might be a nice day today.'

Becky woke up, rubbed her eyes, and threw back the blue duvet. 'Morning, Mum, morning Aunty Rose.' She slowly walked the few steps across the bedroom and sat on the bed next to her mother.

'Did you have a nice sleep?' asked her mother who was stirring her tea.

'Yes. Mum, do we have to go home today?'

'Well, we can't stay here forever, can we, and I'm sure Sooty's missing you. Why don't you go and see if your father's awake?'

Becky knocked on the door but got no answer, so slowly she pushed the door open and turned on the light. 'Dad, are you awake?'

There was a slight movement from him, and a quiet voice said, 'What time is it?'

'It's a quarter to eight.'

'Turn off the light will you, darling, and go and get your father a cup of coffee.'

'OK. How's your head, today, Dad?'

'Not so good. I'll think I'll miss breakfast and have a few extra hours of sleep.' The young girl was carrying a cup of coffee back to her father's bedroom when Alexis saw her.

'How's your father today, Becky?'

'His head is still bad, and he says that he'll miss breakfast and sleep a bit more.'

'Will you tell him please that I'll come and see him at eight o'clock.'

'OK.'

At eight o'clock there was a gentle tapping on Slider's bedroom door. 'Slider, it's Alexis, can I come in?'

'Yes, but please don't put the light on.' On entering his bedroom, she struggled to see him as the blackout curtains were still drawn. She pushed them open slightly.

'Not too much, please.'

Slider was lying on top of his bed, curled up in the foetal position. Alexis realized that he was having a serious problem with his head today. She stroked his hair, kissed him on his cheek and whispered, 'You stay here and I'll see what I can get for you.' She gently closed the curtains and left the room. After talking to his wife, Alexis went to the pharmacy department and spoke to the doctor in charge. 'Good morning, I'm Alexis Polti, and I have a man in my care, a Mr Matthew Slider, who suffers from a chronic head migraine. Today he's having a particularly bad day, and I wondered if you have something which might help him?'

'If you can give me the name of his doctor and the address of the surgery, then I can see what medication he's been given, and I can prescribe something which might alleviate his pain.'

'It's Dr White, and the surgery is at two hundred and ten, Whitchurch Road, Cardiff.'

He took a few minutes to check the details. 'It seems Mr Matthew Slider has had a chronic migraine for more than ten years and has taken quite a few different tablets. And from my information, he is currently being prescribed Nortriptyline. Now, what we do have is something called Erenumab, which is injected into the body and has only recently been made available to the public.'

'We'll take it then.'

'Would you like to know the cost?'

'No, the cost is immaterial, just add it to my bill. I just want it administered as soon as possible.'

'What room number is Mr Slider in?'

'Room number two on the east wing.'

'I'll prepare the injection and a nurse will be there presently to administer it.'

'Thank you, doctor.'

It had just turned a quarter past eight when there was a tap on Slider's door. Alexis opened the door, and a young nurse in a blue uniform and carrying a syringe in an oval tray was standing in front of her. 'Hello, I'm Nurse Adams, and I've been asked to administer Mr Matthew Slider's injection.' On entering his room, the nurse found his whole family either sitting or standing around his bed, and the blackout curtains were only slightly open to keep the light to a minimum. 'Mr Slider, I'm Nurse Adams and I'm here to give you your injection. Could you lie on your back for me, please?'

'I hate injections,' he mumbled.

He rolled slowly onto his back. The nurse opened the curtains, pulled back the blanket on his bed, and asked, 'Can you put your right arm out for me please?' She disinfected his skin and administered the injection into his forearm. A plaster was applied over the puncture wound. 'There we are, all done,' she said smiling. The nurse placed the syringe back in the tray. Alexis thanked her for her help and opened the door for her to leave, then turned back to look at Slider.

'Well, I can't see Slider being able to go to the police station today, especially when he's in this condition. And I don't want to travel back to London when he's unwell, so I'm going to stay another night and travel back tomorrow. It's such a pity that Nurse Walsh had to leave when she did. Anyway, I'll let Irene know what's happening, and I suggest we all go and have breakfast and see what he's like at, say, midday. I'll also tell Babs we're all staying an extra night.'

The morning was a dull affair, with everyone trying to keep the noise to a minimum. The three children were together in one of the bedrooms, and Alexis, Lily, Rose, and Janey, who had joined them from her hotel, were in the lounge area discussing what to do with the rest of the day. Just before midday Slider emerged from his bedroom and walked slowly and steadily into the lounge, where he was confronted by four smiling faces. Lily walked quickly over to her husband, put her arms around him and kissed him. 'How are you feeling now, darling?'

'Surprisingly, a lot better, thank you; my head is a lot clearer.'

'Come and sit down with us, and I'll get you a cup of coffee.'

He was drinking his coffee when Alexis asked, 'What would you like to do this afternoon?'

'As it's a nice day I'd like to go out and get some fresh air, and I wouldn't mind going back to Penarth and have a walk on the pier. The sea air always benefits my head.'

'Well, you go and have a shower and get dressed, and we'll leave at, say, twelve thirty.' Alexis looked at the others, who were all in agreement. She walked to her bedroom where the children were playing and found the three of them constructing a jigsaw puzzle. 'Andy, Becky, you'll be pleased to know that your father is much better and we're all going to Penarth Pier in half an hour.'

At half past twelve two black Carver saloon cars were waiting at the entrance with the doors open. As they all came through the automatic doors Becky asked her father. 'Dad, can I sit in the front today?'

Her father, who was wearing his brown leather jacket, black jeans, and white vee neck T-shirt said, 'Of course you can.' The girl ran around to the front of the car with a large smile on her face. Lily, Andy, and Slider got in the back. In the other saloon car, Rose, Alice, and Janey sat in the back, while Alexis assumed her usual position, which was in the front. The journey to the pier usually took half an hour.

Alexis said to the driver as they pulled away, 'We're not in any great hurry to get there, so don't push it.'

Slider was back to his usual chirpy self, but as the car entered Penarth town centre his mood changed somewhat, and he became quiet. His wife noticed this straightaway and said, 'Are you alright?'

'Yes, don't worry, I'm fine. I'm just having a few flashbacks to the time when I drove along this road.'

The two cars exited the town centre and drove down the steep hill. Penarth Pier in all its glory came bursting into view. Slider's eyes were firmly fixed on the pier: the tide was high again, just like it was on that awful day. The two cars stopped directly outside the entrance to the pier and everyone got out. As the group assembled all eyes were on Slider. They could see that he was full of emotion, but nobody said a word. Janey talked to the two drivers, and the Carver vehicles pulled away.

Becky was staring at the sticks of rock in Ye Olde Sweet Shoppe's front window. 'Dad, can I have a stick of rock?'

'We're going onto the pier now, darling, and we're having fish and chips for lunch. You can have a stick of rock when we're leaving,' answered her mother.

Slider wasn't the only one who was full of emotion. As they walked onto the pier, popular music could be heard from the tannoy speakers which were sited on the roof of the café/restaurant. Alice suddenly broke down and started crying. Her mother knelt on the pier, put her arms around her daughter and quietly said, 'What's wrong, darling?'

'I'm scared, Mum.'

She rubbed her hand gently down her daughter's back. 'There's nothing to be scared of.'

'I'm afraid I might fall into the sea again.'

Her mother laughed. 'Don't be silly, you're not going to fall into the sea.'

On seeing this exchange Slider also knelt beside the little girl and said softly, 'If I carry you in my arms, I promise I won't let you fall into the sea. Would you like that?'

With tears still trickling down her red cheeks she said, 'Yes, please.'

He picked up the young girl and looked her in the face. 'And if you're a good girl I'll buy you some chips for lunch. Would you like that?'

'Yes, please, and can I have a sausage as well?' she asked cheekily.

The whole group was reduced to fits of laughter, which put everyone at their ease. And even Slider had lost his emotional tag and was back to his usual self. As they walked towards the two white kiosks, he glanced at the handrail from where he had jumped. He slowly walked to it and peered down into the sea. 'This is it,' he announced as the others congregated around him.

Everyone was silent and they looked down into the water. Becky slowly said, 'It's a long way down, Dad.'

'You're telling me it is, darling. Now, who would like fish and chips for lunch?'

He took the orders for lunch, and leaving Alice with the others he joined the queue at the same kiosk he'd been at prior to the accident. He was shocked to see the same young woman behind the counter. When he reached the head of the queue, she stood frozen at seeing him. 'Excuse me, sir, aren't you the man who handed me his wallet and car keys, then jumped into the sea to save a little girl?'

'Yes, that's me, I'm Matthew Slider.'

The young woman stopped what she was doing, opened the door, walked out onto the pier and stood in front of him. Looking slightly tearful she said, 'Mr Slider, it's so good to see you again and looking so well. Are you here on your own?'

'No, I'm with my wife and family, and we've also brought the young girl, Alice, who is here with her mother. Alice, come and say hello.' The little girl walked over to him. He scooped her up in his arms, and said, 'This is Alice Polti, the little girl who fell into the sea. Say hello, Alice.'

'Hello'

'Hello, Alice, I'm Amy, how are you?'

She put her arm around Slider's neck. 'Much better, thank you.'

'Please, Mr Slider, it would be an honour if this kiosk could treat you all to lunch on us.'

'Thank you, that's very kind and generous of you.'

'Think nothing of it, you're a hero, but could I have a photo of you all before you leave?'

'Of course you can.'

Andy barged up to them. 'Dad, can I have twenty pence for the telescope?'

'I'll be glad when you leave school and get a job! Asking me for money all the time … here's three. Let your sister and Alice have a look. And Andy …' warned his father, looking into his eyes.

'Yes, Dad.'

'No climbing on the handrail!'

'OK.'

Slider sat on the promenade bench with his wife on one side and Rose on the other. Alexis sat on the bench directly behind, with Janey, which allowed them to talk together. He had his arms around his wife and Rose. 'I love this,' he said, 'just smell that salt air.'

A few moments later Amy appeared carrying a tray with five portions of fish and chips, with plastic knives, forks, and the usual condiments. 'Come on, you three, it's lunchtime,' yelled Alexis, who was shaking vinegar onto her tray of food. The children squeezed in wherever they could. Amy reappeared with their trays of food, and everyone seemed happy and contented as they ate in relative silence, while taking in the views from the pier as well as gazing at the assorted pleasure craft and container vessels which constantly moved back and forth in front of them.

No sooner had they started to eat when out of nowhere a group of twelve boy scouts, dressed in their khaki short-sleeved shirts, dark blue corduroy shorts, wide-brimmed hats and accompanied by two older scouts, filed past them with their fishing gear in hand and proceeded to the very end of the pier. Slider was quiet for once as he ate and watched as the scouts assembled their fishing rods and reels. Memories came flooding back as he remembered when he used to take his son fishing, but the introduction of computers soon put paid to that. 'Andy, do you remember when I used to bring you here fishing?'

'Yes, Dad, and I can remember catching more than you.'

A large ripple of laughter emanated from the group when his father jeered, 'I don't think so; the only thing I remember you catching was a cold.'

'Oh, come on, love, remember that time when you brought home a cod that Andy caught and I put it on a large plate, and Sooty tried to drag it through the cat flap?'

'Yes, I remember – the stupid cat had the fish sideways in her mouth, and she wondered why she couldn't get through the door.'

'Oh, Dad, Sooty's not stupid!' bawled Becky.

'Sorry, darling, I didn't mean to say that, I should have said daft.' His daughter pulled a face at him, then went back to eating her chips. 'Who would like a cup of tea or coffee?' he said as he started to gather up the plastic trays and dispose of them in the litterbin.

'Thank you, darling, I could do with a nice cup of tea, and one for my sister, please.'

'Alexis?'

'Tea, please.'

'Janey?'

'Tea with no milk, please.'

'And what about you three?' He looked at each one in turn. 'Right, three orange drinks.' He placed his order for the drinks and then wandered over towards the scouts, watching as they assembled their fishing rigs and secured the bait to their hooks. Amy handed the teas and orange drinks to his family. High above them were a pair of speakers which were attached to the top of a lamppost which was sited between the two benches.

Madonna's song "This used to be my playground" filtered over the pier. Amy spotted Slider talking to one of the scouts and placed a cup of coffee in his hand.

His family and friends watched him meticulously as he weaved between the group. One of the older scouts suddenly recognized him and shook his hand vigorously. The entire troop suddenly stopped fishing and gathered around him. A large round of applause could be heard, which put a smile on Lily Slider's face.

Slider was helping a young scout to fasten a bloodied piece of fresh mackerel onto his fishing hook when the sight of the blood dripping onto the pier made his entourage grimace. From out of nowhere a shout of 'knock knock' could be heard and a fishing rod could be seen bouncing up and down against the handrail. He walked over, placed his cup of coffee down on the scout's fishing box, leaned over the handrail and waited for the fish to break the surface. The young boy struggled to bring the fish up. Suddenly a dogfish came leaping over the handrail and knocked Slider's cup of coffee over, which reduced his family and friends to hysterical laughter.

He said something to the young boy and patted him on the back, then looked across at his family and friends and noticed them wiping their eyes with tissues. Slider was in his element on the pier. He loved the sight and the smell of the sea air, and symptoms of his bad head had all but vanished. He said his goodbyes to the scouts and walked back and sat back down next to his wife.

'You seemed to be enjoying yourself over there,' she said as she put her arm around him.

'I love it here. It's so relaxing and stress-free and the children seem to be enjoying themselves as well.'

'Yes, they do. How's the head now?'

'I haven't given it a thought; this sea air makes a big difference to me.'

'Well, in that case we'll have to make a point of coming here more often,' replied his wife as she gently cuddled into him.

'We'll have to do a lot of things more often,' he said, staring into her eyes.

'I can see this sea air is making you frisky!'

'Hey, come on you two.' Rose yawned. 'We haven't got time for all this lovey-dovey stuff.'

'Tell me, Rose, when are you going to find yourself a husband and settle down?' snapped Slider, as he kissed his wife.

She looked at Alexis and winked at her. 'I'm quite happy as I am, thank you.'

'Mum, can I have an ice cream?' asked her daughter as she came running over from the telescope.

'Of course you can. Who else would like an ice cream?' said Lily out loud.

There was a mass of hands waving in the air and in unison everyone answered, 'Yes, please.'

Janey, who up to this point had been quite quiet and reserved, stood up and said, 'Please, it's my turn to order you all something.'

As she was speaking to Amy at the kiosk, Lily murmured, 'Janey's a bit quiet today, darling?'

'Well, she was on a yacht in the Indian Ocean only a few days ago, so I suppose she might still be jet-lagged.'

'Um, Alexis has been a bit quiet as well.'

'Well, let's try to keep it that way, shall we?'

'Did I hear my name mentioned?' said Alexis, raising her sunglasses.

'We were just saying that you seem a bit quiet today,' Lily replied, smothering a yawn.

'Well, I'm treating this as a day off, so I'm soaking up the sun and not worrying about anything.'

'You should have more days like this.'

'Slider, are you trying to be funny again?'

With closed eyes his wife said, 'Don't pay any attention to him, he's always like this.'

'Right, wake up you lot, I've got an ice cream for you all.' Janey proceeded to hand around the ice creams.

'Oh nice, a flake as well. Thank you, Janey,' said Lily.

Slider was licking his ice cream when Andy came running over and shouted, 'Dad, come and see what they've just caught!'

He got up and walked with his son to the end of the pier and watched as the wriggling fish had the hook removed. 'Good God, it's a red gurnard. I've never seen one caught off this pier before.'

'Where do they usually catch them, Dad?'

'More down Swansea way, where the water is cleaner. You can see that the water around here is very brown because of all the mudflats that we have.' He approached one of the adult scouts. 'Hello, I just wondered why the scouts are fishing here today.'

'They're all trying to win their angler badge, and to win it they have to catch a fish.'

'I see. Have many scouts caught a fish today?'

'Six so far. We've caught dogfish, eels, a few pouting, and the gurnard, so not too bad, and as you can see the tide is going out, so we haven't much time left.'

'OK, we'll let you get back to it.' Slider draped his arm around his son's neck as they walked slowly back towards their group. 'Have you had a nice afternoon here?'

'Yes, I've loved it. Dad, do you think that man by the handrail looks a bit like James Bond?'

'Yes, he does a bit. I was telling your mother that we'll have to come here more often.'

'That would be great.' He patted his son and Andy ran off and rejoined his sister and Alice who were looking at the brass plaques set into the decking of the pier; they signified important points in people's lives, such as weddings, deaths, and favourite spots.

'What time is it, darling?' asked Slider as he squeezed in between his wife and Rose.

'It's coming up to four o'clock. Why?'

'I just wondered what time we're staying till.'

'Go and get us another cup of tea and I'll talk it over with Alexis and Janey. And don't forget to ask the kids what they want.'

'As if I could forget.'

A few minutes later he returned empty-handed and sat down next to his wife, who said, 'Janey has ordered the cars for four thirty. So, where're the teas?'

'Amy's going to bring them over in a minute.'

'Good, I've told the kids what time we're leaving.'

Amy brought the assorted drinks over, and everyone helped themselves from the tray. 'Would it be OK to take that photo now, Mr Slider?' she asked.

'You can take your photo whenever you're ready.'

'Thank you.' She placed the tray against the bench and stood in front of his family and friends. 'Big smile – thank you so much, this means an awful lot to me.'

'You're welcome.' Slider sipped his coffee and muttered to no one in particular, 'I've really enjoyed this afternoon.'

'Mum, you won't forget to buy me a stick of rock, will you?' Becky said, while also trying to suck the orange juice from the end of her straw.

'As if I could forget.'

Slider finished his coffee and looked at his son. 'I suppose you want a stick of rock as well?'

'Yes, please, Dad.'

'What about you, Alice, would you like a stick of rock?'

The young girl looked at her mother, who nodded at her, and whispered, 'Yes, please.'

'Right, you three, let's go and see what they've got in the shop, and we'll leave the others to catch us up.' With that, he stood up and walked towards the entrance to the pier, with his daughter holding one hand and Alice the other. Andy, as usual, ran on ahead.

Inside Ye Olde Sweet Shoppe there were numerous different colours and sizes of rock, which made it a veritable Aladdin's cave for the children to explore. After what seemed an age they finally decided upon what they wanted and slowly drifted outside, leaving their father to pay at the counter. The children wasted no time in unwrapping their rock, and like hungry little mice they started to devour it.

'Would you like some, Dad?' asked his daughter, who had a purple tongue.

'No, thank you, darling, I'll hurt my teeth if I eat that stuff. For goodness sake, Andy, what made you choose black? Why didn't you have pink like Alice?'

'I like black.'

'Well, you'll never get that colour off your tongue!'

'That's alright.'

'And when we get home tomorrow, you and your sister will have to start doing some homework. I don't want you just lounging around the house all summer, and you're both going to have to have your hair cut before going back to school. I'll have to take you to Jacks and he can give you a peaky blinder of a haircut.'

'Oh, Dad!' shrieked Becky. 'I don't want a peaky blinder haircut! Curtis, who's in my class, has one and it looks awful!'

'Don't go worrying yourself, darling, it's only for boys. Your mother will take you into town to have your hair cut, and then you can go to Gamlin's to look at the pianos.'

Becky looked at her brother, rocked her head from side to side, and gave him a large grin. Andy looked forlorn. His father put his arm around his neck. 'Don't worry, it'll only be a trim – we can't have you frightening your mother.'

'Oh, thanks Dad,' Andy replied sarcastically.

The others finally caught up with Slider and the three children. Andy stuck his tongue out in front of his mother. 'Oh, Andy darling, what on earth made you choose that colour?'

'I've always liked black.'

'Well, don't go eating too much or you won't eat your dinner. Babs told me before we left that we're eating Italian tonight.'

Becky, who had been sucking on her rock, said, 'Mum, what's Italian food like?'

'You know, darling, food like spaghetti Bolognese and lasagne. We ate it when we went out on your father's birthday, and he got Bolognese sauce down his nice white shirt. Do you remember?'

'Yes,' answered her daughter, who looked weary.

'I think you've had too much sea air today, young lady,' her mother said. 'Are you feeling tired?'

Her head was leaning against her Aunty Rose when she muttered, 'Just a bit.'

'Well, when we get back, we can all have a lie-down before dinner. What do you say, Rose?'

Her sister, who was yawning profusely, said, 'That would suit me just fine.'

The two Carver vehicles appeared, and as they were all piling in Slider suddenly said to his wife, 'I'm going to travel back with Alexis. I want to see where she was filming for Channel 5.'

'OK.'

Alexis and Slider both sat in the back of the second vehicle, which was most unusual for both. As the cars climbed up the steep hill onto Beach Road, they crested the road into Windsor Terrace and approached the large roundabout. 'This is a lovely town centre,' said Alexis as the car moved onto Windsor Road.

'I've never given it much thought. When you're a driver, town centres all look very much the same.'

She sighed then pointed. 'This is it here, on the left, Beaver's House B&B.'

'Well, the front door looks like it could do with a coat of varnish. Is it one of those B&Bs that's losing a lot of money?' murmured Slider.

'Trust you to say that. Certainly not, quite the opposite in fact. It was nominated for a national award, and I being one of the judges had to decide whether it could be put forward as a finalist.'

'And did you?'

'Well, I'm not really supposed to divulge anything, but yes, it got my vote as a finalist. It's a beautiful, well cared for B&B.'

The two Carver vehicles arrived back at the nursing home within a minute or two of each other and the exhausted passengers filed into the lounge and plonked themselves down on the sofas. No sooner had they sat down than Barbara wheeled in her trolley containing pots of tea, coffee, milk and sugar, and the cups and saucers. And on the bottom tier were the cold drinks for the children and a plate of cakes and biscuits. 'I saw you arrive and had everything prepared ready for you.'

'Babs,' said Lily, 'you're an absolute star. Whatever would we do without you?'

The teas and coffees were duly poured and handed around. The adults all drank in silence, and all were exhausted from their afternoon excursion to the pier. The children sat together in a small circle on the carpeted floor and quietly sipped their juices and ate their custard slices without saying a word.

Slider looked at his wife's wristwatch. It was a quarter past five. 'I'm going to have a shower and a lie-down for a while.'

'Well, don't forget that dinner is at six thirty.'

'I won't.' He walked slowly with a cup of coffee in hand towards his bedroom and sat on the side of the bed, placing his cup of coffee down on the bedside cabinet. He removed his white T-shirt, which was soaked in perspiration, wiped his body with it and threw it onto the chair that was underneath his window. He let out a deep sigh as he lay on his bed, and said to himself out loud, 'Slider, you're getting old!'

After finishing his coffee and showering, he put on his black and white striped robe and started to think about the following day, when he would be travelling with Alexis's solicitors to Cardiff Central police station at Cathays Park, to answer questions about the assault on Police Officer Juliet Hanson. And the thought of coming face to face with Sergeant Faulkner again was an unpleasant one. Just as he was about to nod off, a gentle tapping on his door roused him.

'Dad, are you awake?'

'Yes, darling, come in.'

'Mum said I should ask you if I could play the piano tonight.'

'Yes, of course you can, provided you're not too tired.' With that, Becky ran out of the bedroom with a beaming smile on her face.

At six thirty everyone had assembled for what was going to be their last night at the Sparta nursing home. There was a buoyant mood around the room, with Irene Asher, Lynn Williams, and Janey O'Mara also present.

Glasses of Alexis's favourite champagne Moët & Chandon Imp⬜rial Ros⬜ were passed around to the adults, who drank it with ease. The children were given chinotto to drink, which was an Italian carbonated soft drink similar in colour to cola, and they loved it. Slider was back to his best and had everyone in stitches when he recounted stories that beggared belief. The starter course consisted of either a light salad or chicken parmesan sticks dipped into a dish of tomato sauce. The children enjoyed it, and so did Slider, judging by the tomato sauce that dripped onto his napkin, which luckily was covering his white shirt.

After clearing away the starter dishes Barbara brought in the main courses on her trolley. When they'd been served, Slider poured a glass of champagne and handed it to her. Standing up he announced, 'Ladies and gentlemen, boys and girls. I'm sure you'll agree that we have all been looked after very well by Babs, and so I would like you all to stand up and drink a toast to her.' Everyone stood up. Slider looked at her, kissed her on her cheek, and called out, 'To our wonderful chef and waitress Babs!'

The room responded 'Babs!' followed by a loud cheer.

He passed her an envelope, which Alexis caught sight of as she slipped it into her apron pocket. With tears rolling down her cheeks Babs said, 'I would just like to say that it's been a privilege and an honour to cook and serve for you all … and I will dearly miss all of you.'

With that, the women in the room all stood up, put their arms around her and hugged her. When everyone had sat down again Lily looked at her husband. 'That was a very nice thing to do, dear.'

'Well, I'm a very nice man.'

'Yes, you are.' She gently kissed him.

Alexis was topping up everyone's champagne glass, and when she reached Slider she said, 'That was a very nice gesture to make.'

'Well, you should always look after people who help you in life.'

'Does that mean you'll look after me?' she asked as she looked at Lily and winked.

He looked up at her, his face expressionless, and slowly said, 'I can never thank you enough for what you have done for me and my family.'

She smiled. 'Ditto.'

Once the dishes for the main meal were all cleared away, the knickerbocker glories were brought in, served in tall, conical glasses with wafers cut into the shape of a fan protruding from the top. The sight of these desserts left the three children open-mouthed. Lily looked at her daughter. 'Do you think you can eat all of that, darling?' Becky was chomping on her wafer and nodding with excitement.

Andy looked at his mother. 'Mum, can we have these when we go home?'

'Well, we only have these on special occasions, so remind me nearer to Christmas.'

'OK.'

Lily leaned towards her husband. 'Rose has just told me that Irene would like a word with you before the night is through. Something about tomorrow, I think.' He looked across at Irene and gave her a gentle nod.

The evening dinner came to its conclusion, and everyone retired to the lounge with their drinks and coffees and sat in readiness as Becky was to perform two pieces from her grade 5 piano syllabus. As she entered the room to a round of applause, she didn't look like a nine-year-old schoolgirl, but someone of a more advanced age. She stood in the middle of the room in her pink and white dress, curtsied, and announced, 'Tonight, I am going to play two pieces that I have learned for my grade 5 piano exam. The first piece is *Slow Air* by Ralph Vaughn Williams and then I'll play Sostenuto in E flat by Fryderyk Chopin. And if we have time, I'll play Mum and Dad's favourite piece.'

She made herself comfortable and started to play. Instantly, her audience felt the emotion of the music. Heads were bowed, eyes were wiped, as her audience was left spellbound at the quality and precision of her playing. At the end of her two pieces, she stood up and took a bow to a thunderous applause. Once the clapping had subsided, she said, 'And this final piece is for Mum and Dad.' The young girl then proceeded to play Prelude no 4 in E Minor by Fryderyk Chopin. Slider looked around the room; everyone was captivated by her performance. Once it had finished, he walked towards his daughter, lifted her up and hugged and kissed her. Soon she was surrounded by everyone, and kisses were distributed by all.

He held his daughter in his arms and asked, 'How did it go then?'

She held out her right hand and moved it gently from side to side. 'Not too bad; I was a bit wobbly in places though.'

'Wobbly! I thought it was brilliant.'

Shortly after, the children retired for the night. The adults then contemplated the following day. Irene Asher sat next to Slider on the sofa and gave him an insight into what to expect from tomorrow's cross-examination at the police station. Rose, Lily, and her two children would be going back to their house in Llandaff North, while Alexis and her daughter would be travelling back to London. Janey O'Mara, the Carver executive, would be staying in Cardiff until Slider's meeting with the police.

TWELVE

The following morning, everyone seemed downbeat, and it didn't help that it was raining and felt cold, which was most unusual for the third week of May. Slider hadn't slept very well. His imagination had been running riot all night, and he was continually yawning as his wife asked, 'So how are you feeling today?'

'I didn't sleep very well, and I'm still tired now.'

'Well, you'll sleep better tonight when we're in our own bed.'

'I'm looking forward to going back home and just doing the simple things for a change, like feeding the fish and washing the car.'

Lily looked around the room. 'It's been like a holiday at times, staying here, but I think our time is up, and I for one will be glad to be going home.'

Barbara was laying out the cutlery when she spotted the Sliders talking together. 'Breakfast will be ready in ten minutes.'

'Thanks, Babs.'

Becky ran towards her mother and asked, 'Mum, can I play the piano before we go home?'

'Well, breakfast will be in ten minutes, and we're all leaving here at ten o'clock, but you can play for a little while after breakfast.'

'Thanks, Mum.'

Alexis and her daughter entered the dining room, and Slider was shocked to see that she was wearing the same red, three-quarter length coat that he had seen her wearing on that frightful day at Penarth. She looked at him, smiled and said, 'Cat got your tongue this morning?'

'No, not really, but that red coat of yours brings back images of that day on the pier.'

'I'm sorry.'

'No, no, it's OK.'

'So how are you feeling today?'

'I didn't sleep very well. My mind was conjuring up all sorts of thoughts, but a walk in the garden after breakfast should wake me up a bit. What time are you leaving for London?'

'We're both leaving at the same time as you and your family.'

They turned to see Barbara wheeling in her trolley. Slowly, Slider's family and friends started to assemble in the dining room for the very last time. 'I'm going to miss your cooking, Babs!' said Andy as he was putting bacon and fried eggs onto his plate.

Laughter and the sound of 'hear hear' filled the room.

'Well, don't think you're having bacon and eggs every morning at our house, young man,' said his mother, who was talking to her sister.

'Yes, it's back on the cereals for you two tomorrow,' stated their father, who was stirring his cup and staring at his children.

'So, Rose, are you coming to stay at the house for a while? Or do you have to rush back home?'

'I'll stay for a few days. I know it's going to be hectic for you and I'm sure you could do with an extra pair of hands around the place.'

Lily hugged her sister. 'Thanks, darling.'

There seemed to be an air of anticipation hanging over everyone as they ate breakfast together that morning. Slider had his forthcoming meeting with the senior officers at Cardiff Central police station, and his wife was hoping their house was not topsy-turvy when she returned home. Alexis, too, was wondering what she would find when she eventually returned to her London home in Kensington. The children, however, seemed not to have a care in the world and seemed sad that they were leaving.

'Alexis, what time does your train leave?' asked Rose, who was staring into her compact mirror.

'We're booked on the ten thirty from Cardiff Central.'

'I imagine your husband will be glad to see you back home.'

'Yes, he will, and I'll be glad to see him again. These past days have been very traumatic for me.'

'Well, you've certainly seemed to have taken everything in your stride.'

'Is that another one of your witty remarks, Slider?'

'No, not at all,' he insisted, laughing. 'I'm just trying to point out that nothing seems to faze you.'

'Well, things do, but I try not to let it show.'

The morning breakfast was eaten in relative silence and slowly, except by Becky who couldn't wait to play the piano one last time. 'You've eaten that rather quickly, young lady,' said her mother, who was buttering her toast.

'I want to have one last play on the piano before we go. Dad, can you push the screen back for me please?' He got up and unlocked the grey screen and pushed it back against the wall.

'There we are. Now, not too loud please.'

'OK.' As she immersed herself in playing, the remainder of the group reflected on their past days together. Although they were once two separate families, the accident to Alice had sealed their friendship forever, and now they were totally bonded together as one happy and loving family group.

At nine fifty Irene Asher and Lynn Williams entered the dining room, and upon seeing the two of them Slider's stomach turned over. 'Good morning to you all,' said Irene as she and Lynn both took a seat at the dining table. Irene looked straight at Slider. 'So how are you feeling today?'

'To be perfectly honest I'm feeling very nervous this morning.'

'Well, try and relax. It's quite possible that you might be let off with a caution.'

'Do you think so?'

'It's possible.'

Alexis re-entered the dining room with Alice and her suitcases. 'Good morning, Irene, I didn't hear you arrive.'

'We've just this minute got here. There are two taxis for you and the Slider family waiting outside.' It was five minutes to ten. All were assembled in the dining room with their cases and bags and the round of hugs and kisses began. Barbara was also there and waved as they all walked towards the reception. As they passed Rachel Rees they all said goodbye and exited the building for the very last time. Outside the main entrance, the Carver drivers wasted no time in putting the luggage into their cars.

Slider looked down at his two children. 'I don't want you both to go worrying about me. I'm only going to talk to the police, and I'll be home in a few hours. OK?'

Quietly Becky said, 'So you won't be going to jail, Dad?'

'No, not today and not at all if I can help it,' he replied, laughing. His children quickly entered the car. He then turned his attention to his wife and sister-in-law. 'Don't you two worry either; this is only an interview so I should be home in a few hours.' He gently hugged and kissed them both. They got into their taxi, and as the car started to move away, he waved to them all until it disappeared at the junction. Once the car was out of sight, he slowly walked the few steps to talk to Alexis, who was waiting patiently at the door of her taxi with her daughter. 'I'll bet you'll be glad to see the back of me for a while,' he said with a smirk on his face.

'To be perfectly honest with you … I won't. You're certainly an enigma, Slider, and you do have the quirkiest sense of humour, and although you wind me up at times, I'm going to miss you.' And with that she hugged him and planted a kiss on his cheek.

He slowly knelt and put his arms around Alice. 'And you look after yourself, young lady.' The little girl, who looked slightly tearful, gently nodded. They got into the taxi and Slider closed the door behind them. As the car gently moved away, he waved at them, and they waved back.

'Right, Mr Slider, if you're ready to go we'll make a move,' said Irene, who was looking at her watch. Lynn was already sitting in the back of the taxi, and he was told to sit next to her. Irene followed and sat next to him. 'I thought it would be easier for us to talk together if we were all sitting in the back. Now, Slider, this is going to be a formal meeting at the police station, so I need you to be bright and alert. Do you understand?'

'Yes, of course.'

'You're going to be asked questions about the assault on Police Officer Juliet Hanson, so think before you speak, and whatever you do, don't let them get to you and try to provoke you. How you handle yourself this morning will have a significant bearing at your trial, which I'm afraid is very probable. If they do ask you something inappropriate, I'll jump in and tell you not to answer. OK.'

'Yes.'

'And for God's sake cheer up a bit. You have to go in there confident in the knowledge that Alice Polti would surely have drowned if it hadn't been for your actions!' Irene turned her attention to her assistant. 'What else have we scheduled for today, Lynn?'

'Well, we had a Mr Stiles phone the office today. He's buying an apartment and was looking for a solicitor, so I've put him in touch with our conveyancer. You also need to phone Mr Brownlee, the driving instructor who was involved in a traffic accident, and claims he has a whiplash injury. There's the ...'

While the two women were talking Slider took in the views as they travelled towards the city centre. The road works hadn't altered very much, and new ones seemed to have sprung up, and a smile lit up his face whenever he saw drivers that he knew and worked with. As the car turned into Edward VII Avenue, he started to become more anxious, and his adrenalin levels rose in response to his stress levels. When the car stopped outside the police station, he took several deep breaths to try and compose himself.

Irene placed her hand on his and looked at him. 'Are you OK?'

'Yes, don't worry, I'm fine.'

As they all exited the taxi, Janey O'Mara was already waiting to meet them. 'Good morning, Irene, good morning, Lynn, how are you both today?'

'We're both very well, thank you.'

Looking at Slider she asked, 'And how are you today?'

'Well, I was feeling a bit on edge earlier, but now I've settled down and I'm fine.'

The four of them walked up the steps and into Cardiff Central police station. Irene Asher was now in her element. She had been in this position hundreds of times in her long and illustrious career and knew exactly what to expect. Having told Slider and Janey to take a seat, Irene and Lynn approached the young policeman behind the counter. 'Good morning, I'm Irene Asher and this is my assistant Lynn Williams. We're here with our client Mr Matthew Slider and we have a ten thirty appointment with Detective Cranshaw.'

'If you would like to take a seat I'll let him know you're here.'

Irene and Lynn had only just sat down when a tall man dressed in a black suit, white shirt, and wearing a red and black diagonally striped tie approached them. 'Good morning, I'm Detective Cranshaw, would you all like to follow me please.'

235

Irene looked at Janey. 'I think it will be more appropriate for you to wait here.'

Janey smiled. 'Whatever you wish.'

The detective led the way along a corridor and through two sets of double doors, then opened a grey door on his right-hand side, which had a white plastic plate with the words Interview Room No 4 written on it. He entered the room and held the door open for everyone, and closed the door behind them. The interview room was quite small, about the size of a small bedroom. It had a brown wooden table in the centre with two chairs on either side. Additional chairs were against the side walls. In one corner of the ceiling was a close circuit camera. The detective would also be recording their conversation.

Just as Slider was getting comfortable in his seat, the door opened, and in walked Sergeant Faulkner followed by Police Officer Hann. The sergeant took a chair and sat at the side of the table, staring intently at him. Officer Hann brought a chair from the side wall and sat next to her sergeant. Slider had come across rough-looking men in his sixteen years as a taxi driver and wasn't going to allow the sergeant the satisfaction of trying to intimidate him. He stared back at him, taking in his guise. He was slightly shorter than he was, but there was a mean streak about him, his face being rough and pockmarked. He looked a brute of a man and was probably old-school in his ways of administering justice, which would reduce his paperwork and was possibly why he had never risen above the rank of sergeant.

'This is Detective Cranshaw, and I'm starting this interview at ten thirty-seven on Thursday, May the seventeenth, two thousand and eighteen. With me are Sergeant Faulkner and Police Officer Hann. Also present is Mr Matthew Slider, who is accompanied by his solicitor Irene Asher and her assistant Lynn Williams.' The detective smiled. 'I trust you are well today, Mr Slider?'

'Yes, I am.'

Sergeant Faulkner moved his face closer to Slider. 'No bloody headaches today then?'

'Thank you, Sergeant, that will be enough of that,' said Detective Cranshaw before asking, 'Would any of you like a cup of coffee or tea?' Slider was about to say something when Irene's shoe hit him hard on the side of his ankle.

'We're fine, thank you,' said Irene.

'Well, Mr Slider, you are here to answer questions into the assault on Police Officer Juliet Hanson on Monday, May the seventh, two thousand and eighteen at Penarth Pier. An assault that has left her with several loose teeth, a fractured jawbone, and a concussion following her fall on the pier. She will probably be off work for several weeks. So, how do you respond to this accusation?'

'Well, there were extenuating circumstances; a child was drowning in front of me.'

'Yes, I am fully aware of that, but we're here today to talk only about the assault on Police Officer Juliet Hanson. So, do you plead guilty or not guilty to the assault on Police Officer Juliet Hanson?'

Slider thought through that question and answered, 'Not guilty.'

'Now I have in front of me the statement from Officer Hanson, who says that without warning and any provocation you attacked her and subsequently beat her to the ground. So, please would you like to explain to us why you carried out this vicious assault on one of our police officers?'

'Well, I've just told you why, but firstly, it wasn't as you described, a vicious assault. I only struck the officer once, and if you've read the newspapers or watched the TV you'll already know why it happened.'

'Well, Mr Slider, we weren't on the pier that day, and newspapers and the media can give a distorted view of events, so please tell us in your own words what happened.'

'I dropped off a passenger at the University Hospital Llandough and drove to Penarth Pier for a cup of coffee and something to eat, and while I was there a young girl had somehow fallen over the handrail and into the sea.'

'That would be Alice Polti?'

'Yes, it would.'

'Continue.'

'I saw the young girl lying face down in the water and ran to the white kiosk to tell the young girl behind the counter to phone nine nine nine and ask for the police, ambulance, and coastguard.'

'Why didn't you phone the emergency services; why leave it to somebody else?'

'My phone was in my car on charge.'

'Go on.'

'I ran back to the handrail with the intention of jumping into the sea to try and help the child.'

'That was a bit brave of you, don't you think?' said the detective, smiling.

'It was certainly a challenge; but have you any children of your own?'

'No.'

'Well, I have, I've got a daughter of a similar age to that young girl. Anyway, I had one leg over the handrail when a hand grabbed my shirt collar and dragged me to the floor. It seems that Police Officer Hanson didn't have the guts to take on the job herself.'

'Just watch your mouth, Slider!' said the sergeant, whose anger was growing.

'Detective Cranshaw, if we have any more outbursts from Sergeant Faulkner, I'm going to insist that he leave this room. Do we understand each other?' asked Irene, whose voice was calm and measured.

'I'm sorry for that, Ms Asher.' Detective Cranshaw looked at the sergeant. 'Careful now, Sergeant.' Faulkner sat back in his chair, crossed his fingers together over his stomach and stared at the ceiling. 'Right, let's carry on. So, what happened when you got to your feet?'

'I shouted at the police officer and asked her why she stopped me.'

'And what did Police Officer Hanson say?'

'She told me to get back to the other side of the pier and that help was on its way.'

'So what did you do?'

'I got to my feet and realized that time was of the essence. So I stepped forward and struck Officer Hanson once on the side of her jaw.'

'Bastard,' said the sergeant quietly.

'What did you do next?'

'Well, that gave me the time to get over the handrail and jump into the sea.'

'Well, Mr Slider. Let me put this to you. The reason Officer Hanson told you to stay away was that she didn't want two people drowning in that sea. From what I've heard and read, the little girl sustained a bad cut to her forehead during her fall. Now imagine that had happened to you, we would have had two casualties to deal with. What do you say to that?'

Slider's solicitor jumped into the conversation and looked the detective straight in the eye. 'Detective Cranshaw, you can speculate all you want, but the fact of the matter is, my client saved the life of Alice Polti, and if he hadn't acted in the way that he did the little girl would surely have drowned. How does that sound to you? And furthermore, Police Officer Hanson informed my client that help was on its way. So please tell me what help was sent that morning to aid in the rescue of Alice Polti?'

The detective looked pensive. 'To my knowledge, there wasn't any other help forthcoming.'

'Quite right. The Penarth lifeboat was in Aberthaw towing back a fishing boat to Cardiff. If it hadn't been for the measures that my client took, the little girl would have drowned. Isn't that the case, Detective?'

'Yes.'

'I'm sorry, I didn't quite hear you.'

'Yes, that's correct,' said Detective Cranshaw, who looked drawn and fatigued.

The solicitor cast her eye towards Police Officer Hann who hadn't said a single word up to this point. 'Tell me, Officer Hann, would you have jumped into the sea to save the life of Alice Polti?'

'Probably not.'

'No, is what you mean,' said the solicitor. 'A lot of you young policewomen and men hide behind health and safety and don't have the guts—'

'That's not fair!' said the detective sharply.

'Yes, it is. A lot of unfortunate men, women, and children have drowned because the emergency services hide behind the health and safety laws and would prefer to watch someone die rather than get their feet wet. Isn't that the case, Detective?'

'We in the police force are governed by rules and must abide by them, just like yourself. And if our officers are not trained in a rescue from the water, they are told not to enter that water.'

'It seems to me that a lot of your officers don't have the spunk that the older generation had, and you would rather chastise my client here, who showed exceptional courage in performing a rescue from the sea.'

'Ms Asher, your client, Mr Slider, was brought here today to answer for the assault on Police Officer Hanson. The rescue of Alice Polti is a separate issue altogether, and although it's very commendable what he did, it doesn't detract from the fact that an assault on a police officer took place. So, and I am sorry to say this, Mr Matthew Slider is going to be charged today with the assault on Police Officer Juliet Hanson.' Detective Cranshaw looked Slider straight in the eye. 'Mr Matthew Slider, you are formally charged today with the assault on Police Officer Juliet Hanson. Normally you would be held in custody until bailed, but because of the swift action that you took in saving the life of Alice Polti you will be released today, and a date will be set for you to appear at Cardiff Magistrates' Court to answer the charges that have been levelled against you. Mr Matthew Slider, do you understand the charges against you?'

'Yes, I do.'

'I am now concluding this interview at ten fifty-seven on Thursday, May the seventeenth, two thousand and eighteen.' With that everyone stood up. Slider looked at Sergeant Faulkner who mouthed something to him which made him grin.

The detective opened the door and they filed out into the corridor. When they reached reception Janey O'Mara, who had been waiting patiently, approached them. 'So how did it go then?'

'Pretty much as I expected,' said Irene, staring at Slider who looked very much like a little boy lost. 'Come on, snap out of it! Anyone would think that you're going to the gallows the way you're sulking.'

'I'm OK, but I've just realized that I now have a police record, and I'm wondering what the Hackney Office in Cardiff will make of that.'

'Listen,' sighed Janey, 'you're too important a person to have your licence taken away from you, and if there are any problems just let me know.'

He gently said. 'OK.'

They left the police station and walked down the steps to where the Carver taxis were waiting. 'Right, Slider, Lynn and I are going to leave you now and travel back to London, and we'll inform Alexis of what's happened today. But we'll be back in Cardiff a few days before your trial, so that we can put together a plan for you.'

'Do you know when that'll be?'

'In a couple of weeks, I would imagine, but it all depends on how busy the courts are.'

'Well, I just want to say thank you for everything that the two of you have done for me.' With that, he shook hands with them before they entered the taxi. As the car pulled away both Slider and Janey waved until the car was out of sight.

Janey said, 'I'll take you back home now, but I'll be staying in Cardiff until tomorrow when I have to travel back to our Carver office in Ireland. But please don't worry about a thing. Take the next few weeks to recover fully and please don't go driving anywhere. Use the taxis that I've supplied for you and your family. The last thing we want now is for you to have a bump somewhere.'

Slider smiled. 'Will do.'

THIRTEEN

The phone rang as Lily and her sister were in the lounge listening to Becky play. Rose, who was closer, lifted the receiver and listened while turning to face Lily. 'Thank you, we'll be ready and waiting.' Putting the phone down she said. 'That was Janey, they'll be here in ten minutes.' They jumped up from the sofa to begin preparations for Slider's homecoming. 'I'll just go and put some lipstick on,' she said, running up the stairs.

'Tell that son of mine to come down straight away.'

'OK.'

Andy came running down the stairs and was met by his mother. 'Go across the road and tell Roger and Pam that your father and Janey will be here in a few minutes, and tell the sergeant as well.'

'Yes, Mum.'

'And watch the road!' The boy was out of the front door before she got a reply.

Rose and Becky came down the stairs together, closely followed by Sooty, who had been sleeping on the bed. Lily finished putting on her lipstick and said, 'Let's go and wait for them on the pavement.' They walked past Slider's car that was parked on the driveway and stood by the sycamore tree. The number of reporters and TV crews had swelled considerably in the previous hour, and neighbours who had spotted the Sliders emerged from their houses and joined them to welcome their hero home.

It was 11: 33 a.m. when Andy, who was standing on top of the garden wall, spotted a silver BMW with its headlights on slowly making its way towards him. Looking down at his mother he shouted, 'He's coming, Mum, I can see the car!'

'Well come down off that wall before you fall down. I don't want to be taking you to the hospital today.' He stood beside his mother and his Aunt Rose, who smoothed over his hair. He held his sister's hand and they were joined by Pam and Roger. The congregation of family, friends, and neighbours had expanded their group into a large gathering.

The Carver driver gave a rat-a-tat-tat on the car horn as it pulled up neatly in front of Rose's MG Morgan, causing a wave of cheering and clapping. As soon as the car stopped, Sergeant Dunscombe moved swiftly to open the rear passenger door, and held out his arms to make some space. Lily, seeing her opportunity, pushed past the sergeant and threw her arms around her husband as he exited the car and kissed him passionately on his lips.

'Welcome home, darling!'

'Thanks, luv, it's so good to be home at last.' She kissed him again, and the rounds of hugging, kissing, and backslapping began. When they finally stopped he reached down and picked up his daughter and put his other arm around his son.

'So, they didn't jail you, Dad?' said Becky as she played with his hair.

'No, they didn't.'

'So will you have to go back to court?' asked his son, who was looking puzzled.

'Yes, I will. Look, why don't we all go inside so we can talk.' Slider, his family, and friends walked up the driveway to the front door. He turned and addressed the large crowd which included the various TV networks. 'Ladies and gentlemen, boys, and girls I would like to take this opportunity to say thank you to everyone who has helped me and my family during this troubled period. The past week will be one that I and my family will never ever forget. Although I stand before you today a free man I will have to return to court at a future date to answer for the assault on Police Officer Hanson. So we would kindly ask you all to give me and my family some time alone together. Thank you.' With that they went inside and closed the front door. Just as Slider was taking off his jacket, a familiar face protruded from between the spindles and gave a meow. 'And it's nice to see you again.' He smiled as he picked up Sooty and carried her into the kitchen.

'I've just made a pot of tea; would you like me to make you a coffee?' asked Rose as she began looking for some cups and saucers.

'Thanks, that would be nice. If you're looking for the cups and saucers, they're in the cupboard on the right.'

'Oh yes, I've found them.'

Slider continued stroking the cat and walked out into the garden and put her down next to a tennis ball, which she immediately started to play with. He stood staring into the fishpond and was joined by his son and Roger. 'The water's looking a lot cleaner, Rog,' he said as he was handed his cup of coffee by Rose.

'I did it yesterday. There is also a surprise for you in that brown bucket by the shed.'

Andy looked into the bucket just before his father and gave an 'argh' of surprise.

'Good God, where did they all come from?' asked Slider, sniggering.

'What is it, Dad?' asked Becky excitedly.

'Don't look, darling, don't look!'

She couldn't resist the temptation to look, and gave out a loud scream and shouted, 'They're horrid!'

'Well, I told you not to look.'

Both sisters were sitting underneath the parasol with Pam and Janey, drinking tea, when suddenly they broke off from talking and put their cups down. Lily turned to look at her husband. 'Whatever is going on over there?'

'It's OK, Mum,' said Andy. 'Roger has taken the frogs out of the pond.'

Rose and Lily got up to have a better look, although Pam and Janey decided to stay put. Lily said, 'Well, don't you dare bring those things into my house!'

'Don't worry, I'll take them to the lake tomorrow and get rid of them.'

'Can I come, Dad?'

'Yes, of course, you can.' Looking at his daughter he said, 'Would you like to come?' Becky's mouth was firmly closed, and slowly she shook her head from side to side.

'Well, darling,' said his wife, who was pouring tea into several cups, 'you haven't told us what happened at the police station.'

'Well, I gave my side of what happened at the pier, and I answered their questions, but they still charged me with the assault on the police officer, and I'll have to appear at Cardiff Magistrates' Court at a later date.'

'Was Sergeant Faulkner there?' asked Lily, who looked concerned.

'Yes, he was there, along with Police Officer Hann, and he did his usual shouting and balling, but Irene took control of the interview and he was soon put in his place.'

'Do you know when your trial will take place?' asked Rose, who was sipping her tea.

'Nobody's exactly sure. It could be in a few weeks, or it might take several months.'

'So, will you be going to work, Dad?' asked his son, who was shaking the bucket with the frogs in.

'No, I'll be staying home to recuperate.'

'What does that mean?' asked Becky, who was playing with the cat.

'It means I'll be resting and trying to recover from my ordeal.'

'So what do we do for money?' asked his wife, who was looking anxious.

Janey jumped in and looking at Lily said, 'I told your husband when we first met that Carver would continue to pay his salary, and we've also given him a generous bonus. So please don't worry yourself about the financial side of things.'

Lily put her hand on top of Janey's. 'Thank you, thank you very much.'

'Well, you can thank me by pouring me another cup of tea; the last one's gone cold. And I don't know if you're aware, but I told your husband that the Carver corporation in New York will be wanting to meet him once this has all been cleared up.'

'Does that mean we're going to America, Mum?' asked Andy, who looked startled.

Janey turned to look at him. 'Yes, it does, you're all invited.' And turning to Rose, Janey smiled and said, 'You're coming as well, Rose.'

'Well, let's not get too excited just yet,' said Lily as she poured Janey another cup of tea. 'My husband has a trial to get through first, and who knows what will happen at that.'

* * *

It was the day of the 2018 men's Wimbledon tennis final. Novak Djokovic was going to play Kevin Anderson and Lily and Rose were eagerly looking forward to watching the final. The previous day they had been on the edge of their seats watching Angelique Kerber overcome Serena Williams 6-3 6-3 in what was a pretty one-sided game. The two women always looked forward to the Wimbledon fortnight: it was the highlight of their year as far as sport was concerned. In their youth they'd played tennis competitively against each other, with Rose, who was eighteen months younger than her sister, usually coming out on top. Her five feet eight inch height coupled together with her long legs and supple body, were more than a match for Lily, who was shorter and heavier than her sister.

Out on their driveway, the children were helping their father to wash and wax the car. Slider was told many times by the drivers he worked with to never buy a black car or you'll be forever cleaning it. But their words fell on deaf ears. He always loved the look of a black car; somehow it looked more elegant and distinguished than, say, a red or a blue car, and as for white, well, that was never going to be an option. Becky, who was dressed in her denim bib-brace, was polishing the front wing when she asked, 'Dad, what time is lunch?'

'I'm not sure, darling.' He looked at his watch; it was nearly quarter to one. 'I can't see your mother moving away from the telly once the tennis starts.' He then tapped on the glass of the bay fronted window to attract his wife's attention. She turned to look at him with a puzzled look on her face. 'What time does the final start?' he shouted through the glass.

Lily came to the front door and looked admiringly at the car. 'That looks really lovely; you've all made a really good job of it.'

'Becky was wondering what time lunch is going to be?'

'Well, I'm sorry to say that the kitchen is closed until the tennis has finished, and the final starts at two o'clock by the way.'

'Oh Mum,' said Andy, who was rubbing wax into the rear wheel arch.

'Look, I'll make you a sandwich if you like, but I'm not cooking until later tonight. Alright.'

'Yes, Mum.'

Slider and his children were all sitting on the mat in the porch when she returned with a plate of sandwiches, two soft drinks, and a mug of coffee. 'Right, you three, don't disturb us again!' They all looked at each other and giggled. No sooner had they started to eat their food when a familiar head appeared around the open front door.

'Oh Sooty, this isn't for you.' Becky picked up the cat and placed her to one side.

'Why is that cat always hungry? Have you fed her today, son?' asked his father, who was looking closely at her.

'I fed her this morning when we all had breakfast, but she's always hungry, that's why she looks so fat.'

'She's not fat!' said Becky loudly.

'Well, perhaps she's pregnant,' speculated Andy, as he touched her stomach.

'Don't say that, son, that's all we need – another three of four cats running around the house.' Slider had finished eating and stood up with his coffee mug in hand and was confronted by the postman coming up the drive. 'I didn't know you guys worked on a Sunday?'

'I'm just doing it for some overtime money. The car's come up nice.'

'Thanks.' The postman handed him a brown official-looking envelope. He immediately knew that this was the letter that he'd been waiting all these weeks for. Today though wasn't the day to be showing it to his wife and upsetting her, so he placed it into the glove compartment and continued waxing his beloved car.

The next morning, he was still tired when the alarm sounded at 8 a.m. The thought of opening that brown envelope had preyed on his mind for most of the night, and all the different courtroom scenarios had been played out in his imagination.

'What time is it, darling?' asked Lily as she turned to face him.

'It's just turned eight o'clock. Would you like me to put the kettle on?'

'In a minute.' She put her arms around her husband and kissed him passionately. 'I've missed this bed.'

'The letter came yesterday.'

'What letter?'

'The letter from the courts.'

'You should have told me.'

'I didn't want to spoil your afternoon watching the tennis. Was it a good final?'

'Well, it went the usual way, the favourite won in the end … Give us a hug, will you?' Slider and his wife consumed each other until the creaking of the door and the sound of the cat climbing all over them led to hysterical laughter. With Sooty purring in his ears he had no option but to get out of bed.

Looking at her he said, 'Trust you to come in when you did.'

'Make us a cup of tea will you and let's have a look at that letter. And don't forget a cup for Rose.'

'Where's Babs when you need her?' he said, laughing.

'We had it too good for too long at that nursing home, and it's made you lazy.'

'Well, they certainly looked after us.'

'Yes, they did, now go and put the kettle on.' A short time later he returned with two cups on a tray, along with the brown envelope from the car. 'Did you get Rose a cup?'

'Of course I did.' Slider sat on the side of the bed and read the letter. 'The court date is set for Friday, July the twenty-seventh, two thousand and eighteen, at ten o'clock which is in eleven days.'

'Let me have a look, please.' Lily read the letter. 'You'd better call Alexis and Janey and let them know the details.'

'I'll phone them after we've had breakfast.'

It was just after half past eight when the Slider family, including Rose, were all seated around the circular pine table in the kitchen. Andy, who was in his black lounge pants and black Harry Potter T-shirt said, 'I wish we were back at the nursing home eating breakfast; these cereals don't taste the same as they did there.'

'Yes, I know, son,' replied his mother, who was staring at him while spreading marmalade over her toast.

'But what you have to remember is, we treated the nursing home like a holiday camp, and things always taste better when someone else cooks for you.'

'Yes, I suppose so.'

'It's called living the good life when someone else cooks and cleans for you,' said Rose, who was filling the kettle. 'And just remember, young man, the good life doesn't last forever.'

'It does if you win the lottery,' said Becky, who was dunking her breaded soldiers into her soft-boiled egg.

'Not even then, darling,' said her father. 'People who win the lottery just get lazy.'

'I wish we could win the lottery,' whispered a tired-looking Andy.

'Well, we may need to win the lottery if your father goes to jail,' smirked Lily as she turned and grinned at her sister.

'Ha ha ha, how very droll,' countered Slider, who was waiting for the kettle to boil. Suddenly, the phone could be heard ringing in the lounge.

'I'll get it,' said Andy, as he rushed out of the kitchen. A few moments later he poked his head around the kitchen door. 'Dad, it's Alexis, and she wants to speak to you.'

'Here we go,' said Slider as he finished pouring boiling water into the teapot.

'Be nice now, darling.'

He took his cup of coffee into the lounge and placed it down on the small table next to the phone. He sat in the armchair, picked up the receiver and said, 'Good morning, Alexis, and how are you today?' He listened carefully as she was talking, and replied, 'That's very kind of you, but my wife and I would prefer to stay in our own house if you don't mind.' There was a long silence at his end, and he finished by saying. 'See you at three thirty. Bye.' He walked back into the kitchen to find his wife washing some cups and plates. He threw the remnants of his coffee down the sink and placed the cup in the beige plastic bowl for her to wash. He put his arms around her waist and said, 'They're all travelling down next Monday and staying at the Park Plaza Hotel in Greyfriars Road, and we'll be meeting them for afternoon tea at three thirty.'

'What else did she say?'

'Nothing really.'

'Well, she must have said something else; you were on the phone for long enough.'

'Alexis wanted us to stay with her at the hotel, but I said we preferred our own bed. She also said that Alice would be staying in London, and her solicitor would be wanting to meet with me to talk over preparations for the trial. Janey will also be there.'

Becky was sitting at her piano in her Peppa Pig pyjamas and had just started working on her final piece for her forthcoming piano exam, Waltz in E Minor by Grieg, when she noticed a postman coming up the drive. She went to the door, opened it, and was asked politely, 'Hello, is Mr Matthew Slider here?'

'I'll go and get him for you.' Finding him in the kitchen, she said, 'Dad, there's a postman at the door with a funny voice.'

He went to the front door with his daughter standing beside him and was asked by the postman, 'Are you Mr Matthew Slider?'

He was immediately struck by the postman's accent, and replied, 'Yes, I am. You've got a strong accent.'

'Yes, I'm Polish. I have a registered letter for you. Could you sign here please?'

After signing for the letter, he thanked the postman, closed the front door and went into the lounge to open it. After reading it, he stood up, letter in hand, and walked very slowly towards the kitchen where his wife and her sister were putting the plates and cutlery away. 'Darling, you'd better read this.'

Lily was placing the eggcups on the top shelf of the cupboard and could clearly see that her husband was distressed. 'Whatever's wrong?' She took the letter from his hand, looked at him, and sat at the table to read it. As she did so she broke down, with floods of tears cascading down her face.

'Mum, Mum, what's wrong?' Becky called out, 'Aunty Rose, come quickly!' Rose dashed back into the kitchen and was quickly followed by Andy. Upon seeing her sister, Lily stood up and threw her arms around her shoulders. Tears gushed down the back of Rose's pink silk dressing gown. Rose took the letter from her sister and read it out aloud.

'Dear Mr Slider,

You have been strongly recommended for an honour for your brave and valiant act in saving the life of Alice Polti, rescuing her from the sea on Monday, May 7th 2018. It has been decided by a panel of distinguished members to award you the Queen's Gallantry Medal.

The ceremony will take place in the ballroom at Buckingham Palace at 11:30 a.m. on Wednesday, 29th August 2018 and the Investiture will be performed by Her Majesty Queen Elizabeth ll.

Family members and close friends are most welcome.

Yours sincerely,

The Rt Hon. Charles Hamilton CVO'

The whole room disintegrated into a mass of joyful tears and for several minutes everyone hugged and kissed each other, which spread to laughter and cheering. 'Oh, darling, I'm so proud of you,' said Lily as she kissed her husband again.

Andy, who was reading the letter asked, 'Dad, are you going to be meeting the real queen?'

'Yes, I am.'

'Dad, will the queen be wearing her crown?' asked an excited Becky.

'No, darling, the queen only wears her crown on very special occasions like the opening of Parliament.'

Word had spread like wildfire that Slider was to receive the Queen's Gallantry Medal. The phone immediately started ringing with people congratulating him on his award. That same evening the family were gathered around the TV when it was announced on the national news programme, with Lily commenting, 'Here we go again.'

'Don't worry, at least you'll have me with you this time.'

'Yes, I will.' With that, she arched her head to kiss her husband gently on the side of his face.

The following days seemed to be repeating themselves, with the Slider household being inundated with 'Congratulations' cards and well-wishers arriving at the door with chocolates and flowers, and the phone never stopped ringing. Andy and Becky loved opening the cards and more string lines were put across every conceivable wall to hang them on. The day before their meeting with Alexis and her solicitor, the Slider family were finishing their lunch when the doorbell rang. And then it rang again.

'Is somebody going to answer the door?' said Lily, who was reading a magazine.

'I'll go,' said Slider, who was closest to the kitchen door. Their aluminium front door had a pane of autumn-leaf-patterned glass, through which he could just make out the contours of someone with black hair.

'I thought you were never going to let me in.'

'Alexis, it's so good to see you again.' He hugged and kissed her. 'We're all in the kitchen, why don't you go through.'

'Who is it, darling?' came a call from the kitchen.

A familiar voice answered, 'It's only me.' As she put her head into the kitchen.

'Alexis!' screamed everyone as they congregated around her. Hugs and kisses were distributed by all. Even Andy gave her a kiss, which was most unusual for him.

'We all thought you were arriving tomorrow,' said Lily, who was looking for a vase to put the tulips in that she had just been handed.

'Well, I saw the news report about your husband receiving the Queen's Gallantry Medal and I just had to travel down to see you all. I would have arrived sooner, but I've been away filming for Channel 5.'

'Is that your silver Audi outside?' asked Slider, as he turned to face her.

'Yes, it is. And I just want to say how proud I am that you are to receive a medal; nobody deserves it more than you.' With that, she kissed him on the lips.

'Steady now, Alexis, the wife's watching!'

'You carry on, he deserves all the attention he can get,' said Lily, as she trimmed the flowers.

'Have you got any plans for this afternoon?' asked Alexis, as she was taking her red jacket off.

'Well, over lunch we were talking about going to the lake. Would you like to come with us?' asked Lily, as she poured her a cup of tea.

'I'd love to. Rose and I drove past the lake on our way back from town after buying your husband his suit, and it looked beautiful. By the way, I hope you've got your suit hanging up nicely.'

'Of course I have,' he answered with a sigh.

265

'Don't worry, I made him put it in a plastic suit bag and hang it up,' said Lily, as she handed Alexis her tea. 'And while you're drinking your tea, we'll all get ready.'

'Mum, can I bring my scooter?' asked her daughter.

'Of course you can.' Fifteen minutes later they all filed out of the house, and with Alexis's car blocking their driveway, they decided to travel in her Audi.

'Can I sit in the front, Dad?' asked Andy.

'No, I'm going to sit in the front to show Alexis the way; you can sit in the front on the way home.'

'OK.'

No sooner had they pulled away than Slider started to press a few buttons on the dashboard. 'I wouldn't have taken you for a Radio 4 listener?'

'Will you leave things alone. I don't want you messing up my radio stations!' He started to laugh, and so did the others in the back seats. The journey to the lake passed through the Heath area of Cardiff. Alexis was taken with the pink cherry blossom covering the majority of trees in the area.

'Alexis, do you have trees like this where you live?' asked Becky, who was squashed between her mother and her Aunty Rose and could barely see through the side window.

'In the parks we do, but not usually on the main roads like this. This is beautiful.' Once the car had pulled onto Lake Road West the search for a parking space began. The afternoon sun had brought many people to the lake. Slider spotted a parking space close to the main gates where a car was trying to pull out. 'Well spotted,' said Alexis, as she threw him a stare. A red Rover pulled out, and she started to reverse into the vacated space.

'Would you like me to guide you in?' said Slider, as he turned and grinned at her.

'The day I need you to help me park the car is the day I'll give up driving for good,' she replied and slotted the car perfectly into its space. 'There … is that good enough for you?'

'Perfect, I couldn't have done better myself.'

'No, darling, you would have hit the kerb as you usually do,' said his wife, as she was trying to open the rear door. A wave of laughter infected them all, as Slider got out and opened the doors.

'I'm not that bad.'

'Dad, can you get my scooter out of the boot please?' He opened it, and lifted out his daughter's red scooter, which had been a Christmas present from her Aunt Rose.

No sooner had they passed through the gates than the sight of the ice cream kiosk brought out the usual requests. They all walked towards it, leaving Slider to place the order. Alexis then tried to push a twenty pound note into his hand. 'No, no, Alexis, I have enough money, thank you.'

'Are you sure?'

'Yes, perfectly.'

Quietly she said, 'Irene phoned me this morning and it seems that the courts are bringing out the heavy guns at your forthcoming trial.'

Looking pensive he said, 'So what does that mean?'

'It means that your trial may not be as straightforward as we all hoped it would be. But please don't go worrying yourself; Irene will give you more details tomorrow.'

'Thank you for letting me know.' Slider distributed the ice creams which were accompanied by chocolate flakes.

As they sat on the promenade benches eating their ice creams, Alexis commented on the white lighthouse which was to her right. 'So what does that lighthouse in the lake signify?'

'Well, we did a project in school about the park and lighthouse,' said Andy, who was spooning his ice cream out of a tub. 'Would you like me to tell you all about it?'

'Yes, young man, I would be fascinated to know about it,' she said with a smile.

'Before you start … darling, keep an eye on your daughter please, I don't want her going too far on her scooter.'

'Don't go worrying yourself, I'm keeping my eyes on her.'

After finishing his ice cream, Andy launched into the story. 'Roath Park was donated to the city in eighteen eighty-seven mainly by the Marquis of Bute, and it was opened to the public in eighteen ninety-four. The lake was created from marshland, and the lighthouse was constructed in nineteen fifteen to commemorate Captain Scott's ill-fated journey to the Antarctic which was in nineteen ten. And if you look at the very top you can see a small ship and that's the *Terra Nova* which was his ship, and it set sail from the docks here in Cardiff. In the nineteen sixties and seventies, the lake was used for water-skiing, water carnivals, and swimming and that was until they found the lake water to be too filthy to carry on.'

'Why thank you,' said Alexis, as she smiled at him and ruffled his hair. 'That was a lovely story.'

Without warning, Lily stood up and waved her arm at her daughter, who she could see in the distance. Becky came scooting back and stopped right in front of her mother. 'I wish you wouldn't go so far, darling, you'll have me worrying about you.'

'Sorry, Mum. Mum, are we going on the swings and slides?'

Lily looked at her sister, who had her eyes closed and was napping. 'Rose, wake up!'

Rose opened her eyes, yawned, and muttered, 'I could do with a nice cup of tea at this moment.'

'So could I.' Looking at her daughter she suggested, 'I'll tell you what, darling, why don't we go and have a cup of tea and a piece of cake, and then we'll go and feed the swans. And when we get home you can play your new piece of music for Alexis. Is that OK for you?' But just as the young girl was about to answer, a shower of rain descended upon them, leaving them to make a hasty retreat to the Terra Nova café/restaurant which was a short distance away by the rowing boat station. Once inside Alexis took charge and started to take the orders for the teas, coffees, and cakes.

'Well, that was lucky, wasn't it,' said Slider as the rain lashed against the outside of the window.

Rose, who was using a serviette to dab the rain from her face, said, 'Well, that's woken me up.'

Lily picked up two trays and helped Alexis to carry the food and drinks to the tables. Once they were all seated around the tables she turned to face Alexis and said, 'So, how did your husband Roberto react when he saw Alice again?'

'Well, he was waiting to meet us in the underground car park that we have at our townhouse, and as soon as he saw her he burst into tears, and has vowed never to let her out of his sight again, which is why Alice is not with me today. And she won't be attending Slider's trial either. But Roberto's very eager to meet the whole Slider family, and in particular your husband.'

'Yes, I can understand that,' said Lily as she spread butter over her Welsh cake. The two children were staring intently at the swans who were swimming just outside the window, when their mother said to them, 'I'm sorry that you couldn't go on the swings or feed the swans today.'

'That's OK, Mum,' whispered her daughter, who looked a little despondent.

'Dad, can I still sit in the front of the car on the way home?'

'Yes, son, of course you can.'

The rain continued to fall, and it didn't look like it was going to stop any time soon. More drinks and cakes were consumed and then Alexis suggested, 'Why don't I take a photo of you all?' That idea seemed to perk everyone up and brought some life and jollity back into the group. Alexis stood up and away from the table and

271

uttered those immortal words, 'Smile, please.' Looking at the picture she said, 'Thank you, I'll print this photo and put it in my dining room when I get home.'

As they gazed across the lake the sky suddenly turned brighter, and the rain started to ease off. 'We could make a dash for the car if you want,' said Slider as he was finishing his coffee.

'Well, I'm not getting my hair wet,' stated Rose bluntly as she was putting her coat on.

'Don't you remember when we used to play tennis in the rain?' laughed Lily, who was helping her daughter with her coat.

'I remember when I used to pick the two of you up after playing tennis, and if it was raining, you'd sit in the back of my Ford escort and the seats would be soaked!' snapped Slider.

'Well, we were younger and fearless back then. Right, sis?'

'Yes, I remember. And stop moaning, you!' said Rose.

Alexis looked at Slider, raised her eyebrows and said, 'Let's go.'

By the time they got outside the rain had stopped, causing Rose to say, 'Thank goodness for that.'

'Dad, can you carry my scooter please?'

Andy quickly barged in. 'I'll push it for you.'

'Well, don't you dare break it or we'll never hear the end of it,' his mother said sternly.

'I won't.'

When they got back to the car, Slider put the scooter in the boot. They all piled into the back, leaving Becky to scream, 'Dad, you're squashing me!'

'I'm so sorry, darling, but there's not much room in here compared to my car.'

'Having problems, are we?'

'No, we're fine. These Audis don't have so much room in the back compared to my Skoda.'

'Do you want me to stop so you can change seats?'

'No, thank you, Becky can sit on my lap,' said Slider. Once back at the house Andy helped to pull his giggling sister out from the back of the car and helped his father out.

'Andy, darling, go and open the front door and put the kettle on, will you, please?'

'Yes, Mum.'

Eventually, they were all able to extricate themselves from the back of Alexis's car and breathe a sigh of relief. 'I'm sorry that you were all a bit squashed back there.'

'That's OK. I don't think sports cars are designed to carry large family groups.'

Slowly, and looking tired, they all made their way up to the front door and into the house. No sooner had Lily sat down than her sister brought in the teas and coffees on a tray. 'Thanks, darling, that's exactly what I need.'

Rose looked at Alexis. 'And what would you like to drink?'

'Tea, please.'

'Do you take sugar?'

'No, thank you.'

'Now where's the other lot gone?' murmured Rose.

'Well, I can see Slider through the kitchen window. Shall we join them in the garden?'

'You go on, Alexis. I'll stay here for a moment and finish my tea,' said Lily, who was covering a yawn.

Alexis left the lounge and said, 'This is a lovely garden that you have, and I love your fishpond.'

'Thanks, we built it earlier in the year,' said Slider.

'What type of fish do you have … oh, is that a goldfish I can see?'

'Yes, we have quite a few goldfish. We also have a few baby goldfish as well,' said Andy.

'And what's the green netting for?' she asked, looking at the young boy.

'That's to keep the birds and the cats away.'

'Right ... I like this pond, in fact, I like it a lot.' Lily wandered into the garden, closely followed by Becky who had been upstairs to change into a dress.

'That's a lovely dress,' said Alexis, as she put her cup and saucer down on the white patio table.

'Thanks, my Aunty Rose made it for me.'

'Did she indeed?'

Lily intervened. 'Our mother was a dressmaker, and she taught both her girls how to make dresses and other garments. In fact, when we were much younger both Rose and I would be wearing identical dresses or skirts when we went out together. Do you remember, Rose?'

'Yes, I remember,' answered Rose, who looked a little dispirited.

'So, what's this new piece of music that you're learning?' asked Alexis.

'It's called Waltz in E Minor by Grieg.'

'Well, let's all go into your lounge and you can play it for us. Have you learnt the whole piece?' Alexis asked.

'Just about.'

'She's been practising day in and day out in readiness for her exam in September,' said her mother.

Everyone gathered and made themselves comfortable in the lounge, while Becky prepared herself quietly at her piano. As she began to play, the beauty and exuberance of the piece shone through, making it a livelier piece than the previous piece that Alexis had listened to. When it finished everyone gave her rapturous applause, leaving her to stand up and give a curtsey in her new yellow and ivory dress. Once the applause had subsided Alexis said, 'I'm afraid I will have to make a move now.'

'That's OK,' said Lily. 'It was very nice of you to call on us.'

Alexis gathered up her red clutch bag and walked to the front door, which was being held open by Andy. As she passed him she gave him a peck on the cheek. They all followed her out towards her car. 'Now, don't forget, the Carver taxi will be here at three o'clock tomorrow and tea will be at three thirty,' she said as she got into her car. The engine started and Alexis could be seen waving as she gently pulled away.

'Well, that was a very unexpected visit, wasn't it,' said Lily, as they all trooped back into the house. In his mind Slider knew her visit wasn't totally unexpected. He had the measure of the woman and knew that her arrival was to warn him about his imminent trial and what he

276

could expect. Tomorrow's meeting with Irene would finally answer his suspicions, and if he was going to be jailed, he could start making plans for that eventuality.

FOURTEEN

The Carver taxi arrived right on time, and everyone was looking forward to going to the Park Plaza Hotel for an afternoon tea as it was generally regarded to be one of the finest hotels in Cardiff. Everyone, that is, apart from Slider, who couldn't get the thought out of his head that he might be going to jail. The afternoon sun shone brightly, and hardly a cloud in the sky could be seen, which for many marked the end of a beautiful day, but for him, it could be marking a day that he would never ever forget.

'How's the head now, darling?' asked Lily, who was looking into the mirror adjacent to the front door, while putting on her red lipstick.

'Not too bad.' This afternoon wasn't the time for upsetting his wife, and although in turmoil, he had to keep a lid on it until his meeting with Irene. 'Come on, you two, hurry up!' he shouted up the stairs to his two children. 'And tell Rose to hurry up, the taxi's outside! Last again, Rose?' he huffed, as she finally came down the stairs looking like something out of a glamour magazine.

'Well, you should know me by now. I always want to look my best, as you never know who you'll meet at these hotels.'

'Well, just remember we're going out for afternoon tea, so I don't want you parading around as if you're on the catwalk,' said her sister.

Rose just had to have one last look in the mirror before leaving, and nearly went flying when her black stiletto heel caught on the door's threshold strip, but luckily for her Slider was on hand to catch her. 'Steady now, we don't want you falling out of that dress and giving my son a view of your assets,' he said with a large smile on his face. She huffed at him as they all filed out, leaving Slider to lock the door behind them. Once they were inside the six-seater Ford Galaxy the mood was a happy one, with the children especially looking forward to going to the hotel for the first time. The journey into the city centre was a slow laborious chug. They were caught in the afternoon traffic, something that Slider knew only too well.

'Dad, why are there so many cars on the road?' asked Becky, who was still in the dress that her aunty had made for her.

'Well, this is what it's like every afternoon when children are going home from school.'

Once they had moved onto North Road the taxi started to make some headway when Lily's phone rang. 'It's Alexis,' she said to everyone. She listened intently then said, 'We're almost there.' After putting her phone away she turned to her husband and straightened his tie. 'She was wondering where we were.'

The taxi turned into Greyfriars Road and pulled into the parking bay in front of the hotel. Alexis was dressed in a short, light blue dress and was patiently waiting. 'You weren't worrying about us, were you?' asked Slider as he exited the car first.

'You should know that I always worry about everything,' she replied, with a slight frown on her face.

'Nice dress by the way.'

'Thank you, and it's nice to see you finally wearing one of my ties.'

The group made its way up the marble steps, through the doors, and into the foyer of the hotel. The cool of the air conditioning was especially welcomed by Slider. As they made their way into the lounge, they were warmly greeted by Irene Asher, Lynn Williams, and Janey O'Mara who had flown in from Ireland earlier that morning. Slider immediately made a beeline for his solicitor and whispered gently in her ear, 'I'm very worried.'

'We'll talk about it later.'

As the group made themselves comfortable on the leather sofas, a waiter came over and took the order for the drinks. Rose, Lynn and Irene all ordered a gin and tonic while Janey ordered a glass of red wine. Alexis asked for a red spritzer, while Lily, who was a recovering alcoholic, settled for a mineral water, as did her husband. The two children were ordered a yellow fizzy lemonade. The conversation moved back and forth across the coffee table with Slider, as usual, giving accounts of stories which had everyone in stitches.

Finally, Alexis had to ask, 'Are you making up these stories?'

'You wouldn't believe what happens in the back of a taxi, or what people leave in the back of my car,' he said, gazing into her brown eyes.

Just as he finished speaking, a young lady in black pinstripe trousers and a white shirt and whose name was Sophie informed Alexis that their table for nine was ready. 'Thank you, Sophie,' she replied with a smile. Once the party had moved into the dining room, the problem arose of who was going to sit where.

After some deliberation, Alexis sat at the head of the table and the others worked themselves in, giving the seating a veritable mix of ages and professions. Slider had Irene sitting in front of him and wondered if this was by luck or by design. He had a strong feeling as he looked at her that trouble was in the air, but that would have to wait till later when he could speak with her alone.

The menu for the afternoon tea consisted of freshly cut finger sandwiches, Welsh cakes, warm savouries, and sultana and buttermilk scones with clotted cream and strawberry preserve, which would be followed by an assortment of fruit dishes and finished by a tier of small individual cakes.

'So, how are you filling your days?' asked Janey, who was sat on Slider's right-hand side.

'Quite well. I must have the cleanest private hire vehicle in Cardiff,' he answered as he leaned back to allow the waitress to place a tier of miniature pastries and cakes in front of him.

'Well, I don't want you overdoing it now; you still need to take things easy.'

'Don't worry, I had my children to help me wash and wax the car last week, which was a big help, while someone else was watching the Wimbledon tennis final,' he said quietly, as he looked at his wife and winked at her.

'Dad,' said his daughter, who was sitting on his left-hand side, looking at the menu. 'Are these fruit cocktails the same as we had at the nursing home?'

He looked at the dessert menu. 'Almost the same, darling; there pieces of fruit in a tall glass which is topped with ice cream and a wafer.'

She looked across the table at her brother. 'Dad said they are the same!'

'I thought you might have worn your new suit today,' said Lynn, who was sat next to Irene.

'No, I'm saving that for the big day.' His attention was caught by Rose, who was standing at the bar and talking to a well-dressed man in a suit. He looked towards his wife, but her head was turned away from him. He then looked towards Alexis and caught her eye and mouthed the words, 'Keep an eye on her,' as he nodded in Rose's direction. She looked back at him, smiled, and gently nodded.

As the three-tier silver stands with more assorted small cakes were being placed around the table, Alexis approached Slider and whispered in his ear, 'I've had a word with the duty manager, and apparently they have a piano bar here. I was thinking that while Becky is entertaining us, you and Irene can have a chat together.'

He looked up at her. 'Perfect, thank you, but please keep an eye on Rose for me.'

'Certainly.' Alexis then spoke quietly to Becky, who started beaming with excitement.

Slider had just consumed a miniature cake and was stirring his coffee when he turned to his daughter and spoke quietly in her ear. 'I'll be having a chat with Irene while you're playing the piano; is that OK with you?'

'Yes, Dad,' she replied, looking into his eyes.

He'd just polished off yet another small cake when Alexis stood up and tapping on a wine glass to attract everyone's attention announced that Becky would be providing the afternoon's entertainment with a selection of piano pieces, including one or two pieces that she had learned for her upcoming piano exam. With that, a generous round of applause emanated from around the table. 'Alexis has told me it's a baby grand piano that they have here. Have you played on one before?' asked her father, as everyone was starting to leave the table and wander in the direction of the piano bar.

'We have one in the school assembly room, and I sometimes play it during lunchtime,' Becky replied, as she pushed her chair underneath the table.

He stood up, and after kissing his daughter on the cheek said, 'I want you to enjoy yourself in there.'

'I will.'

He watched as his daughter walked towards her mother who was waiting by the dining room door.

Glancing further to his right, Alexis and Rose were linked arm in arm and were giggling like schoolchildren as they too were leaving the room. Slider sat back down in his chair with his solicitor on the opposite side of the table. Janey O'Mara had decided to stay and sat on Slider's right-hand side. Turning to look at her he asked, 'Are you sure you want to stay?'

'Yes, you're a VIP in the Carver organisation, and our CEO has taken an interest in you.'

Irene intervened into the conversation and looking across at Slider said, 'Are you quite happy for us to talk here or would you prefer to move somewhere else?'

Brushing some demerara sugar off the table he replied, 'Here's fine.'

'My sources have informed me that the District Judge is going to be Rebecca Etherington. I haven't come across her personally, but my sources have informed me that she's a formidable judge. Apparently, her daughter Catherine was mugged and beaten by a man in the street nine months ago. To make matters worse I have been reliably informed that the prosecution barrister is Rosemary Howard-Stott, and she is someone who I have crossed paths with in the past. She's a feminist and she is not going to take kindly to you so–'

'So, where does that leave me?'

'Well, you've already pleaded not guilty to the assault on Police Officer Juliet Hanson at an earlier interview with Detective Cranshaw, and an assault on a member of Her Majesty's police force does carry a fixed-term sentence of six months. But the picture is not as black as it appears to be.'

'Well, it's looking pretty grim from this side of the table!'

'Look, Slider, I told you once before that you must keep your emotions under control. If you can't control yourself in the courtroom, you surely will be jailed. Do you understand?'

'Yes … I'm sorry for that outburst.'

'I know jail seems a frightening prospect, but you must trust me when I say that all is not lost. I'm bringing in Mr Nicholas Harrington, who is an excellent defence barrister, and he's someone who I've worked with in the past.'

'Can I just say something?' asked Janey.

Irene lowered her glasses to look at her. 'Yes, you may.'

'Police Officer Juliet Hanson didn't do anything morally wrong on the pier, did she? Now, she might be lacking in morale fibre, and she might be regarded as a coward by many, but are we going to tarnish her for her inability to help?'

'Whose side are you on?' argued Slider, as he stared her in the face.

'I'm just looking at the facts, that's all.' Janey could see that Slider was angry with her.

'Let me say this,' Irene responded. 'Police Officer Hanson did absolutely nothing to help in the rescue of Alice Polti. She lied when she said help was on its way, she did nothing to alert other emergency services. And she could have gone to the yacht club, which was two hundred metres away, to get help, but she chose not to. The people of this country deserve better from their police force. Don't you agree?'

'Yes, you're right,' said Janey, who was looking slightly flushed.

'And furthermore, we all need to pull in the same direction and give Slider all the help we can.'

Turning to face him, Janey said, 'I'm sorry if I've upset you in any way.'

'That's OK,' he gently murmured.

'Now, where was I?' Irene looked at her case notes. 'Ah yes, as you have already pleaded not guilty, the trial should start by putting you into the witness box to be cross-examined. Slider was momentarily distracted by the sound of applause emanating from the piano bar. Irene continued. 'Your trial is in two days, so I want you to make the necessary preparations just in case you are jailed. Do you understand?'

'Yes.'

'And I want you here by nine o'clock on Friday morning, so that we can go over any last-minute details which may have come to light.'

'I won't be late,' said Slider, who seemed lost and bewildered by Irene's comments. As he stood up the dining room door opened and his smiling family came in to meet him. Scooping up his daughter in his arms he asked, 'So, how did it go then?'

'I loved it, Dad, I've never played on a white piano before.'

'Dad, can I have something to drink?' asked his son, who'd rushed up to him. It suddenly impacted on him that he'd been neglecting Andy somewhat in recent days, and if he were jailed times would be especially difficult for his son, who would have to put up with the playground taunts.

'Of course you can.' Together they walked towards the bar, with Slider asking, 'And who else would like a drink?'

'Yes, please,' came the chorus of replies. Once everyone had been handed a drink, he said, 'I would just like to say a few things while we're all together. Firstly, a big thank you to Irene and Lynn for their hard work, and if it goes badly for me in court, then so be it. I would also like to thank Alexis for everything that she has done for both myself and my family, for without her I certainly wouldn't be here today. Also, many thanks to Janey and Carver for supporting me. And last but by no means least, my wife Lily, Rose, and my children who have been my rock and who I will always love.' His wife put her arms around him and kissed him passionately on his lips. This was followed by a large round of applause.

Alexis joined them and asked Slider, 'What do you want to do now?'

'I want to go home and reflect on a few things.'

'I'll get Janey to order you a taxi while you're saying goodbye to everyone.'

'Thank you, I would appreciate that.' Lily spoke to Rose and her children, and told them that they were leaving, while her husband had a few last words with Irene.

A few minutes later, Slider spotted a familiar face through the glazed dining room door and went to investigate. 'Alan, what are you doing here?' he said, smiling at him.

'I'm your lift home. How are things progressing with your upcoming trial?'

'I'm fucked,' he said quietly. 'I had a meeting with my solicitor a short time ago, and she thinks there's a good chance that I'll be jailed.'

'Fucking hell, and after all that you've done. I'm so sorry for you.'

Slider sighed deeply and said, 'Come and pick me up about nine thirty tomorrow morning and we'll go to Elmer's Café for breakfast. We can talk about it there, and bring a few of the boys with you.'

'Yes of course.'

'And please, don't say anything on the way home.'

'Of course not.'

With their coats on, and the customary goodbyes duly taken care of, they filed out of the hotel and down the steps to Alan's car. 'Hello, Alan, it's very nice to see you again,' said Lily, as she waited for her sister to extricate herself down the steps in her stiletto heels. 'Why you have to wear those things on your feet, God only knows!' she chirped, as Rose slid into the back of the car.

'Well, you know me.'

'Don't I just,' she said, grinning and rolling her eyes. The two children followed their aunty inside, and just before getting in herself Lily kissed Alan on the side of his face and said, 'I just wanted to say thank you to yourself and the other drivers for their kind donation that they gave us.'

'Our pleasure, Lily.'

Slider and Alan got into the car, and it slowly started to move away and all smiled and waved at Alexis, Irene, Lynn, and Janey who were waving from the top of the steps. 'Dad, there's much more room in here than in Alexis's car,' said Becky, who was surveying the car's interior.

'Why thank you, young lady,' said Alan. He threw a quick glance at Slider. 'What type of car does Alexis have?'

'She has an Audi, and we were packed in like sardines when she took us all to the lake.' The journey back to Llandaff North took far less time than it took to travel to the hotel. Once outside their house Slider thanked his good friend and reminded him, 'Nine thirty tomorrow morning.'

'I'll be here on the dot.'

The Carver taxi drove away, leaving his wife to ask, 'And what was that about nine thirty tomorrow morning?'

'I'll tell you about it later,' he replied as they all walked up the driveway and into the house. After changing out of his shirt and tie and back into his black jeans and T-shirt, he asked his family to join him in the lounge. Sitting on the sofa with his wife on one side and Becky on the other he said in a quiet and fatigued manner, 'After my talk with Irene Asher, my solicitor, it appears that there is every likelihood that I will be sentenced to six months in jail for the assault on the police officer. She also said that all is not lost, but for the life of me I can't see how I'm going to escape not going to jail.'

As he said that his two children along with Rose broke down in floods of tears. His wife threw her arms around him and kissed and hugged him. Andy and Rose both sat closer to Slider and put their arms around him. A few minutes passed and nobody said a word. After the initial shock had worn off Lily commented in a whisper, 'Well, if Irene thinks that all is not lost then we'll just have to trust her.'

'Yes, we will.' Turning to look at his two children he said, 'I don't want either of you getting upset. I haven't been jailed yet, and until that time comes, I want to see happy smiling faces.'

They nodded and said, 'Yes, Dad.'

'Go upstairs and get changed, and we'll all have a quiet night in together. And I'll unplug the phone; we don't want that going off tonight!' While the two children were upstairs getting changed, Rose took Becky's place on the sofa and Slider placed his left arm around her. With both women in his arms, he quietly said, 'I don't want either of you two going to pieces; we're all in this together and until something changes, we carry on as normal.'

'Yes, darling,' said his wife.

Although visibly upset Rose quietly agreed too.

'You two stay put, and I'll go put the kettle on.' He walked into the kitchen, began filling the kettle and caught sight of Sooty's head poking out of her cardboard box, which sat atop the fridge/freezer. 'Whatever are we going to do, girl?' he said, stroking her head while lost in thought.

Becky wandered into the kitchen looking for her favourite Peppa Pig mug. 'Dad, will it be like Shawshank Prison that you might have to go to?'

Slider burst into loud laughter. 'Oh, darling, you really have put a smile on my face.'

'What's all this laughter?' asked Lily, as she wandered into the kitchen, closely followed by her sister.

'Your daughter was wondering if it's going to be like Shawshank Prison if I'm sent to jail.'

'I hope you're not watching films like that,' her mother said sternly.

'I only saw a little bit on the Film 4 preview.'

'Well, that's all right then,' she said, while looking for a new box of teabags.

Later that evening they were all in front of the TV watching the *Mama Mia* film, which had Lily, Rose, and Becky up on their feet and joining in with the songs. Slider and his son were sat together on the sofa and were trying to join in. Andy, who was considered by his family to be the world's worst singer, simply mimed the words. This was a happy evening for all of them, and in the back of his mind, Slider was hoping that in the future he and his family would have many more evenings like this one.

The following morning, Slider was up early and was washed and dressed just after eight o'clock, which came as a surprise to his wife, as she flung her arm across an empty mattress. 'You're an early one this morning,' she said, yawning.

Slider was sat on the side of the bed stroking her long dark hair. 'Did you ever think of going blonde like your sister?'

'No, not really … why, would you prefer me to be blonde?' she asked, while rolling onto her back.

'I like you just the way you are,' he said, kissing her gently on her forehead.

'Why are you up so early?'

'I wanted to get a few things done before Alan arrives.'

'Oh yes, I remember you were saying last night. Off to Elmer's for breakfast.'

'Yes, well, I want to see a few of the boys just in case things don't work out very well tomorrow.'

'What time is it now?'

'It's twenty past eight and the kettle's already boiled. Will you be alright if I go and see the boys?'

'Of course I will.' Slider left the bedroom and could be heard rattling down the stairs. Lily slid her legs out of the bed, stood up and put on her purple and black silk dressing gown which was hanging on the back of the bedroom door. As she gazed out of her bedroom window, she noticed Sooty looking bemused as she stared into the fishpond. As she entered the kitchen the cat bolted through the cat flap and started instantly to meow. 'If he catches you near the fishpond there'll be trouble,' she whispered, while stroking her head.

'Here you are. I thought you were still in bed,' said Slider, who had his wife's favourite cup in his hand.

'I thought I might as well get up; lazing in bed doesn't feel the same when you're alone.'

He stopped what he was doing to hug his wife passionately, just as Andy and his sister entered the kitchen and sat down at the table. 'What are you two going to do when I'm out?' he asked, as they poured cereals into their dishes.

His son shook his head. 'Not sure, Dad.'

'Well, just remember, son, Alexis is going to help you if you get the right exam grades, so I don't want you falling behind with your schoolwork. They don't take just anyone at universities. And that goes for you as well,' he added, looking at his daughter.

'Yes, Dad,' they said in unison.

The kitchen door slowly opened and Rose entered, yawning profusely. 'My head's not so good this morning,' she announced, while looking for a cup.

'Sit down and I'll pour you a nice cup of tea,' said her sister with a smile.

'I'm not surprised after what you drank yesterday,' grinned Slider, who was opening a tin of cat food.

'Well, you have to enjoy yourself when you go out,' blurted Rose, who looked bleary-eyed and tired. 'What time is it anyway?' she asked, while spreading marmalade over her freshly grilled toast.

'It's five past nine,' said her sister. 'And I think you'd better have a shower to wake yourself up.'

'I'd better feed the fish before I go,' said Slider, who was followed into the garden by his son. As he was throwing the fish pellets into the water he spoke candidly to him. 'You're going to have to look after things if I'm jailed, and that means looking after the car and the pond and not feeling sorry for yourself. Do you understand?' he whispered, while looking into his son's eyes.

'Yes, Dad.'

Throwing his arm around his shoulder he said, 'You're going to have to learn to be the man around the house.'

'Dad, Alan's arrived!' shouted Becky from the kitchen door.

'OK, I'll be right there.' Andy and his father went back inside the kitchen and Slider grabbed his brown leather jacket which was hanging on the back of his daughter's chair.

'What time do you think you'll be home?' asked Lily.

'I'll be back by midday, so don't worry.' As he stepped out of his house and into the morning sunshine, a familiar face was standing underneath the sycamore tree. 'Sergeant Dunscombe, back again are we?'

'If it's any consolation to you, I would have done exactly as you did,' he replied in a serious tone.

'Well, that's something we'll never know.' With that, he got into the car, and waved to his wife and family as it pulled slowly away. Looking at his friend Alan he asked, 'Have you told the boys I'll be at Elmer's today?'

'Don't worry, I put the message out as soon as I dropped you off yesterday.'

'Good.'

The journey to the café had him on the edge of his seat. Alan had always been a fast driver, and always liked to talk, especially when he had young women in his car, and although he was a few years older than Slider and possessed grey hair and a moustache and was happy with his partner, he still considered himself to be a bit of a ladies' man. As the car rounded Gabalfa roundabout and moved onto Whitchurch Road, Slider became rather unsettled, which Alan picked up on right away. 'Are you alright?'

'I'm getting a bit nervous, that's all.'

'Fuck off. You nervous? In all the years that I've known you, nerves are not something you suffer with.'

'Well, I'm starting to feel it now, and I only hope I can keep it under control for tomorrow.'

'Don't worry, we'll all be coming to support you.'

The car moved onto Crwys Road, and the Co-op supermarket came into view. It was here that the drivers would park their cars and make the short walk to the café. Slider spotted a few drivers who had parked on the main road, and laughed. 'They haven't changed, have they?' he remarked as the car turned off Crwys Road and headed for the supermarket car park.

'Drivers never change, you should know that.'

As the car made its way into the car park Slider said, 'This brings back memories.' He recognized a number of taxis, and his nerves suddenly disappeared, knowing he was again amongst friends. As he exited the car he threw his leather jacket onto the back seat, and the drivers who had just arrived vented their feelings upon seeing him.

'Slider, how are you?' It was Les, the Capita driver. Les was a bear of a man and didn't give a rat's ass who was around. He would always speak his mind, and sometimes drivers had to remind him to be careful of what he was saying, especially when women and children were close by.

'It's good to see you, Les,' he said as the two men shook hands. 'Still with Capita, I see. When are you going to join us at Carver?'

'Fuck Carver!'

The three drivers walked towards the café, where a number of taxi drivers had already congregated outside to welcome home their hero. There were handshakes and backslapping as he entered the café to a tumultuous round of cheering and clapping. Frosty, Hugh, and Gary were all sat at a table that had a place reserved for their good friend and were joined by Alan and Les. Slider felt at ease with all the drivers, and it took some time to shake hands with everyone. Cliff, the owner of the café, came from the kitchen after hearing the cheering and warmly greeted a familiar face. 'Slider, my good friend, so how are they treating you?' he asked, while taking his order and shaking his hand.

'Well, I don't know if you've heard, but there's a strong possibility that I'll be jailed tomorrow.'

'I'm shocked to hear that, and after you saved the life of that young girl. Life's not fair, is it?'

'No, it isn't, saving the life of that girl means nothing to the courts, all they're interested in is the assault on that police officer.' As Slider ate his breakfast, drivers came and went, and all wished him well for his upcoming court appearance.

'What time does it start tomorrow?' asked Les, who had been talking loudly to someone at the next table.

'Ten o'clock in courtroom number two, at the Magistrates' Court.' Slider caught the eye of Jess the female waitress and ordered himself another coffee.

'Coming right up. Do you boys want more tea or coffee?'

'Yes, why not, we're not in any rush this morning,' said Hugh, who was staring at his phone.

'So, who's going to take your kids to school if things go badly for you?' asked Gary, who was looking concerned.

'Carver I imagine, although we haven't talked about it yet. You wouldn't believe it, but Janey the Carver executive said yesterday that she didn't think that the police officer had done anything wrong.'

'What!' Expressions of disbelief echoed round the room.

'I could have jumped down her throat. It was only because my solicitor was there that I held back.'

'I wouldn't have let her get away with that,' said Les quietly. Laughter went around the table as they all imagined what he would have said. As they ate breakfast, Slider was brought up to date about what had been happening, and who'd be where and with whom. Feeling relaxed, he started to imagine what life would be like if he wasn't with his good friends.

'Is there anything we can do for you?' asked Alan, who had been staring at him.

'Well,' said Slider, who seemed distant and out of sorts, 'some support would be much appreciated tomorrow, because, and being honest with you all, I can't see a way out of this, and I can't afford to go to jail and lose my licence.'

Alan reached across the table and put his hand on his arm. 'Don't worry, we'll all be there.'

Slider smiled, and looking at Alan said, 'And if I'm cleared, you're all welcome to come to the Park Plaza for a celebration drink. Alexis has told me that her husband has made a celebration cake for me.'

'No pressure then,' Frosty said, laughing.

'I owe that woman everything,' said Slider. He looked at the clock on the wall: 11:40. 'Look, guys, I'm going to have to get going, I promised the wife that I'd be home by twelve.' He finished his coffee and took out his wallet.

'And you can put that away!' Alan said, forcefully.

'Oh, thank you.' Slider stood up and waved his goodbyes to the drivers who were still eating. Cliff walked over, shook his hand, and wished him all the best for the following day.

Outside, he said his goodbyes to Hugh, Gary, Les, and Frosty then walked backed to the car park with Alan. The drive to his house was a quiet affair with Slider looking somewhat subdued. Once they had arrived back at his house, Alan turned off the engine and looked him in the eye. 'If there's anything we can do, just let me know.'

Slider looked at his good friend. 'Yes, OK.' But deep down inside he knew there was nothing anyone could do to help him – the next day would bring him either pain or relief – and so he shook Alan's hand, closed the car door, and waved as his good friend drove away. Across the road, he could see Roger cutting the grass with his rotary mower and went over to talk to him. 'Hi Rog, the grass is looking nice.'

'Yes, I just sharpened the blade, and it made a hell of a difference.'

'I just wanted to have a word with you about tomorrow. I had a meeting with my solicitor yesterday and there's a strong possibility that I may be jailed. If that happens Lily may need some help as Rose may soon have to return home.'

Pam came out and along the footpath, after seeing them through the lounge window and said, 'What time do you have to leave tomorrow?'

'Irene, my solicitor, wants me at the hotel at nine o'clock, and the trial starts at ten.'

'Slider was just telling me that he might be jailed,' said Roger, in a subdued voice.

'Goodness gracious, no!' Pam looked shocked. 'Well, if that does happen, you know you can rely on us to help your wife and the children.'

'Thank you, that means a lot to me.' With that, he hugged them, turned and crossed the road, and went back inside his house without a word to the police sergeant.

FIFTEEN

The sun was slowly appearing above the horizon and it was going to be another long hot day, and for some in more ways than one. Slider had been sitting on the side of the bed drinking coffee for over half an hour and was looking aimlessly out of the bedroom window. Below, in the pond, several goldfish pecked at the surface, and the flowers in the borders looked radiant in full bloom.

Today's trial at Cardiff Magistrates' Court could put an end to all his hard work, and today's date with destiny would all be over in just a few hours. The red illuminated figures on the clock showed 06:57 when he placed his hand on it to cancel the alarm, which had been set for seven o'clock. After finishing his coffee, he put on his black and white striped cotton robe and quietly crept downstairs and into the kitchen. After filling the kettle and switching it on, the sound of the cat flap brought in a welcome face. 'And how are you today?' he asked as he picked up his tortoiseshell cat and stroked her head.

After making a pot of tea and feeding the cat, he slowly climbed the stairs, with the cup rattling in its saucer, and placed it down on the bedside cabinet next to his wife. Pulling back the curtains revealed the sun in all its glory, and the bright sunlight awakened his wife, who yawned loudly. 'What time is it?' she asked, reaching for her cup of tea.

'It's twelve minutes past seven, and the sun's already up.'

'Are the children awake yet?'

'I'm not sure.'

'How's your head today?' she asked while placing her cup back in the floral saucer and pulling back the pink duvet cover.

'I've had better days, but if I can get through this day then perhaps we can all have a few days away by the coast somewhere.'

'Well, let's get through this day first.' With that Lily put on her dressing gown and knocked on the children's bedroom doors. Pushing her daughter's door ajar she called out, 'Time to get up, darling!'

'OK, Mum!'

Slider put his head around his son's door and was relieved to see him out of bed. 'Big day, son, so let's not dawdle please.'

'Dad, what time do you have to leave?' he asked, while putting on his Harry Potter dressing gown.

'Half past eight, and Becky's out of the bathroom, so you'd better get in there quick before Rose.' Andy bolted for the door and made it into the bathroom just before his aunty.

'Here you are, Rose, have this cup of tea,' Lily said as she reached the top of the stairs. She followed her sister into her bedroom and said quietly, 'He won't be long in there.' The two women sat on the side of the bed, with Lily's arm around her sister's waist. 'I don't know what I'll do if they jail Slider.'

Rose stood up and placed her cup and saucer on the dressing table next to her hairbrush. 'How can they jail him? He has to travel to London to receive the Queen's Gallantry Medal from Her Majesty the Queen.'

'Do you know, I'd forgotten all about that.' With that the two women burst into laughter.

'I'm out of the bathroom!' shouted Andy.

Lily met her son on the landing. 'Hurry up and get dressed, and I'll start cooking the bacon and eggs.'

'Ah, thanks, Mum.'

Down in the kitchen, the aroma of bacon and eggs filled the morning air. Becky was busy laying out the plates and cutlery, while her father stood over the frying pan. 'How is it going?' asked Lily as she entered the kitchen.

'It won't be long now.'

'Well, you make the tea and coffee and I'll take over, and give Rose and Andy a shout.'

He walked to the bottom of the staircase and shouted, 'Rose, Andy, breakfast in five minutes!' The sound of feet scurrying down the stairs brought them both into the kitchen. Slider poured the teas, and all were happy as they ate breakfast together.

'What time are you going to get dressed?' asked Lily, looking at her husband.

'Well, I had a shower and shave while you were asleep, so I'll get dressed just after eight,' he replied, while covering his egg in brown sauce and checking the clock above the kitchen door: 07:44.

'Are we coming with you, Dad?' asked Andy, who was fiddling with the top on the salt cellar.

'No. I'm leaving here at eight thirty. Your mum and Rose will be leaving at nine o'clock and will meet me at the court at nine thirty. You two will be travelling with Pam and Roger to the Park Plaza Hotel, where we will all meet later in the day. And as a special treat, you and your sister can feed the fish this morning.'

'Thanks, Dad.'

'But don't forget to lock the shed. Now, I'm going upstairs to clean my teeth and get dressed.' After leaving the bathroom, he walked into his bedroom and saw his wife taking out his new blue suit from its protective suit bag.

'What tie would you like to wear with it?' she asked, holding all three aloft for him to look at.

'Choose me a lucky one.' Just after a quarter past eight, Matthew Slider walked down the stairs and into the lounge wearing his new blue suit and brown shoes and was greeted by his family.

'Oh, darling, you look fantastic,' said his wife, who hugged him and had tears in her eyes.

'Careful now, darling, I don't want any tears down my new suit.'

'Dad, you look great,' chorused his children.

Rose, who was sitting next to her sister, said, 'You really do look the part.' And kissed him on the side of his face.

'Dad, there's an awful lot of people outside our house,' said Becky, as she lifted the piano lid.

'God, will it never end?' gasped her mother.

A few minutes later. 'Dad, the taxi's outside,' said his son, who was looking red-eyed and tearful.

'Time to go I suppose. Come on, you lot, happy faces now. I'm not going to be jailed and I want to see you all smiling when I step outside.' With that, he walked to the hallway and kissed everyone before opening the front door. As he walked to the taxi with his wife on his arm and his family surrounding him, many neighbours and friends were cheering him and wishing him well.

Sergeant Dunscombe, who had been standing outside on the pavement for several hours, was trying desperately to hold back the reporters who were bombarding Slider with questions. 'I'll see you at the court at nine thirty,' he said to his wife before giving her a final kiss and dipping his head inside the car. The sergeant closed the door, and he could be seen waving to his family and friends as it slowly moved away.

'Come on, let's get back inside,' said Lily.

'Mum, the phone's ringing!' screamed Andy as he ran inside.

'Answer it then!' she yelled.

'Hello, this is Andy Slider, how can I help you?' The young man listened, then said, 'Just now … here's my mother … It's Alexis, Mum.'

Lily took the phone from her son and breathing heavily said, 'Hi, Alexis, nice to hear from you.' As Alexis talked she stared at her family. 'Yes, see you at nine thirty.' She put the phone down. 'She just wanted to know if everything was OK.'

The rush-hour traffic was heavy, which it always is on any Friday morning. Slider sat quietly behind the driver and opened the window slightly to form a breeze. The journey into the city centre was slow and measured. He spotted a few drivers that he knew, but kept a straight face and thought only of his impending court appearance. The Carver taxi pulled up in front of the Park Plaza Hotel at eight minutes to nine. He gave the driver a two-pound tip. Getting out of the car, Slider thanked the driver and closed the door. The heat from the sun was quite intense even at this hour. After walking up the steps and into the foyer the air conditioning brought a welcome respite. Sitting together around a black glazed coffee table were a few recognizable faces. 'Good morning, Irene, good morning, Lynn.' And looking further to his right. 'Good morning, Janey. How are we all today?'

'Good morning, Slider. I must say you look very smart. In fact, you look every inch the politician in that blue suit.'

'Thank you, Lynn. Where's Alexis?'

'She left something behind in her room and will be joining us shortly,' said Irene, who was handed some papers by Lynn.

'How are your nerves today?' asked Janey, who was still not in Slider's good books.

'Fine. I feel a lot less nervous than when I spoke to Detective Cranshaw.'

'Good, good,' remarked Irene who was staring down at some papers.

'Well, well, well, and what do we have here? Is it a politician? Or is it a business executive?'

Slider turned around and was confronted by Alexis, who was dressed in a black business suit and had a large smile on her face. 'Good morning, Alexis, and it's so good to see you again.' And with that, he placed a kiss on her cheek.

'Nerves OK?'

'Yes.'

'If I may, I think Slider and I should have a few minutes together,' said Irene.

'Come on, Janey, we'll leave them for a minute and you can tell me all about your holiday in the Indian Ocean.' Alexis led Janey away.

Slider sat down next to Irene, who had Lynn sat on her opposite side, and listened intently to what she was saying. From a few metres away Alexis could see Slider nodding and saw him look up at the clock above the reception area to check the time: 09:22. A few minutes later all three stood up and rejoined Alexis and Janey who were chatting together by a black marble pillar. 'If we're ready,' Irene said, 'we'll make our way outside.'

'I'd rather wait until the car arrives if you don't mind; it's too hot for me outside,' said Slider.

'Yes, whatever you wish,' replied Irene, who looked every inch the solicitor in her black matching jacket and skirt.

Janey had been standing by the main entrance door when she spotted the arrival of the black six-seater BMW. 'It's here.'

As they filed through the doors and down the steps Slider smiled at Alexis and whispered, 'Who's riding shotgun today?'

'I knew you'd say that, I just knew it,' she replied, exhaling strongly. 'Go on, you can sit in the front.' Irene and Lynn entered through the sliding side door and sat together, while Janey and Alexis sat on the opposite seat, allowing them all to see and talk to each other. 'Men … they're like bloody children.'

Irene laughed. 'Tell me about it.'

Slider turned and winked at Alexis, who poked out her tongue at him and continued looking out the side window. The journey to the Magistrates' Court took longer than expected, as traffic on Dumfries Place was especially bad. As the car pulled up outside the steps, clusters of reporters and TV cameramen could clearly be seen. At the top of the steps, sheltering in the shade, were his wife and Rose.

'Don't anyone say a word when we get out, and let's make our way inside as quickly as possible,' said Irene. At the top of the steps, Slider greeted Lily and Rose and told them to stay close to him and not to say anything. Once inside, Irene spotted her defence barrister straight away and approached him. 'Good morning, Nicholas. I trust you are well.'

'Very well, thank you, Irene. If you and your party are all assembled, I think we should make our way quickly to a room we can use.' A cold shiver ran down Slider's back when he spotted Detective Cranshaw and Sergeant Faulkner, along with Police Officer Juliet Hanson and Police Officer Hann, entering the building. Irene spotted them too and quickly moved to deflect Slider's gaze and bundled him into the waiting room.

'What's the matter,' asked Lily when she saw her husband's angry expression.

'It's OK, I've just noticed the police contingent entering the building.'

'Get a grip of yourself, Slider, and don't whatever you do go looking for them in the courtroom!' said Irene forcefully, and then turned to speak quietly to her defence barrister.

Slider was sitting in between his wife and Rose when the court usher opened the door and asked, 'Are we all ready?'

Tears started to stream down the faces of both Lily and Rose. On seeing this Slider hugged them both and said, 'I don't want either of you crying in court. We must go in there looking strong and defiant and not showing signs of weakness.' Both wiped their eyes and followed Slider towards court number two. Inside the court, he was shocked to see it packed to capacity. As he took his seat next to Irene he noticed a large gathering of friends and drivers high above him in the public gallery. Gently, he touched the right-hand side of his nose with his index finger to signify that he had seen them.

'Court will all rise,' commanded the court usher.

Everyone in the court stood up and Slider got his first look at the District Judge, Rebecca Etherington. This was a woman he took an instant dislike to. She wore dark-framed glasses and had dark shoulder-length hair which, together with her pale skin and unflattering features, marked her out to be an uncompromising and soulless looking judge, and not the type to give anyone the benefit of the doubt. While on his feet he noticed the prosecuting barrister Rosemary Howard-Stott, who was standing to the left of his own barrister. From his sideways view of her, she looked tough and unflinching, and not the sort of woman who'd give a taxi driver a tip.

After everyone had sat down the presiding judge opened the trial with a statement. 'Ladies and gentlemen of the court, we are here today to conclude the case against Mr Matthew Slider who on Monday, May the seventh, two thousand and eighteen, launched an unprovoked assault on Police Officer Juliet Hanson in the execution of her duties. An assault which left her with a fractured jaw, several loose teeth, and several facial issues, and this has resulted in the police officer being unable to return to work due to severe panic attacks. But I must emphasize that we are not here today to discuss the rescue of Alice Polti from the sea as, although commendable, it does not have any bearing in this courtroom today.'

With that, loud booing could be heard from the public gallery.

'And if I hear any more remarks from the public gallery, I will insist on it being cleared,' said the judge. 'Mr Matthew Slider has already pleaded not guilty to this charge at an interview at Cardiff Central police station on Thursday, May the seventeenth, two thousand and eighteen.'

The prosecution barrister stood up and said, 'I would like to call Mr Matthew Slider to the witness box.'

'Steady now,' urged Irene. 'Take your time.'

He stood up, and noticed Alexis sitting between his wife and Rose and threw them a wink as he walked to

316

the witness box. Standing in the witness box he confirmed his name and swore the written oath in front of him on the Bible. Feeling at ease he cast his eye around the court and could see his friends in the gallery grinning at him, and to his left Sergeant Faulkner, who was looking pleased with himself. He turned and focused his eyes on the prosecution barrister.

'Mr Slider, you pleaded not guilty to the charge of assaulting Police Officer Juliet Hanson at an earlier hearing at Cardiff Central police station. Do you now wish to change your plea?'

'No, I don't,' he replied firmly.

'Mr Slider, are you a man who hits women?'

'Judge, this is speculating,' said Slider's Barrister.

'Please answer the question.'

'No, I am not.'

'So, you would want us to believe that this was the first and only time that you have assaulted a woman?'

'Yes, that's correct.'

'Mr Slider, have you ever spanked your wife?'

A wave of laughter echoed around the court, with Judge Etherington again calling for order. 'I will not have this court descend into bawdiness!' Slider stood resolute and bit his tongue, in defiance of the laughter.

'I'm sorry for that, Judge. Mr Slider, have you ever slapped your wife?'

'Judge, my learned friend is deviating from the case.'

'Judge, I'm merely trying to establish if Mr Slider is a man who strikes women.'

'You may answer the question.'

He looked directly into the eyes of the prosecution barrister and answered firmly and slowly, 'No, I have never, ever hit my wife.'

'Mr Slider, why did you punch Police Officer Juliet Hanson on the pier? Why didn't you just push her out of the way?'

'That is the question that's been continually on my mind, and the answer to your question is, I honestly don't know. It was something that happened in the heat of the moment.'

'It seems to me that you have demonstrated to the court today that you are the type of man who would use his fists first before thinking the matter through. No more questions, Judge.'

Slider's defence Barrister Mr Nicholas Harrington stood up. 'Mr Slider, how long have you been a taxi driver?'

'Sixteen years.'

'So, in your sixteen years, you must have met some awkward and aggressive passengers.'

'Yes, I have.'

'Did you ever come to blows with any of them?'

'No, never.'

'What action would you take if, say, a passenger refused to pay you.'

'If that was to happen, I would let them walk away.'

'Without payment?'

'Yes, but I would report it to my operator who would blacklist that passenger.'

'So, how often does that happen?'

'In my sixteen years, it only happened on three occasions.'

'So, is this why you work for Carver?'

'It is one of the main reasons, yes.'

'What were the other reasons for joining Carver?'

'I had good feedback from other drivers who had joined them. To be perfectly honest, it was like a breath of fresh air compared to other taxi companies that I've worked for.'

'Thank you, Mr Slider, there will be no more questions.'

Slider stepped down from the witness box and gave his wife a quick smile. Irene took his arm and quietly said, 'You did well.'

Turning to face Judge Etherington Mr Harrington said, 'Judge, I would now like to ask Police Officer Juliet Hanson to enter the witness box.'

'Judge, Police Officer Juliet Hanson is not on trial.'

Slider's defence barrister quickly rose to the challenge. 'Judge, I think it only fit and proper that the court should hear testimony from the injured party.'

Judge Etherington looked down in front of her and pondered the question for a few seconds before saying, 'Continue.'

All eyes were on Police Officer Hanson as she made the short walk to the witness box. In Slider's eyes, she looked weak and feeble, and not the type of police officer you would call on in any type of emergency. Police Officer Juliet Hanson stated her name and read the oath she had in her right hand while holding the Bible in her left.

Mr Harrington asked, 'Police Officer Hanson, how long have you been a serving officer in the South Wales Constabulary?'

'Four years.'

'Do you consider yourself to be a good police officer?'

'Yes, I do.'

'Well, Officer Hanson, I put it to you that on Monday, May the seventh, two thousand and eighteen, you were derelict in your duties when Alice Polti fell into the sea and you did absolutely nothing to help.'

'Judge, we are not here today to discuss the accident to Alice Polti!'

'I did say at the start of this trial that the accident to Alice Polti would have no bearing in this trial. We are here today solely for the purposes of determining if Mr Matthew Slider is guilty of the assault on Police Officer Hanson. Please strike that last question from the records. Continue.'

'Officer Hanson, you informed my client Mr Matthew Slider that help was on its way, so what help was sent to aid in the rescue of Alice Polti?'

'Mr Harrington, you are beginning to try my patience. Continue.'

'A lot of people consider you to be a coward; do you think you are?'

'Judge, my learned friend is speculating.'

'You may answer.'

'No, I don't.'

'It seems to me that you were a very frightened police officer that day on Penarth Pier. It was as if you were a rabbit caught in the headlights and didn't know where to turn.'

'I wouldn't agree with that.'

'Have you ever been assaulted while on duty?'

'No, never.'

'So, you've never been involved in any late-night skirmishes when the pubs and clubs are closing?'

'I've never been punched in the face.'

'Have you ever attended any traumatic incidents?'

'I've been at the site of several car crashes and house fires.'

'Have you ever witnessed any murders or dead bodies?'

'I've seen a few murder victims.'

'Did viewing a murder victim affect you at all?'

'Only slightly.'

'No more questions, Judge.'

The prosecution barrister stood up and asked, 'Police Officer Hanson, can you swim?'

'Judge.'

'Judge, I'm just trying to establish a fact.'

'Continue.'

'Not very well.'

'Have you been trained to rescue people from the water?'

'Judge, this has no relevance here.'

'Judge, again I am merely trying to establish a fact.'

'Continue.'

'No, I have not received any training in retrieving people from the water,' she stated firmly.

'No more questions Judge.'

'Police Officer Hanson, you may step down from the witness box, and I would like to say thank you for your testimony in what must be a difficult time for you.' Irene looked at Slider and raised her eyebrows.

District Judge Etherington addressed the court. 'We have heard testimony today from the accused Mr Matthew Slider and we have also heard testimony from Police Officer Juliet Hanson, and I am left in no doubt that Mr Matthew Slider is guilty of the assault on Police

Officer Hanson on Penarth Pier on Monday, May the seventh, two thousand and eighteen.' A large disturbance emanated from the visitors' gallery and other sections of the court upon hearing this verdict. Judge Etherington appealed for quiet. Once order had been restored the judge started her summing up. 'Mr Matthew Slider, would you please stand.'

He stood up and was addressed by the judge.

'Mr Matthew Slider, you strike me as a man who is vicious in his demeanour. A man who would lash out at the least provocation, and would think nothing of assaulting either a man or a woman. The striking of one of Her Majesty's police officers in uniform means little to you, and I am disgusted by your behaviour. You leave me little choice but to jail you for the maximum sentence allowed, which is six months.'

Pandemonium ensued and shouts and screams echoed round the court. In the upper gallery drivers and others were leaning over the balcony shouting and verbally abusing District Judge Etherington. Crunched up pieces of paper and cushions were sent flying through the air as the court bailiff struggled to keep order. Security officials and police were rushed in to regain order. Finally, after a few minutes, order was again restored, and Judge Etherington, who was looking shell-shocked, spoke. 'Ladies and gentlemen of this court. In all my years as a Judge I have never known such terrible and unruly behaviour once a verdict's been reached, and you should all feel thoroughly ashamed of yourselves. Now, earlier today a courier travelled from London to deliver to me a letter. The letter was addressed to me, and I was instructed to read out this letter that I now hold in my hand once the sentence had been passed. I shall now read the contents of this letter to the assembled court.'

'I have been following the events involving Mr Matthew Slider with much interest. All human life is precious, and the life of a young child is especially a precious one.

Sometimes in life we are forced to make difficult decisions about life in the blink of an eye. During the Second World War, I saw many acts of courage that moved me to tears. For many years London was bombarded by the German bombers and although many people died, the will to survive remained.

Mr Matthew Slider had to make such a life or death choice on Penarth Pier and although, sadly, a young police officer was injured, a child's life was saved.

Therefore, it is my solemn wish to grant Mr Matthew Slider a Royal Pardon.

Elizabeth R'

The cheering and clapping that followed was truly deafening and reverberated around the whole court. Slider was tearful as he put his arm around his solicitor and with his voice breaking he said, 'Thank you, thank you very much.'

Once the cheering had subsided District Judge Etherington addressed the court. 'This has been a truly extraordinary court case and one that will never be forgotten. I would like Mr Matthew Slider to stand again please.' He stood up and faced Judge Etherington. 'Mr Matthew Slider, I am truly lost for words, and it remains only for me to inform you that you are now a free man and may leave this court.'

There were cheers and backslapping as Slider moved slowly through the throng of reporters, friends, and well-wishers. He eventually found his wife who was overcome with tears and kissed her passionately.

'Oh, darling, I'm so happy for you, and I'm struggling to find the right words.'

'Say nothing, Lily; I'm also in a state of shock.'

As they slowly filed out of court number two and into the atrium, Slider was greeted by Rose, Alexis, Irene, Lynn, and Janey where kisses and hugs were in abundance. Reporters and microphones were everywhere as everyone tried to get close to their hero. Nicholas Harrington, his defence barrister, put his arm around his shoulder. 'Congratulations, Slider, I'll be dining out on this case for years!'

Making their way down the stairs was a large contingent of taxi drivers who were all hollering and shouting as they made a beeline towards their man. The women took a step back as Slider was engulfed by his most special friends. 'You lucky bastard!' hollered Les as he picked up his good friend in a bear hug.

'You had us all worried for a moment,' said Alan, who eyes were red and swollen.

'If you were worried imagine how I felt; I really thought I was going down.' Slider had his arms around the shoulders of Hugh and Gary and looked like a man who had had the weight of the whole world suddenly lifted from him. 'I'm just going to use the toilet, then we'll go over to the Park Plaza and have a good drink,' he said to his friends. He entered the toilet, and after relieving himself started to wash his hands.

The sound of the door opening seemed insignificant, until a meaty right fist narrowly missed his jaw and smashed into his right shoulder, causing him to yell in pain. He fell to the side of the wash-hand basins and saw the grotesque features of Sergeant Faulkner screaming at him. 'You lucky fucker! If you think you're going to walk out of here, then think again!' Slider managed to stand up. He clenched his fists and gritted his teeth.

The sergeant didn't hear the door being pushed open, but he felt a massive right fist slamming into the side of his head. He turned in shock as Les's left fist caught him flush on the right-hand side of his jaw, sending him sprawling to the floor. Alan, Frosty, Hugh, and Gary stormed into the toilet to see Les finish the sergeant off with a right-hand punch which tore open the nose of the sergeant, and blood spattered across the cubicle door and floor. Hugh and Gary restrained Les from giving the sergeant any further punishment and dragged him unconscious into a cubicle and locked the door, while Alan and Frosty put their arms around Slider to hold him back. The six men huddled together, with Slider looking at Les and thanking him for his intervention.

'Well, you can thank me by getting the drinks in!' he said in his usual loud voice.

With that, they moved towards the door, but were stopped by a court usher trying to enter, who asked, 'What's been going on in here?'

'Nothing,' said Alan. 'Our friend here slipped on the floor.

Slider and his mates, accompanied by the court usher, re-entered the atrium of the building. Lily and Rose spotted Slider through the large melee of reporters, cameramen, friends, and other taxi drivers. On finally grabbing hold of him and kissing him, his wife asked with a large grin on her face, 'Whatever have you done to your tie?'

'You know me, darling, I'm not used to wearing a tie.'

Slider regrouped with his family and friends and exited the Magistrates' Court to a rapturous sound of cheering and clapping. At the bottom of the steps, Janey was waiting by the open doors of the Carver vehicles which would take them all back to the hotel. She hugged him and said quietly, 'I hope I've been forgiven for those unfortunate remarks that I recently made?'

He kissed her. 'Yes, all's forgiven.'

Alexis hugged and kissed him. 'I'm so pleased for you.' Slider was hugging Alexis, when he caught sight of Irene who was standing behind her, and he couldn't help but wonder if somehow she knew all along that this was how it would end. But a chat with Irene would have to wait till later. This day was still developing, and some serious celebrations were about to begin.

As Slider and his entourage entered the reception area of the hotel, they were guided into a large room that was especially designated for partying. It had a large wooden sprung dance floor, and around it were circular glass tables for diners. At one end of the rectangular room was a stage with speakers to one side and a microphone stand which was placed in the centre. At the opposite end of the room was a bar where young ladies dressed in green waistcoats were busy serving the hotel's guests. Once inside he found Becky and Andy and as soon as they spotted their father they rushed over to him. He knelt on the wooden dance floor and hugged them both.

'They didn't send you to jail, Dad?' asked Becky, who had her arms around her father's neck.

'No, darling, they didn't jail me,' he replied laughing.

Andy put his arms round his dad too. 'So, will you have to go back to the police station again?'

'No, son, I'm a free man, and tonight we're staying at this hotel so you can both stay up as late as you wish.'

After seeing his children and after being congratulated by Roger and Pam, who had brought them here to the hotel, Slider looked for his wife through the masses of guests. He eventually found her along with other family members and friends sitting around a table which had seating for ten. No sooner had he sat down than Alexis appeared and poured champagne into a glass for him, and topped up the glasses of others. 'Steady now, you don't want to be getting me drunk too early,' he said, laughing.

'Now that it's finally all over, I think you deserve a night of exuberance,' she replied, smiling. Slider was the centre of attention, and rightly so. The rescue of Alice Polti from the sea, and his subsequent trial at the

Magistrates' Court, had taken its toll on him, and although he was greatly relieved not to be going to jail, he wondered if he would ever be the same again.

The party continued in full swing throughout the afternoon, with laughter and merriment abounding. Around the bar many taxi drivers had congregated, and their loud antics were being kept in check by Alexis, who was patrolling the room and making sure everyone was having a good time. At two thirty she asked the DJ to stop playing records, and a large cake was wheeled into the room by a stocky middle-aged man and a young girl. It was pushed directly towards Slider's table, and as it drew closer he seemed to recognize the little girl. He stood up, open-mouthed, and started trembling when he recognized her. The little girl was Alice Polti. He pushed past a few chairs with tears flowing down his face and knelt in front of the young girl and held her close. He planted a kiss on the side of her cheek. 'Oh Alice, it's so good to see you again.' The whole room erupted with cheering and clapping.

The young girl quietly said, 'Nice to see you, Slider, and this is my daddy.' She looked up at the man who was holding her hand.

He stood up and the two men hugged each other. 'You've certainly surprised me today. I'm Matthew Slider and I'm so pleased to meet you at last.'

The stocky man had short curly hair and was wearing a light cream suit with a white open-neck shirt. Tearfully, with a slight Italian accent, he said. 'Mr Slider, I'm Roberto Polti, and I can't thank you enough for what you have done for me and my family. You will always be like a brother to me.'

Alexis, who was also tearful, joined the two men. Slider kissed her and said, 'I should have known that you would do something like this.'

'Well, this is a very special day for you, and I wanted to mark it in a very special way.'

'You've really caught me out. I never expected anything like this,' he said, wiping his eyes.

'Well, are you going to cut your cake?' asked Alexis, who had linked arms with her husband.

'Just give me a moment please.' Slider was joined by his wife, their children, and Rose. He took a deep breath, wiped his eyes again, and stared down at his beautiful, iced cake. It was rectangular in shape and was decorated with a large black car in the middle. It had the word Carver on its side in white icing, and a face looked out from the car. 'Is that supposed to be me?' he asked, pointing at the face.

'No, he's better looking than you,' joked his wife as she hugged him.

'Before I cut this cake I would like to say that this has been one of the happiest days of my life. And it was made so by the Polti family, who have looked after me and my family, and who have baked for me this beautiful cake, and who I now regard as my family. So, I would like to ask Roberto to help me cut this cake which will seal our friendship.' Roberto stood by Slider's side and the two men looked at each other as the knife sliced through the cake. A wave of clapping filled the afternoon air.

The Slider family and the Polti family were helping to distribute the cake around the room to their guests when Slider noticed several drivers waving to him. As he approached them his good friend Alan said, 'We're going to have to go now, we've got the school run to do.'

Slider glanced at the clock on the wall. 'Well, I want to thank you all for the help that you have given me, and in particular to you, Les,' he said looking at the man.

Les smiled. 'Any time, Slider, any time!' He walked with them to the main entrance and waved as they disappeared into the afternoon crowd.

Back in the ballroom Slider was handing out more portions of his cake when Alexis approached him. 'I thought you might like to know that Irene and Lynn will have to leave at two forty-five to catch the train back to London. Also, Janey's mother has been rushed into hospital, and so she's had to leave for the airport.'

On hearing the news Slider searched the room, looking for Irene, and found her in a quiet corner far away from the loud music. 'Here you are. Alexis tells me that you have to leave.'

'Yes, I'm afraid so, we have a busy day in London tomorrow.'

'Where's Lynn?'

'She's upstairs, packing.'

'Well, before you leave, I would like to talk to you about that royal pardon that was bestowed on me. Because in the back of my mind I can't help but feel that you were somehow instrumental in its award to me.'

'Well, if you remember, I did say that the picture wasn't as black as it appeared to be.'

'I do, and if I remember, I said that it looked pretty grim from my side of the table.'

'Firstly, I must warn you that if you ever breathe a word to anyone about what I'm about to divulge to you, then you'll be jailed, and they'll throw away the keys. Do you understand?' she warned, looking deep into his eyes.

'Yes, I do.'

'Very well. You were given a royal pardon because of a special favour that was bestowed on me many years ago. During the spring of nineteen forty-four, the German army was close to capitulating when a senior

German officer put forward an audacious plan to kidnap both Princess Margaret and Princess Elizabeth from Buckingham Palace and ransom them for Winston Churchill. The German enigma typists were very sloppy, thinking that no one could crack their enigma codes, but the code breakers at Bletchley Park were reading them as quickly as the Germans were typing them. The Germans used an eight-man team from the Brandenburg, which was a German special forces unit proficient in foreign languages and capable of blending in wherever deployed. The unit was dropped off by submarine on the south coast on the seventh of August nineteen forty-four, and quickly made its way to London where we at MI5 first located them. The plan was to kidnap the girls on August the twenty-first, which was Princess Margaret's fourteenth birthday. On the said night, I, along with a detachment of commandoes, was lying in wait, while the princesses had been moved to Windsor Castle for safety. A running gun battle ensued throughout the palace, with only minor injuries to the commandoes while all eight Germans were killed. Two weeks later both I and the commandoes were summoned to the palace where we received, in privacy, the George Cross from King George VI, although, and according to official records, this plot never happened. The two princesses were also in attendance and bestowed on us a special favour for saving them from kidnap. I contacted the palace last week and used a code to activate my special favour to prevent you from being jailed.'

'I'm stunned,' said Slider. 'So you were an MI5 agent during the war?'

'Yes, I was, and don't look so surprised; lots of young women were either MI5 or SOE agents during the war.'

'Has anyone else ever been given a royal pardon?'

'In two thousand and thirteen, Alan Turing was given a posthumous royal pardon.'

'Does Alexis know about you?'

'No, she doesn't, and please, let's keep it that way!'

'I don't know what to say.' Slider, who looked shocked, said, 'So why did you choose to help me?'

'Because you've got something called grit and it's sadly lacking in a lot of men these days, and unfortunately, I'm not getting any younger.'

Lynn poked her head around a pillar. 'I'm sorry to have taken so long, I mislaid a shoe.'

'That's alright, we had a nice chat while you were packing,' said Irene, who was staring into Slider's eyes.

Alexis walked up to where Slider, Irene, and Lynn were sitting. 'Irene, Lynn, your taxi has arrived.'

Slider wheeled their cases to the car and placed them in the boot, then firstly hugged and kissed Lynn and then Irene, who handed him her business card. Quietly he said to her, 'I will never forget what you have done for me.'

Irene smiled. 'And when you receive your medal from Elizabeth don't forget to mention that Irene said thank you.'

'I won't forget.' The two women entered the car and both Slider and Alexis could be seen waving as it pulled away. 'Irene is an extraordinary woman,' he said as the car disappeared into the distance.

'Yes, she certainly is, and you wouldn't believe it to look at her, but Irene is ninety-four years old.'

'I'm shocked. But there again, she's one of a kind. If you don't mind me asking, how did the two of you first meet?'

'Some years ago I was asked to refurbish a large country mansion which had been requisitioned by the army during World War Two for training purposes. At the time it was derelict and almost beyond repair, and I was looking for a good no-nonsense solicitor and was put in touch with Irene by its owner.' As they re-entered the hotel Alexis asked, 'So when will you and your family be travelling to London to come and stay with us?

'Well, I'm receiving my medal on Wednesday the twenty-ninth, so I was thinking of bringing the family to London on the Sunday beforehand.'

'Yes, that's fine. It will give me a few days to show you and your family the sights of London. Oh, and please ask Becky to bring her music with her.'

'OK, I won't forget.'

Slider and Alexis re-entered the hotel and celebrations continued well into the late evening, with joy and happiness in abundance.

SIXTEEN

The train pulled into Paddington railway station only two minutes behind schedule at 11:47 a.m., on what was another hot sunny morning in August. This was the first time that the Slider children had ever visited London, and both were eager to see the sights. In fact, Slider could count on the fingers of one hand the times he had visited the city. As the train pulled in slowly and stopped at platform number two, everyone was happy, and it was very noticeable to him how his wife Lily seemed more youthful and full of life now his trial was finally over. And with Rose in tow, they were like a pair of naughty girls on a day out.

As they all made their way down the stairs and towards the concourse of the station, the number of people jostling to leave the station made it a slightly unnerving experience for the whole family, who weren't used to being confined into such a small space with so many people surrounding them. Finally, they reached the concourse with Slider saying, 'I'll phone Alexis and see where she is.' Putting one finger to his ear to deaden the station's noise he listened then replied, 'OK, see you in a few minutes.' Looking at his family he said, 'She's standing outside the WH Smith store.'

Everyone starting to look around for the shop when Rose pointed. 'It's down the other end by the photo booth.'

'Got lost, did you?' asked Alexis, who was smiling and hugging them. Looking at Slider she said, 'I didn't think a taxi driver could get lost in here.'

'And it's very nice to see you again.' And with that, he hugged and kissed her.

'I thought it would be better to use a taxi rather than my own car.'

'Well, that's a relief,' he whispered.

'What did you say?'

'Nothing. I was just thinking how nice it would be for us to ride in a London black cab.' She looked at him, her eyes slowly narrowed, and a smile crept round her mouth.

The line of black cabs seemed to stretch as far as the eye could see, and the line of people who had just left the station was equally as long. Eventually, they found themselves at the head of the queue, and the driver of a silver eight-seater Volkswagen Caravelle opened the doors. They got in, leaving the driver and Slider to struggle with the luggage. 'St Mary's Gate, please, driver!' said Alexis as the car performed a U-turn. After leaving the station the car moved onto London Street which would take them across the Serpentine.

'Dad, what's that fountain over there?' asked his son, who was pointing.

'That's the Princess Diana memorial fountain,' replied the driver. Slider could see from his badge that his name was Harry Cumming. 'Are you here visiting our capital?' he asked, while staring at Slider in his mirror.

'My friends are here for a few days and have business at the palace,' replied Alexis, who had her back to the driver.

'If you don't mind me saying so,' said the driver, who was still focused on Slider, 'your face looks very familiar.'

'Well, Harry, if you've been reading the papers, or watching the TV then probably you will have seen my face.'

Then out of the blue it happened. The penny suddenly dropped into the driver's mind. 'You're Slider!' he screamed.

'Yes, that's me,' he replied as everyone started to laugh.

'Don't forget to turn right towards Kensington,' said Alexis as they approached the junction. The driver didn't forget and as they headed towards the Borough of Kensington, everyone was struck by the beauty of the architecture.

'So, when are you receiving your medal?' Harry asked.

'Wednesday morning.'

'Well, good luck to you. You deserve it after what they put you through.'

'Thanks.'

The cab moved slowly into St Mary's Gate and stopped outside a three-storey red-brick Edwardian townhouse. 'We're here,' said Alexis as the driver started to open the doors.

'Do you think I could have my picture taken with you?' asked Harry, who was helping everyone with their cases and bags.

'Certainly, you can.'

He gave his phone to Alexis and stood next to Slider, and put his arm around his shoulder. 'Big smile.'

'Thanks, this means a lot to me.'

'Any time.'

Slider was massaging his forehead when Alexis said, 'You're going to have to get used to people asking you for a photo.'

'My husband doesn't like having his photo taken, do you, darling?'

He rolled his eyes. 'The things I have to do for people!'

As they entered Alexis's home they were warmly greeted by Roberto, who was wearing his black and white striped chef's apron. 'Welcome, welcome to our home. Please let me help you with your bags.'

Alexis showed the Slider family into their spacious lounge, which had a beautiful wooden floor that was covered in oriental rugs. 'This is a beautiful room,' said Lily as the whole family plonked themselves down on the leather sofas.

Roberto entered the room carrying a large china teapot and placed it down on the brass serving trolley which had several cups and saucers on it, as well as the milk jug and sugar bowl. On the lower tier, several small cakes were in evidence. 'I've made you a nice cup of tea.' Then looking at Slider he said, 'My wife she says you like coffee.'

'Thanks, white coffee with demerara sugar will be fine.'

Looking at the children Roberto said, 'I have some nice Italian chinotto for you two.'

'You'd better make him a pot of coffee darling,' shouted Alexis as her husband was leaving the room. 'And go and find Alice and tell her Becky and Andy have arrived.' Just as Roberto was leaving the room, his daughter poked her head around the door. 'Did you fall asleep, darling?' asked her mother, who was pouring the teas.

'Yes, Mummy.'

'Well, go and sit next to Becky, and I'll get you a chinotto.'

After they'd finished their drinks the Slider family was given a tour of the house. From the third-floor bedroom windows they could just make out the Shard building to their right. Once they were settled back in the lounge, Alexis informed them that lunch would be ready in twenty minutes and that her husband had made an Italian light salad.

'Would you like us to help lay the dining room table?' asked Lily, who felt rather uncomfortable doing nothing.

'Well, I've almost finished, but the cutlery and wine glasses need to go on the table. There is also a surprise for Becky in the alcove.' As they entered the dining room a large ruby-red cut-glass vase had a prominent position in the middle of the smoked glass table. It was goblet-shaped and filled with pink tulips, and around its surface was a map of the world in gold leaf.

As Becky entered the room, she discovered a white digital piano in the alcove. The young girl beamed with delight and asked Alexis, 'Can I play it now?'

'Of course you can.' With that, the young girl rushed upstairs to fetch her music from the bedroom that she would be sharing with her aunty. While they were all eating their Parma ham salad, Alexis put forward some ideas for activities to entertain them. 'Tonight, we're going to have a river cruise on the Thames, and after the cruise we're going on to an Italian restaurant that I know. Tomorrow, I'm taking you all to the London Eye.'

Looking at his children Slider said, 'So, what do you think about that?'

'Sounds great, Dad,' said Andy who seemed genuinely excited.

'And what about you, darling?' he asked, looking at his daughter.

Becky was drinking through a straw and nodding in approval then said, 'Alexis, where do they keep the dinosaurs?' Laughter went around the table.

'Would you like to see them?' she asked, smiling at the young girl.

'Yes, please.'

Turning to Andy, she said, 'Would you like to see them as well?'

'Yes, I would.'

Looking at Lily and Rose she said, 'Would you two like to come with us to the museum?'

'It's very kind of you to ask us, Alexis, but if you don't mind Rose and I would prefer to do some shopping while we're here.'

'Well, in that case on Tuesday we'll drop you two off at Harrods in Knightsbridge, and the rest of us will travel to the Natural History Museum, and later we can all meet up for lunch somewhere. So, how does that sound?' Everyone seemed in agreement and looking at Slider she said, 'Would you prefer to go shopping with your wife or come with us to the museum?'

He sat rigidly in his chair and said in a single word, 'Museum.'

'I'm afraid my husband's not a lover of the shops, are you, darling?' He didn't answer that question, but merely moved his head from side to side. More laughter went around the room as his wife planted a kiss on his cheek. The remainder of the lunch was eaten in a jovial spirit, with Roberto giving an account of how he first met Alexis when she was studying at the London School of Economics while he was working as a head chef at an

Italian restaurant on the Thames waterfront. While the teas and coffees were being served, Becky took the opportunity to play a few pieces from her piano syllabus. Lily noticed her husband massaging his head again. 'Is everything OK, darling?' she asked softly so as not to disturb her daughter's playing.

'My head's giving me a few problems … so I might have to lie down before we go out tonight.'

Later that afternoon Slider was lying on the bed, massaging his temples, when his wife, who was lying next to him, said, 'Have you had your injection today?'

'Yes, I did it this morning before we left, but I'm getting these stabbing pains every so often.'

'Well, look, if you're not feeling well we won't go out tonight.'

'No, no, I'll be OK, it's probably linked to the trial, and this hot weather doesn't help me either.'

'Well, you stay here and have a nap, and I'll go downstairs and rejoin the others.'

She returned to the lounge and found the children watching a *Star Wars* film on the wall-mounted TV while Alexis and Rose were deep in conversation and giggling over some item in a fashion magazine. The two women turned their attention to Lily who sat next to her sister, with Alexis asking with concern in her voice, 'How's your husband?'

'He's OK. His head's been troubling him, and he's still very tired, and this hot weather doesn't agree with him.'

'Well, let me get you a drink. Would you like a glass of wine?'

She looked at her sister. 'Am I allowed another glass of red wine today?'

'Well, just one more!' replied Rose sternly.

Looking at Alexis she said, 'Just a small glass, please.'

While pouring wine into her glass, Alexis said, 'If you don't mind me asking, what brought on your alcoholism?'

Turning her eyes to the ceiling she said, 'Him upstairs. I was left at home with two young children to look after while Slider was working all the hours day and night and we hardly saw each other. So I took comfort in a few glasses of wine every night.'

'Is your drinking under control now?'

'Yes, it is. The champagne at the nursing home was the first alcoholic drink that I've had for several months.' And with that, the women toasted each other and turned their attention to the important topic of shopping in Knightsbridge.

Shortly after, Roberto entered the lounge with some glasses of chinotto for the children as well as some pink coloured ice cream, which was served in a white dish and had a wafer on the top. On seeing the three women drinking red wine, he disappeared back into the kitchen and reappeared a few minutes later with a selection of cheeses, along with some Italian cheese biscuits and red grapes. 'I thought you might like some cheese and biscuits to go with your wine,' he said, removing some cups and saucers from the table.

'Thank you, darling,' said Alexis. 'What are you doing in the kitchen?'

'I'm making some pastry for tomorrow.'

'He's a real treasure,' sighed Rose. 'I wish I could find a man like that.'

'Well, you keep your eyes off him,' said her sister, and with that the three women broke down into fits of laughter.

'So, what's all this laughter about?' said Slider, who had just entered the lounge and plonked himself down on one of the reclining armchairs.

'Rose has got her eyes on Roberto,' smirked his wife. 'How's the head now?'

'Not too bad. I could do with a cup of coffee though.'

'Well, you put your feet up and I'll make you one,' Alexis said, as she headed towards the kitchen.

'And you'd better warn your husband that Rose is on the prowl.'

'Oh, darling.'

'Well, Rose is always chasing some bloke.'

'I can't help it if I find men attractive,' said Rose, who was sipping her wine.

'The problem with you, Rose, is the men you chase are usually already married.'

Alexis returned with a cup of coffee for Slider. 'Will you be OK for tonight?'

'Yes, I'm looking forward to it.' The film finished and the three children descended upon their parents, with them all asking Slider if he was alright.

Roberto appeared with plates of small squares of toast which were covered in several different types of pate. The children wasted no time in devouring them, and between mouthfuls Becky asked, 'What time are we going out?'

'Well, the boat leaves the Tower Pier at six thirty, so we're leaving here at six o'clock,' replied Alexis, who was looking at the young girl while deciding on what piece of toast to eat.

Slider looked at the gold carriage clock which sat on a small table next to the fruit bowl. It was twenty past five. 'I'm going to have a shower and get changed.'

Andy, who had been unusually quiet all day, suddenly asked, 'Alexis, where am I sleeping tonight?'

'Well, my daughter's sleeping in our bedroom for the next few nights, so you're going to have to sleep in Alice's bedroom, which I'm afraid is all pink.'

'Great,' he replied in a whisper.

The two black taxis arrived within a few minutes of each other, with the Slider family taking the rear car while the Polti family entered the front cab. The journey from Kensington to the River Thames took in a lot of the sights that most of them had never seen before, and it appeared to Slider that the drivers were taking the scenic route to the river. Lily and her sister were thrilled when the cab drove past Harrods and the two children were glued to the window when the cab passed the London Eye and drove past the Shard, which even to Slider looked very impressive.

They joined the queue of people waiting to board the river barge and eventually it started to move. On board, everyone was happy with their seating as a large party of Chinese students had cancelled their trip at the last minute. Roberto decided to sit next to Slider and his son. Soon the three men were deep into a conversation about football, while the five women, who were also sitting together, were admiring the sights of the river from the port side of the barge.

As the vessel made its way down the river, famous landmarks were pointed out to Slider and his family, and the evening cruise was turning into a delight for everyone. Glasses of a sparkling drink and various kinds of cold canapes were served. On the return journey an Elvis impersonator belted out various songs which went down very well with his audience. As the barge returned to the Tower Pier after its ninety-minute cruise, a line of cabs were eagerly awaiting some business.

The journey to the *Cantina Del Ponte* restaurant, which was situated on the opposite side of the river Thames, took only a few minutes on this sultry Sunday evening. Once inside, Roberto wasted no time in greeting the staff and its manager. This was Alexis's favourite restaurant, a place that she had frequented many times over the years. Their table which had been reserved for them had stunning views over the Thames and everyone was delighted with what they could see.

When the menu arrived Slider and his family were slightly disconcerted to discover it was in Italian. It was left to Alexis and her husband to take charge of translating and ordering. Slider was back to his jovial best, telling stories which defied belief. Rose couldn't keep still and was wandering around as if she was on a catwalk. The three children loved the restaurant and as the evening turned to dusk, the lights along the banks of the Thames turned the river into a very atmospheric arena. The Slider family had had an exhausting day, and everyone was starting to yawn, so at ten o'clock the taxis were ordered. Everyone slept very soundly on that Sunday night.

The following morning, they all woke slightly late and bleary-eyed. Except for the children that is, who were especially looking forward to visiting the London Eye and had been awake for the last hour. While seated at the dining room table eating breakfast with her family, Lily stared at the vase in front of her. 'This is a beautiful vase.'

Alexis, who was passing the dining room with a tray in her hands, said, 'Yes, isn't it, my husband bought it for me as a wedding present when we were on our honeymoon in Venice. Roberto thinks of me as "his world", and every week he buys me flowers to put in it.'

'I think Slider bought me a set of saucepans when we got married.'

'No, I didn't!' he said. 'If I remember correctly, I bought you that beautiful gold watch that you have around your wrist.'

'Oh yes, darling, you are right.'

'Saucepans indeed!' Slider shook his head in disbelief, then changing the subject he asked his children, 'Did you two sleep alright?'

'Well, it's a bit noisier here than at our house,' said his son, who was finishing his breakfast of Parma ham and eggs.

'Well, you have to expect more noise when you're living in the middle of a major city like London. Some shops and bars stay open all night.' Casting his eye towards his daughter he asked, 'And did you sleep alright?'

'Not too bad, although Aunty Rose does snore a bit.'

'Oh, what a cheek!' Rose poked out her tongue at her smiling niece.

'Does anyone want any more tea or coffee?' asked Roberto, who was starting to clear away the breakfast dishes.

'Yes, please,' said Slider. 'I haven't seen your wife this morning.'

'When she's busy, she takes her breakfast up to her office, which is next to our bedroom.'

Later

'Good morning,' said Alexis, as she entered the dining room with her breakfast tray in hand. 'I'm sorry I couldn't join you for breakfast, but I'm away filming in a few days and certain preparations had to be made.'

'Let me take your tray, and I'll get you a cup of tea,' smiled her husband as he kissed her and then returned to the kitchen.

'Thank you, darling. So, what time would you all like to leave?' she asked looking around the table.

Slider looked at his wife's wristwatch. It was nine fifteen. 'Shall we say ten o'clock?'

A line of nodding heads smiled back at him. 'Ten o'clock it is then.'

'Alexis, can I play the piano please?'

Looking into Becky's bright blue eyes she said, 'You can play the piano whenever you wish, but just make sure we're all awake first.'

'OK.'

Becky was still sitting at the piano when the taxi announced its arrival by beeping its horn. 'Time to go, darling!' said her mother, who was putting her lipstick on. The young girl turned the digital piano off and looked for her lilac-coloured jacket, which was in the downstairs cloakroom.

Inside the taxi, the driver was given instructions from Alexis to take the scenic route to the London Eye. It was another beautiful warm morning in London, and Slider was somewhat shocked at the congestion of traffic on the roads. 'I couldn't work in all this traffic,' he said to Roberto, who was sitting opposite him.

'You'd get used to it after a while.'

As the taxi approached Buckingham Palace, Slider got his first look at the gate he would have to enter. Goosebumps ran along his arm at the splendour of the palace. 'That's where we have to go on Wednesday,' he said to his family.

As they all looked at the palace, Becky asked, 'Dad, is that where the queen lives?'

'Yes, that's where the queen lives.'

'Getting nervous are we now?' asked Rose, who was smiling at her brother-in-law.

'Just a bit.'

Lily put her arm around her husband and whispered, 'Don't worry, you'll be fine.'

The view from the top of the London Eye was spectacular on this cloudless morning. They were fortunate to have a pod to themselves. As it slowly turned, many landmarks, and even Alexis's home, were pointed out. As they crested the top of the Eye, Andy said to his father, 'Dad, could we go to the top of the Shard?'

'If you want to, yes. But as soon as we get off we'll have something to eat and drink.' The waterside eateries were all doing a fine brisk business on this Monday morning. The two families were sitting at a traditional English café/bar eating and drinking when Slider said, 'I still can't get over the number of people who congregate around the waterside.' Looking at Alexis he said, 'Are all these people tourists?'

'The vast majority of them are. London is one of the major capital cities in the world, and people flock here for our history and tradition.'

He was nodding in response when he winced and moved his left hand to the back of his head then exhaled slowly. Everyone spotted it, which made his wife ask, 'Is your head giving you problems again?'

'I'm getting this stabbing pain in the back of my head every now and then, and it's a bit different to what I've had before.'

Alexis looked directly into his eyes and said, 'If this is too much for you, we'll return to my home right now!'

'No, no, I'll be fine, it only lasts a second or two, so please don't worry.' Alexis looked at his wife and raised her eyebrows. Slider finished his cup of coffee, stood up, and said, 'Are we going to the Shard or not?'

'Only if you're sure,' said his wife, who looked concerned.

'Look, darling, I've had problems with my head for years, so let's not make a drama out of it, please.' As they all walked along the Thames embankment, the morning temperature started to rise, forcing Slider to take off his brown leather jacket and hold it over his right shoulder with his index finger. Just ahead of them was a silver eight-seater taxi which was dropping off passengers. He crossed the road and spoke to the driver. 'Morning, mate, could you take our party to the Shard please?'

'Yes, no problem.' Trying to cross London on this busy morning was easier said than done. Cars and lorries were everywhere and no one seemed interested in giving way to anyone. Cyclists seemed to have a death wish, turning sharply in front of vehicles and ignoring pedestrian crossings and traffic lights. Slider was used to that, but this was on an unimaginable scale and was shocking.

The three children were in awe as they stood below the Shard and tried to look at its very top, so much so that Alice caused a minor scare when she leaned back so far that Slider had to move very quickly to prevent the little girl from falling backwards onto the paving. 'That's twice I've saved you now,' he gasped, taking a breath.

'Sorry,' said the little girl, who looked slightly dazed.

'Whatever would we do without you?' Alexis put her arm around his neck and kissed him. Inside the Shard, the scene from the open air sky deck was a truly wondrous sight, and one could see to infinity. Everything looked so small, and the pedestrians below were like dots on a page. As they moved around the viewing gallery every part of London was visible. After everyone had seen enough, Alexis asked, 'Does anyone want a cup of coffee or tea?'

'Yes, please,' said Rose. 'My feet are killing me, and I could do with sitting down for a while.'

'Why you choose to wear high heels every time we go out, God only knows ... I think tomorrow you'd better wear some flat shoes when we go shopping.'

'Perhaps you're right, sis.'

The lift only took a few seconds to take them down to the sky lounge on level thirty-four. Inside Alexis took the orders. Slider was quite shocked at the exorbitant prices, but reflected that this was London and this was the Shard. Andy was drinking his orange when he asked his father, 'Dad, what's that ship down there?'

'I'm not sure, son.' Looking at Roberto he asked, 'Do you know what ship that is below us?'

'Ah yes, that is HMS *Belfast*.'

'Dad, there seems to be lots of people going on the ship, do you think we could go on it?'

'Well, we'll have to see, son.'

Rose was sitting at a table massaging her foot. Watching her, Becky asked, 'Aunty Rose, will I wear shoes like yours one day?'

'Well, let me tell you, young lady, always make sure you get yourself a good comfortable pair of high heels to wear.'

Picking up Rose's shoe, her mother said to her, 'These are not for walking in, darling, these are for special occasions.' She put her arm around her sister's shoulder and kissed her gently on the cheek. Rose slowly exhaled.

'Your son has just given me an idea,' said Alexis, who was staring at Slider.

'And what's that?'

'Well, with Rose being unable to walk very far, and with HMS *Belfast* being so close, I was just wondering, why don't we go on board the ship and have lunch?'

Andy stared open-mouthed at his father. 'Can we, Dad?'

'Well, only on one condition,' he said, looking at Alexis.

'And what's that?'

'You allow me to treat you all to lunch.'

'You don't have to pay for anything, you're our guests,' said Alexis sternly. 'But if it makes you happy, then yes.' After finishing their drinks they left the Shard, crossed Tooley Street, and walked the short distance down Morgan's Lane to the water's edge. The ship was not as large as HMS *Deacon*, but it did bring back fond memories to Slider of his time on that warship.

'Keep your eyes to yourself now, Rose, we don't want you running off with a sailor!' said Lily as they boarded the ship.

'I've always fancied a sailor, especially an officer,' said her sister, who was again struggling with her high heels.

'Well, not today, if you don't mind.'

HMS *Belfast* allowed its visitors to view all areas of the ship. With Alexis, Rose, and her sister preferring to have a drink, the two men and the children set off to explore. Wax dummies took the place of crewmen and gave the party a sense of what life was like aboard this ship. This was the highlight of the day for Andy, and standing next to the ship's guns on the deck filled the young man with delight. After touring the ship, they all returned to the café.

'Well, did you see everything?' asked Lily.

'It was great, mum!' said her son, who was overcome with emotion.

'I saw where all the sailors sleep,' said Becky, who was a bit puffed out.

'And what about you, Alice, did you see everything?' The little girl, who seemed tired, just nodded her head.

'I suppose you two were like big kids?' said Alexis as she looked at the men.

Slider, who had a large smile on his face and an arm round Roberto's shoulder, said, 'Of course we were. Now, what are we all having to eat?' Lunches were duly ordered and everyone was happy and smiling as they ate, except that is for Slider, who was having another stabbing sensation in the back of his head. He focused his gaze on the far side of the Thames and after a few moments the pain faded.

'Are you alright, darling?' Noticing that her husband seemed a bit distant for a moment.

'Yes, I was just taking in the view.'

Alexis caught his eye as he was talking to his wife and could see he'd had another troublesome moment, so she said, 'Once we've finished lunch, I'm afraid we're going to have to return home. I've got some filming in a few days, and some calls need to be made.' No one seemed displeased at this news. The day had been enjoyed by all. Alexis could see that everyone was just a bit tired and worn out from all the walking. With the sun beating down, it was some relief when the taxi dropped them off at St Mary's Gate.

'I'm going to have a shower and have a lie down for a while,' said Slider as he entered the house.

'Would you like me to make you a coffee?' asked Alexis, as she entered the kitchen.

'Yes, please.'

'You go and lie down, and I'll bring it up to your room in a few minutes.' The women were drinking their teas that Roberto had just made, and the children were all looking tired as they were drinking their juices, which Alexis observed with her keen eyes as she passed the lounge and made her way to Slider's room with his coffee. 'I saw you grimace on the ship, and wondered if you had another painful moment.'

'You don't miss much, do you?' he said. 'I'm going to need a quieter day tomorrow. Wednesday's going to be a hectic day, and I need to be at my best for my investiture.'

'Absolutely. Well, once we drop your wife and Rose off at Harrods, we'll have a gentle stroll around the museum.'

'Yes, that will be fine.' After showering and shaving, Slider lay on the bed and closed his eyes. He cast his mind back and tried to imagine Irene being involved in a running gun battle through Buckingham Palace. He conceded to himself how fortunate he was to have had such an extraordinary woman defending him. That thought put a smile on his face as he gently fell asleep.

The next morning it was again sunny, and everyone was starting to get used to the daily routine. Becky had discovered that she could use her brother's headphones while playing the digital piano, which allowed her to play early in the morning and avoid her auntie's snoring. By half past eight everyone was assembled in the kitchen, eating breakfast. Lily and her sister were discussing where to go shopping and what to see and buy, while the children were talking about what dinosaurs they wanted to see.

Slider was quite happy to just sit back and listen to the discussions taking place. The previous night's sleep had been undisturbed, and he felt fresh and wide awake, and his head was clearer than it had been for some time.

'So, how are you feeling this morning?' asked Alexis, who was still concerned about her guest.

'I'm fine, I slept very well, and my head's a lot clearer this morning.'

'Good, I'll order the taxi for nine thirty which should give your wife and Rose plenty of time to do their shopping.' The eight-seater Mercedes arrived only a few minutes late, with the driver apologizing for the heavy traffic. 'First stop Harrods, please, driver, and then onto the Natural History Museum.' The traffic was again horrendous as the car moved slowly through it, but it gave everyone a chance to see the various sites and to people watch. As the car pulled up outside Harrods, a doorman was on hand to help Lily and Rose, who was wearing flat shoes today, out of the car. 'We'll meet you both here at twelve thirty,' said Alexis as the car door was closing, and everyone waved at each other as the Mercedes pulled away. The journey to the museum was only a short one, and Slider had the distinct impression that it would have been just as quick to have walked.

The museum was packed with schoolchildren, and what looked like international students, which made it a noisy environment for all of them. Slider had picked up a guidebook before entering and handed it to his daughter who was taking the lead and directing them on which way to go round. As Becky entered the dinosaur gallery, a huge Iguanodon left them all speechless at its vast size. 'Imagine being chased by that, darling,' Slider said to his daughter.

'I don't think he would see me.'

'No, but he would probably smell you,' giggled her brother.

'Will you tell him, Dad!'

'Well, lots of dinosaurs had bad eyesight and used scent to find their prey,' said her father, looking down at her. Becky instinctively poked her tongue out at her brother and walked on.

'Take us to the café will you, please?' said Alexis. 'Alice needs the toilet.'

Becky studied the map and pointed with her finger. 'There's a café in Hintze Hall, which is up here.' As they walked along the hall a Mantellisaurus skeleton took their breath away. They all stood motionless, while Alexis took her daughter to the loo.

'Who would like a cup of coffee and a piece of cake?' asked Alexis as she returned with her daughter. Nobody declined the offer, so they walked to the Central café and were lucky to find an empty table with six chairs. Roberto gave his wife a hand to carry the trays back to the table and sat next to Slider.

'So, what do you do when your wife is away filming?' asked Slider.

'I have a business making cakes for all different kinds of occasions, but I specialize in making wedding cakes.' After sipping his coffee, he continued, 'I also make cakes for some of the larger stores in Knightsbridge.'

'Well, the cake you made for me was delicious.'

'Thank you, I'm glad you enjoyed it.'

Slider looked at his daughter, who was studying the map. 'Where to now, darling?'

She pointed and said, 'Down there.' The assembled group continued their tour around the museum under Becky's guidance, and the sight of so many different species of mammal, bird, reptile, and insect overwhelmed them. The children were especially excited at what they saw, which put smiles on the faces of the parents.

They were at the far end of the museum when Alexis said, 'It's quarter to twelve so I think we should start making our way back to the main entrance.'

As Becky led them around the skeleton of a large prehistoric crocodile, and in the general direction of the main entrance, her father remarked, 'He's a big one, isn't he?'

'I don't like crocodiles.'

'Neither do I, darling, neither do I.' Andy was lagging slightly behind so his father stopped and waited for him. 'Have you enjoyed yourself today?'

'I've loved it, Dad.'

He put his arm around his son's shoulder and said, 'We'll come again next time we visit Alexis.'

'When would that be?'

'Oh, perhaps Christmas time.' Outside the museum, several cabs were lined up waiting for passengers, but all were too small. Suddenly Slider saw a large Mercedes indicating that he was pulling up on the far side of the road. Without hesitating, he ran across the road and spoke to the driver, then jumped in, and it pulled up neatly in front of his party.

'Well, you've certainly got your uses,' said Alexis as everyone got in.

The car did a U-turn in the road and headed towards Harrods with Becky saying, 'I wonder what Mum's bought?'

Laughter went around the cab, and her father said, 'I dread to think.'

'Does your wife buy lots of clothes?' asked Roberto.

'You wouldn't believe it ... I just don't know why women want so many clothes.'

'Me too.'

Alexis slapped her husband on his thigh. 'As if I have!' He began laughing, and gently hugged her.

As the Mercedes pulled up and stopped in front of Harrods, there was no sign of Lily Slider or Rose Harper. Slider sighed. 'Trust them to be late.'

'They're probably trying on more clothes,' muttered Andy, who was looking grumpy.

'Well, let's all wait inside and hopefully they won't be much longer,' Alexis said as the store door was held open for them.

'I don't believe it!' said Slider as the two women, carrying copious amounts of bags, walked towards them. 'What on earth have you two been buying?'

'It's not all mine, darling, this all belongs to Rose. Mine is the small bag,' she said as she kissed him.

'I might have known.'

'Well, you know I want to look nice when I go out.'

Slider shook his head from side to side and said, 'Let's go and have some lunch, shall we?'

The decision was taken to have fish and chips for lunch. Alexis knew a place just down the road from Harrods. The party settled in across two long benches, and no sooner had they sat down than Rose started pulling out the clothes that she had just bought. Standing up, she held them against her body, which drew admiring glances and whistles from other diners.

'God almighty, we can't take you anywhere, can we?' barked her sister.

'Well, I'm just showing Alexis what I've bought.'

Everyone was reduced to fits of laughter when her sister then said, 'And everyone else in here. Can't you wait till we get to the house?'

'Well, you know I don't like waiting.'

Lily turned her attention to her children. 'So, did you two have a nice time at the museum?'

'I loved it, Mum,' said her son, who couldn't keep still and gave his mother a full account of what they saw.

Becky was squirting red ketchup onto her chips when she said to her mother, 'Dad said we can go again next time we're here.'

'Did he indeed? So you enjoyed it as well, darling?'

'For me, it was the highlight of our visit here.'

'Apart from tomorrow, you mean?'

'Well, yes, obviously apart from tomorrow.'

Alexis broke into the conversation. 'We do have a slight problem for tomorrow. I've been doing some checking and apparently only three guests are going to be allowed into the ballroom to witness Slider's investiture. But we can all go inside Buckingham Palace to wait for him,' she said, looking at everyone.

'So why do they insist on only three to witness the investiture?' asked Lily, who had considerable concern in her voice.

'Well, around sixty people will be receiving a medal or an honour, and there is only a certain number of seats in the ballroom,' she said as she wiped ketchup from her daughter's mouth. The rest of the lunch was eaten in relative silence, as everyone was doing the sums and wondering who the three would be. After stirring her tea for some considerable time, Alexis said, 'Well, tomorrow is after all Slider's investiture, so I personally think that Lily, Becky, and Andy should be present to see their father awarded his medal.'

Lily reached out across the table towards Alexis. 'Thank you.'

Looking at him, Alexis said, 'And for God's sake try not to trip over the red carpet!' This remark brought about laughter which went around the table, with Slider staring at her and mouthing the words, 'Thank you.'

'I do hope it doesn't rain tomorrow,' Lily said as the taxi made its way back to Kensington.

'No, I've checked the forecast, and we can expect another sunny day,' replied Alexis, who'd become rather quiet and distant. No sooner had they arrived back at the house than a Selfridges delivery man was knocking on her door. 'Give us a hand, Slider,' she shouted.

'What's all this champagne and food for?'

'It's for your party tomorrow.'

As he placed the box of champagne down on the kitchen's black marble worktop, Slider could see that her eyes had clouded over. He put his arms around her and quietly said, 'I'm sorry that you can't be at my investiture tomorrow.'

'Well, it would have been nice, but rules are rules.' While holding her in his arms, a sudden thought came into his head, and after unboxing the champagne he left the kitchen and went upstairs. The rest of the afternoon was spent listening to Becky play the piano. Glasses of Alexis's favourite champagne were handed around as well as plates of gateau.

It rained during the night, and the following morning the pavements were still damp as autumn started to rear its head. Everyone was up especially early, and a lively atmosphere could be felt throughout the house. In the kitchen, Roberto and his wife were busying themselves with demands for breakfasts and pots of tea and coffee.

'Good morning, and how are we all today?' said Slider as he entered the kitchen.

'I thought you were never getting up,' said Alexis as she placed a fried egg onto Andy's plate.

'I would have been down sooner, but I had a few calls to make.'

'Well, join the others, and I'll bring you in a coffee.'

In the dining room, everyone was chirpy, and when Slider entered, they turned their attention to him, with his wife embracing him and asking, 'Good morning, darling, and how are you on this special day?'

'I'm feeling really well today, though I can hardly believe that today I'll be meeting the queen.'

'Well, you will be,' said Alexis, giggling, as she placed Andy's breakfast in front of him.

After sipping his coffee, Slider looked at the wall clock which read 08:47. 'So what time are we going to be leaving?'

'We need to be at the palace by eleven o'clock, so I've ordered a cab for ten thirty,' she affirmed while cutting the top off her daughter's egg. 'So, sit down and I'll get you some breakfast.'

'How's your head today, Dad?' asked his son.

'Fine, son, and how are you today?'

'I'm good thanks, Dad.'

Casting his eye towards his daughter, he said, 'And how are you today?'

Becky was sprinkling salt onto her hard-boiled egg as she smiled and said, 'Good, Dad.'

'My head's not so good this morning,' said Rose who was yawning.

A round of laughter went around the table with Slider commenting, 'I'm not surprised after guzzling down that champagne.'

'You haven't asked how I am today?' said his wife as she stared at him.

'Well, I know that you're always alright.' With that, he kissed her gently.

After her breakfast, Becky played the piano while the remainder of her family were still eating. Slider had just finished his last mouthful when Alexis walked into the dining room and stood in front of him holding a suit bag. 'I've got a present for you,' she said, with a smile beaming wide across her face. 'I remember you saying at the nursing home that a black suit always looks more distinguished.' She removed the suit from its protective bag and held it up in front of him.

'I don't know what to say,' he said in a quiet voice.

'Well, you can say thank you and try it on. There's also some white shirts and ties on your bed.' He took off his robe that was covering his white T-shirt and slipped the jacket on. It fitted perfectly. The jacket had two pockets on the left side and one on the right as well as a top pocket. It also had a beautiful red lining. He put his arms around Alexis, hugged and thanked her. 'As time is now getting on I suggest that we all start getting dressed and getting ready to go.'

They all slipped away to their bedrooms to get dressed. Slider was talking to his wife when their daughter knocked and entered. 'Mum, can I use your bathroom? Aunty Rose is taking all day and won't come out.'

'Of course you can. You can also help me to decide which tie your father should wear.' She held up the three ties and asked her daughter, 'Which one?' Becky pointed to the one on the left. 'I thought that one as well.' Turning to her husband, she handed him the maroon silk tie.

At ten fifteen nearly everyone had gathered in the lounge, with Roberto who was dressed in a black suit handing glasses of champagne to the adults. Becky was wearing a pink and white dress, while her brother was wearing his school uniform, which he loved. Alice, who was sitting next to Becky, wore a dark blue dress.

Alexis had chosen a red and black sleeveless dress, and was popping in and out of the kitchen to check on things when Slider and his wife entered the lounge. She said, 'You both look gorgeous.' Slider looked stunning in his new black suit and his beautiful wife was dressed in a short cream dress which had a large sapphire and diamond broach pinned to it. 'So, who are we waiting for now?'

There was laughter all round when Slider stated sarcastically, 'As if you have to ask.'

'Oh, Rose.'

Eventually, she entered the lounge wearing a short white dress covered with yellow polka-dots, yellow stilettoes, white gloves, and a large white brimmed hat. She capped her appearance with dark shades. 'I hope I haven't kept you all waiting,' she said in a rather grand voice.

'Well, I've seen it all now!' said Slider, who was shaking his head.

'Rose, you're not going to Royal Ascot!' her sister said.

'Well, you know me.'

'The taxi is here,' Roberto called from the kitchen.

'Oh well, this is it,' whispered Slider to his wife.

'Don't worry, you'll be fine. How's the head?'

'It's OK.'

The dark blue eight-seater Mercedes was right on time, and once everyone was settled in and belted up Alexis said to the driver, 'The main archway at Buckingham Palace please.' The journey was only slightly further than the previous day's journey to Harrods, and surprisingly the traffic was much lighter today. As they passed Harrods, Buckingham Palace came into view. On seeing it, Slider used his handkerchief to wipe his brow.

'How are you feeling?' asked his wife.

'I'm fine. I'm just a bit hot wearing this suit.'

As the car stopped outside the main archway, a large crowd of people had already gathered and were waiting their turn to enter the palace grounds. Finally, they all entered under the archway and were greeted by the Lord Chamberlain. As they entered the palace, they ascended the main staircase and were met by an usher who informed the party that the rule allowing only three to enter the ballroom had been waived for their group. Slider had a large grin on his face when Alexis said to him, 'Did you have something to do with this?'

'Well, let's just say it helps to have friends in high places.'

Everyone apart from Slider was escorted to the front row of chairs in the ballroom and took their seats which had been reserved for them.

Slider was ushered into a room to meet and greet other dignitaries who were receiving their medals and honours, and was given his instructions for the ceremony. At precisely eleven thirty an usher opened the door, and his group was led into the ballroom. Everyone stood still, in a line, as the National Anthem was played. He watched in silence as the man in front of him received his medal, and with his heart pounding in his chest, he heard his name called: 'Mr Matthew Slider!'

The Slider and Polti families sat rigidly in their seats as he walked past them and along the red carpet and approached Her Majesty, Queen Elizabeth II. Turning to face the queen he bowed his head, stood upright, and the Queen's Gallantry Medal was pinned to his jacket. Slider listened intently as the queen said, 'Mr Slider, I have been following the events surrounding you for several months, and it gives me great pleasure to finally meet you and to award you the Queen's Gallantry Medal.'

'Thank you very much, Your Majesty. I would just like to say thank you for everything that you have done for me, and Irene Asher would especially like to thank you for your help.'

'How is Irene, Mr Slider?'

'Irene is very well, Your Majesty.'

'Good, I'm glad to hear it. Well, congratulations again, Mr Slider, and my best wishes go with you.' With that, the queen smiled, extended her right arm, and gently shook hands with Matthew Slider. He smiled back, bowed, then turned to his right and continued walking along the red carpet, then stopped and waited as everyone in his group received their honours.

Once the investiture had finished he met his family at the top of the main staircase, where hugs and kisses were generously lavished on him.

'Oh, darling, I'm so proud of you,' cried his tearful wife.

Looking at Alexis he asked, 'Did you enjoy yourself in there?'

'I'm so glad to have seen it all, but you must tell me why we were all allowed into the ballroom.'

'That, I'm afraid, is not possible.'

'Why?'

'I made a solemn promise to someone, and it's a promise that I can never break!' he said, looking deep into her eyes.

In the palace courtyard, Slider was having his photo taken by Alexis, who had elected herself chief photographer, and everyone had their photo taken with him and his medal. They were especially grateful when a palace official offered to take a group photo, which they duly accepted.

'Dad, can I look at your medal?' asked his excited son.

'Of course you can.' He slipped off his medal and handed it to his son, saying, 'Don't drop it.'

As they made the short walk to the main archway of the palace, everyone was in high spirits and looking forward to the party back at Alexis's house. Outside the palace, several black cabs were picking up passengers, but with eight in their party, it took several minutes before a silver Mercedes capable of taking them all was flagged down. Everyone was excited as the car drove back, with requests to have a closer look at his medal being granted.

Back at the house, Roberto wasted no time in popping the champagne corks and distributing glasses to the adults in the lounge. Even Becky and her brother were given a small glass each. Alice, though, was given fizzy lemonade to drink, which she loved. Feeling hot Slider removed his black jacket and placed it on the back of a chair, then started to give an account of what happened behind the scenes at the palace. Alexis, who was bringing plates of food in from the kitchen, looked at him and sharply asked, 'Is everything OK?'

Slider took a few seconds to reply, turning slowly to look at her, and in a slurred voice said, 'What … did you s-say?'

Everyone stopped talking and watched in horror as he missed the coffee table with his champagne glass and collapsed onto the wooden floor. 'Slider!' screamed his wife. There were screams from everyone, as Lily patted the side of his face without getting any response. Alexis reached for her mobile phone and immediately phoned for an ambulance while instructing her husband to take the children into the dining room. Lily, Rose, and Alexis were engulfed in floods of tears as they knelt beside

Slider and spoke loudly to try and get some response from him.

'The ambulance is here!' shouted Roberto from the front door. The paramedics rushed up to the door and were guided into the lounge. Alexis moved Lily and Rose onto a sofa and all three watched as the paramedics went to work.

'Is my husband still alive?'

'He's still alive, but only just. Does your husband suffer from any ailments?'

'His head is always bad, and he was diagnosed with a tension headache over ten years ago,' she said, wiping her eyes.

'We're taking your husband to the Chelsea and Westminster Hospital in Fulham Road. You can come with us; the others will have to follow us.'

'Mum, is Dad dead?' cried Becky, as the stretcher carrying her father passed her.

'No, your father is still alive,' Alexis said, as she looked into the girl's watery eyes.

The wheeled stretcher was pushed into the ambulance. Lily sat opposite her husband and held his hand. As the ambulance left, Alexis ran to her car. 'Rose, you get in the front; Becky, Andy, you two get in the back and put your belts on!' Looking at her husband she called out, 'You stay here with Alice and I'll call you when I can!'

The ambulance accelerated along Marloes Road with its siren screaming and its blue light flashing. Alexis's Audi was only a short distance behind and at the junction turned right into Cromwell Road. The ambulance moved swiftly onto the main road, and as it turned left into Earls Court Road it accelerated away at a frantic speed, leaving the Audi struggling to keep up. At the junction with Old Brompton Road, Alexis very nearly collided with a pedal cyclist who didn't see her as she tore over the junction into Redcliffe Gardens. 'Don't worry, we're almost there,' she said. As the ambulance turned left into Fulham Road the hospital was just in front of them. As it came to a halt outside the accident and emergency department, the two paramedics were out immediately and removed the wheeled stretcher and pushed it inside, with Lily hurrying beside it. Alexis regained sight of the ambulance as she entered the hospital and her Audi screamed to a halt a few metres away from it. 'Follow me, you three.'

Once inside the accident and emergency department, they struggled at first to find Lily, with Becky shouting out, 'Mum, Mum, where are you?'

Emerging from behind a curtain Lily tearfully cried, 'We're in here.'

'Can we see Dad?' asked a tearful Becky.

'No, not at the moment, the doctors and nurses are with him.' Andy and Rose had said nothing since leaving the house, and both seemed in a state of shock, with Alexis comforting them both.

Frantic voices could be heard from behind the curtain, and curious sounds emanated from the lifesaving apparatus and other pieces of equipment. A tall doctor who was probably in his early thirties emerged from behind the curtain and with a very solemn-looking face stated, 'I'm so very sorry to inform you that your husband has died.'

The screams and bawling tears echoed around the corridor in disbelief at what they had just been told. The group hugged each other for several minutes, and when the tears subsided, Lily Slider, who was crying and shaking noticeably, asked, 'Can we please see my husband?'

'Of course you can.'

They entered the cubicle and gathered around Slider, who looked peaceful and at ease. 'How did my husband die?'

'I'm afraid your husband suffered a massive brain haemorrhage. There was nothing anyone could have done to save him.'

Lily and her sister kissed and said their goodbyes. The children, who were in shock, gently kissed their father and said their goodbyes for the last time too, then they were led out into the corridor by their mother.

Alexis, who was standing in the corridor and was openly trembling, re-entered the cubicle. Standing over Slider's body she wept openly and bawled, 'I loved you, Slider … I really loved you.' After kissing him on the lips, she turned and left.

SEVENTEEN

The Gods were angry. It had been four weeks since Slider died, and today was his funeral. Lily had been trying hard to coax her daughter into playing the piano, but the sudden death of her father had left the young girl devastated. She seemed lost in a world of her own and would sit for hours with Sooty sitting on her lap. Her brother was also heartbroken by the loss of his father, and after his death had locked himself away in his bedroom for several days and didn't want to see or speak to anyone.

Rose Harper had remained at her sister's home to give comfort to her and the children. Alexis had also stayed in Cardiff since his death, and was instrumental in arranging the funeral. A post-mortem on Slider later revealed that a bleed on his brain had led to an epidural hematoma, which, they were told, could quite easily have happened long before he received his medal.

'I wish this rain would stop,' said Rose, who was sitting on the piano seat staring out of the window.

'Do you know, Rose, Slider always said that he wanted it to pour down, with thunder and lightning, on the day of his funeral. He used to say, "Sunny days are for getting married and rainy days are for funerals."'

'Well, he's got his wish today. Oh, Pam and Roger are coming across the road.'

'Let them in, will you please?'

Rose went to the door and opened it. 'Come in,' she said, while holding a tissue to her eyes.

'Hi Rose, how are Lily and the children?' asked Roger, whose eyes were red and watery.

'So, so. Lily's in the lounge.'

Pam and Roger went in and sat on either side of Lily on the sofa. Pam put her arm around her, kissed her and said, 'I've never seen so many flowers and cards in one room.'

A smile crept round Lily's mouth as she said in a tired voice, 'People have been very good … I always had it in the back of my mind that something like this would happen.' And wiping her eyes and nose she cried, 'But you're never prepared for when it does happen!'

'What time will the hearse be arriving?' asked Roger, who had stood up to look at the cards on the mantlepiece.

Rose, who looked stunning in a black dress, said, 'Midday.'

'How are the children today?' he further asked.

'Well, Becky's in the dining room, lost in thought, and Andy's upstairs in his room. I would be grateful if you could go upstairs and speak to him.'

Roger did as Rose suggested and knocked on his bedroom door. 'Andy, can I come in please?' He pushed open the door and found Andy sitting on the side of his bed, staring out of the window. He sat next to him and put his arm around his shoulder.

The young boy burst into tears. 'What am I going to do now my Dad's died?'

Roger handed him a tissue from a box on the bedside cabinet and spoke softly. 'Let me tell you something. When I was fourteen my brother Carl was knocked down and killed by a driver while doing his paper round, and I was just like you. But it's been a month since your father died and you can't go on like this. Imagine what your father is saying when he's looking down on you from heaven … He's probably saying. "Enough's enough, son."'

Andy stopped crying and wiped his eyes. 'Yes, you're right, Rog.'

'Nobody will ever forget Slider; he was a hero. Now go and wash your face and come downstairs, the hearse will be here soon. And by the way, have you fed the fish lately?'

'No.'

'Well, you'd better do it before we go, and you can get your sister to help you. That pond was your father's pride and joy, and he wouldn't want you to neglect it.' He left the boy and went back down the stairs and sat next to Becky, who was in the dining room with Sooty on her lap. 'Have you played your piano today?' The young girl stayed silent and shook her head slowly from side to side while stroking the cat.

'Your father loved listening to you play. We all did. He'd be heartbroken to learn that you have stopped playing. Can you write music?' Becky, who was looking down at the cat, nodded her head. 'Well, why don't you write a piece of music for your father. You could call it *Slider's Tune* or something else. And by the way, those fish in the pond need feeding.'

That idea seemed to register with the young girl, who put the cat down and stood up just as her brother, who was looking more composed, came into the dining room. 'Let's go and feed the fish, sis.' Andy took his sister's hand and led her into the garden, where they were observed by other members of the family feeding the fish.

'Thank you, Rog, thank you so much.' Lily smiled as she watched through the lounge window.

The doorbell rang. Roger opened it and was handed a large bouquet of flowers and a card by the delivery woman. 'Thank you.' As he closed the door he was met by Andy and Becky. 'Why don't you two go and find a vase for these flowers and bring them into the lounge?'

A few minutes later Becky and her brother entered the lounge with a vase of beautiful mixed flowers. 'Those look lovely,' said their mother, with a weak smile.

'Where shall we put them, Mum?'

'Where indeed, darling? There're not many places left to put another vase.'

'Shall I put them on top of the piano?'

'Yes, that's a good idea darling. Why don't you play something for us as well?'

'OK. What shall I play?'

'Something lively, darling, nothing sad. And let's have another pot of tea, Pam.' The Slider household seemed to be slowly getting back to normality, with the two children hopefully over the worst of their grief. Although it would still take many more months, the green shoots that indicated life was slowly returning to normal seemed to be appearing.

'Mum, there are two big black horses outside our house!' yelled Becky, as she stopped playing.

'Oh my God!' gasped Lily. 'Whatever has Alexis gone and done?' Outside on the road was a beautiful horse-drawn black hearse, pulled by two large Belgian black horses with black plumes attached to their heads. Along both sides of the carriage were white wreaths which spelt out the name, S L I D E R

Even though it was still raining, the two children couldn't resist the temptation to go and have a look at the horses and each gave a horse a piece of apple to eat. A crowd of interested neighbours had also gathered to admire them. Alexis, who was acting as groom to the driver and was wearing a traditional Victorian costume, stepped down from the carriage and walked up to the front door, to be greeted by the Slider family and friends.

'Alexis, it's so nice to see you. Slider would have loved that hearse,' said Rose, who was sheltering under an umbrella.

'I'm so glad that you like it. I thought it would be in keeping with Slider's sense of humour. Are you all ready to leave?'

Lily looked at her gold wristwatch; the time was approaching midday. 'Just give us a few minutes to put our coats on.' The Slider family assembled on the road, and all were admiring the black hearse and horses, which had brought out virtually all the neighbours from College Road. Lily was arm in arm with her sister and was staring at her husband's coffin, and after a few minutes she wiped her eyes and said, 'Let's go, we don't want to keep people waiting.' The black Daimler with the family in it slowly followed the horse-drawn hearse, with Lily saying, 'Look at all these people.'

'Everyone loved Slider,' said Rose, putting a comforting arm around her sister.

As the hearse made its slow journey up College Road and towards Whitchurch Common, the sight of so many people paying their respects was a truly wondrous sight. It was as if the whole of Cardiff had descended upon Whitchurch, and tears flowed down the faces of both Rose Harper and Lily Slider, in acknowledgment of their respect for the hundreds of people who were paying their last respects to her husband, who was regarded as a very heroic man. As the hearse approached St Mary's Church, several junctions had been sealed off to accommodate the vast numbers of people who were unable to find a pew inside the church. Many were forced to stand on the pavement, as well as on the road, and would listen to the service via speakers. As they waited for the service, the rain fell even harder.

Once the hearse had stopped, the coffin was slowly and carefully taken out and lifted onto the shoulders of the pallbearers, Alan, Frosty, Hugh, and Gary, who were Slider's best friends. Alexis followed directly behind the coffin and was accompanied by Slider's family and friends, while the Reverend Kenneth Mumford led the way slowly along the path and into the church. The coffin was set down onto a white marble plinth, and everyone took their places, with the minister starting the proceedings with a prayer.

During the service, several of Slider's friends stood at the pulpit and recalled stories of Slider's exploits, which drew howls of laughter from the congregation. One story told by Alan was of a young Chinese student who was getting into Slider's car and asked him to be careful with her suitcase. At the end of the journey Slider was taking the case from the boot and felt it move. Suddenly the lock on the case snapped open and the car boot was filled with rabbits.

Although this was a sad day, the minister addressed the congregation and asked them to rejoice in the fact that Matthew Slider was a true hero and would never be forgotten. He concluded the service with a final prayer. While seated, the congregation watched as the pallbearers gently lifted Slider's coffin and carried it through a side door to the churchyard and slowly set it down on wooden bearers next to his burial plot.

His family were inconsolable and wept openly as belts were placed under the coffin and slowly it was lowered into its final resting place. Many people were weeping beneath their umbrellas as the rain continued to fall, and could only just hear what the minister was saying.

'For as much as it hath pleased Almighty God of his great mercy to take unto himself the soul of our dear brother here departed, we therefore commit his body to the ground. Earth to earth … ashes to ashes … dust to dust, in sure of certain hope of the resurrection to et … ern … al … lif … e …'

Suddenly, something very strange began to happen. The minister's voice was slowly fading away.

EIGHTEEN

Somewhere, in the deepest recesses of his mind, a very faint voice which had been lost in time started to reveal itself, and gradually it started to awaken him. It was still far away, but as he slowly exhaled it grew louder and louder until he was engulfed by it. The voice at first seemed alien but slowly his mind adjusted to it, and the sound he could hear was the sound of his daughter's voice calling to him.

'Dad, Dad, wake up … Please, Dad, wake up.'

Deep inside his head, he looked for the way out. It was as if he was lost in a maze and couldn't find the route to the sound. His mind turned various corners, looking for an exit. He heard his daughter calling again and at last found the light and slowly his eyes began to open. The light was blinding as he took his first breath. He could feel his eyelids being lifted, and again the light hurt him as he blinked and coughed for the first time.

Another voice he could hear was foreign to him and it just kept repeating itself: 'Come on, Mr Slider, wake up please.' He could feel his whole body being shaken.

'Where am I?' he mumbled as his arm was being tugged. He was able to turn his head slowly on the white-fringed pillow, and through bleary eyes could just make out his daughter staring at him. 'What's happened to me?' he said, weakly.

'Oh Dad, we all thought you were dead,' said his daughter, who was sitting on the bed next to him.

'Where's Andy?'

'He's gone downstairs to fetch Mum.'

Slider slowly rolled onto his back and after wiping his eyes saw the contours of a man in green fatigues staring down at him. 'Who are you?' he said softly.

'I'm Mr Hopkins, and I'm with the paramedics. You've given us all quite a scare.'

'Why, what's happened to me?'

'Well, it seems you've taken an overdose of Nortriptyline and it very nearly killed you.'

The bedroom door slowly opened, and his tearful wife and son approached the bed and gazed down at Slider, who was still coming to terms with what had happened. 'Do you know, you've frightened the life out of this family, you've been unconscious for nearly half an hour and we all thought you were dead.'

'I'm so sorry.'

'Well, you can say you're sorry to the paramedic team, who pumped your stomach and brought you back to life.'

Looking at the man in the green fatigues he whispered, 'Thank you. Thank you for saving my life.'

'That's OK, Mr Slider, but you must be more careful in future.' Looking at his bottle of pills he said, 'It does state no more than two tablets to be taken in any twenty-four-hour period, so you must have swallowed quite a number.'

'Will you be taking my husband into hospital?' asked Lily, who had now calmed herself.

'No, that won't be necessary, but I would advise your husband to visit his doctor, just to be sure.'

Slider's breathing was now more relaxed, and slowly he was able to focus more clearly on the people around him. Catching sight of his son sobbing he asked, 'Are you OK, son?'

'I was really scared, Dad, I thought you weren't going to wake up.'

The paramedics put all their equipment away, and before leaving the bedroom Mr Hopkins said, 'Goodbye,

Mr Slider, and please try be more careful in future.' He nodded and waved feebly as the paramedics left the room.

The next day Slider woke late. He looked at the red illumination on his bedside clock: 09:22. For a few minutes he just lay there, trying to fully awaken himself, when he heard someone on the landing. 'Hello,' he called out.

The door opened slowly and his wife entered the bedroom. 'So, how are you feeling today?'

'Not too bad. Could you get me a glass of water, please, so that I can take my medication?'

'I'll get you some water, but I'm holding on to your tablets from now on,' she said sternly.

'Whatever you say, darling.' After taking his tablets he pulled back the duvet and sat on the side of the bed, looking out of the window. The morning sun was already high above the roof ridges of the opposite houses, and the wet pavements were beginning to dry out. As he took his first tentative steps, Slider slipped his black and white dressing gown on and paid a visit to the loo. After leaving the bathroom, he knocked on his son's bedroom door. Gently pushing the door open he found Andy, as usual, playing his computer games.

On seeing his father, he said, 'How are you feeling, Dad?'

'Tired. Where's your sister and mother?'

'Downstairs. Why?'

'Well, I want you to come downstairs and sit with us in the lounge. I have something important to tell you all.'

The Slider family had all gathered in the lounge when Slider said, 'You may all think I'm mad, but I've seen so much and experienced so much that you'll think I'm making it up. But to me, it was very real.' He slowly gave them a full account of everything he had experienced and seen.

When he had finished talking, Andy said, 'Wow, Dad, perhaps you were teleported in your dream?'

'I don't know, son, but it was as real as you are sitting in front of me.'

'So who was Alice, Dad?' asked Becky, who was playing with an elastic band.

'Alice was the daughter of Alexis, and she is the little girl who fell into the sea.'

Lily put her cup down and sighed. 'Well, I don't know what to make of it all.'

Looking at his wife Slider asked, 'You do have a sister Rose, don't you?'

They all laughed when she said, 'Of course I have a sister named Rose.'

'And she drives a maroon MG Morgan car?'

'Yes, she does.'

'And do we have a cat named Sooty?'

Another wave of laughter went around the lounge when Becky said, 'Of course we have.'

The cat flap rattled, and a welcome face entered the room. 'Well, at least I got that part of the story right,' he said, stroking the cat.

The following afternoon, Slider and his wife paid a visit to their doctor. After a thorough check-up and after giving him a full account of what he'd experienced, the consensus was that it was nothing more than a bad hallucination. The fact that it seemed so real was a result of his large overdose of Nortriptyline. The next few days were spent taking the doctor's advice, which was to rest and take things easy. His medication was reduced, and life seemed to be getting back to normal, with Slider deciding to go back to work the following Monday, which was in four days' time.

* * *

It was Monday, May the seventh, two thousand and eighteen and Slider was looking forward to going back to work. He had put behind him the events of the past few days and was feeding the goldfish when Becky shouted from the kitchen, 'Dad, it's time to go.'

His daughter was right. It was eight thirty and the traffic would be bad if he left it much later. Slider returned the fish food to his shed, locked the marigold-coloured ledged-braced door, and walked back into the kitchen. After taking his bottles of water out of the fridge, to keep himself hydrated, he asked his children, 'Have you both got everything?'

'Yes, Dad,' replied Becky, who was putting an apple into her pink backpack.

'And what about you?' he asked, looking at his son. Andy, as usual, looked tired and just nodded his head.

'Have you all got everything?' asked Lily, as she entered the kitchen.

'Yes, Mum,' came the reply from her children.

'Well, you all have a nice day.' And turning to face her husband, she said, 'And you be careful out there today.'

He hugged and kissed his wife. 'Of course I will.'

As they all walked towards the front door, Lily held it open for them, and they all filed out. Slider opened the car and Andy went straight for the back seat, so that he could sprawl across three seats. Leaving his sister to say, 'Thanks, Andy,' as she put her seat belt on.

As the car pulled away they all waved and smiled at Lily, who was holding Sooty in her arms. The journey to Cardiff Middle School took slightly longer than expected. Roadworks had suddenly sprung up which Slider hadn't known about, but he managed to drop off his children just in time, before saying, 'I'll pick you up at the usual time.'

On leaving the school grounds he logged on for work and drove past Roath Park Lake. Memories came flooding back of the time he fished the lake as a schoolboy. The lake was now covered in a green algae over most of the surface, and the water at the far end had almost disappeared, leaving the rowing boats able to use only half the lake. He could remember back to the 1970s, when heavy plant machinery would dredge the lake, but this was May 2018 and councils have no money for luxuries like that.

After giving the lighthouse a cursory glance as he passed it, the Carver app offered him his first job of the day. The job was to pick up Jena from the concourse at the University Hospital of Wales. A thought ran through his mind that this name was somehow familiar. As the car approached the pick-up point, a woman in green fatigues could be seen waving her hand at him. After stopping, the woman got into the back of his car.

'Is it Jena?' he asked.

'Yes,' she replied, smothering a yawn.

Slider was full of trepidation when he pressed his smartphone to start the journey and realized the job was to take Jena to the University Hospital Llandough. He could remember quite distinctly taking an ambulance driver from the University Hospital of Wales to the University Hospital Llandough in what his doctor called an hallucination, but to him it was something else. Looking at the woman in his mirror he said, 'Have I picked you up before?'

'No, you haven't. I've only just started work as an ambulance driver, and this is my first day on the job.'

'Well, good luck to you in your new career.'

'Thanks,' she said, and rested her head against the back of the seat.

Throughout the journey, he had the distinct impression that he had seen this traffic before. He remembered the scaffolding lorry parked outside the Holiday Inn Hotel on Castle Street, and as he drove past the Cardiff City Stadium, he could remember seeing the National Express coach having its tyre changed.

After clearing the fare and dropping off his passenger, he parked up, turned off the engine and turned on the radio, just in time to catch the start of the ten o'clock news on Radio 2. The news started with the story that Sir Alex Ferguson was still in hospital in a serious condition, after suffering a brain haemorrhage on Saturday at his home in Wilmslow, Cheshire. This news report confirmed to him that this day was a repeat of what he'd already experienced.

'What's happening to me?' he said to himself.

After the news had finished, he turned the engine back on and started to leave the grounds of the hospital, but braked sharply when he saw a bright yellow restored Ford escort in a parking space to his right. Slider drove past the car and pulled into an empty parking space close by and turned off the engine. After undoing his seat belt and pushing the seat back he closed his eyes and took several deep breaths. Something had happened to him when he was in a comatose state, and it wasn't an hallucination, as his doctor had told him it was, and it certainly wasn't a dream. This was real, and it was happening right in front of him, here today on Monday, May the seventh, two thousand and eighteen. Minutes passed by, then a Premiere Taxi pulled into a parking space close by. As he looked at the car something about it kept niggling away at him. He was finding his mind drawn to the car, and as he looked at the blue and white magnetic sign he kept repeating its name over and over to himself very slowly.

'Premiere … Premiere … Premiere … Premiere … Premiere … what is it?' He knew this was a major clue. He closed his eyes again, bowed his head, and exhaled slowly. He took the top off his water bottle and had a mouthful of water, while looking at the magnetic sign. 'Come on, what is it?' he shouted to himself while replacing the screw cap.

Looking at the sign again he slowly continued to repeat its name: 'Premiere … Premiere … Premiere.' He reduced the name and slowly whispered, 'Prem … Prem … Prem … Prem.' He could sense that he was getting closer to what he was looking for, and suddenly it was as if all the planets in the universe were aligned in perfect sequence, and the sudden realization came that the one word that he had been striving for had hit him right between the eyes, and he slowly said it: 'Premonition'. He sat for a few moments with tears streaming down his face, then lifted his head, wiped away the tears, and started to laugh openly. Everything that he had experienced now made perfect sense. Saving the life of Alice Polti wasn't something that had happened: it was something that was *about* to happen.

Slider looked at the clock in front of him and realized he was way behind time. He started the engine and roared away at a frantic speed towards Penarth Pier. He was caught up in a line of cars all trying to leave the hospital and time was ebbing away, so instinctively he overtook the line of cars and met a lorry trying to enter the hospital at the T-junction. He slammed on his horn and just scraped the wheel arch and smashed his door mirror on the lorry as he tore right onto Penlan Road.

Racing down the hill towards the Merrie Harrier pub/restaurant he again got caught in some traffic and weaved in between two cars at the junction who were blasting him with their car horns. Luckily, he was able to turn left onto Barry Road without any problem, and as he accelerated, he spotted the concrete lorry dispensing its load and pushed the car even faster, as he was way behind the point where he had spoken to the road worker. As he approached the crossroads his temper was starting to rise and he shouted, 'Not again!' In front of him was a learner driver who was trying to turn right at the lights. 'Come on, come on!' he exploded.

On seeing the learner driver stall her car, he accelerated into the middle lane and overtook the learner on her nearside, which made the driver jam on the brakes. This put a large grin on Slider's face. Racing down Cogan Hill brought the small roundabout into view which he cleared easily, and once onto Windsor Road he started to look for Beaver's B&B where he knew Alexis would be filming. Up ahead he could see a bright lamp which was illuminating the location, and standing on the pavement, with a cameraman filming her, was Alexis Polti, who was wearing her bright red, three-quarter-length coat.

Slider pushed his car even harder and steered it sharply towards the opposite side of the road. He screeched to a halt, causing other drivers to move out of his way, and pedestrians stared in amazement at the lunacy of the driver. Once out of the car he barged in between the cameraman and Alexis. Looking at her, panting for breath, he said, 'I need you to come with me right now.'

'Do you mind, we're trying to do some filming.'

'I know this seems very strange, but you have to believe me when I tell you that your daughter Alice is in grave danger.'

'How do you know my daughter is in danger?' she replied angrily.

Trying to stay calm, Slider said, 'I know everything about you. Your husband's name is Roberto. You live in Kensington, and your favourite champagne is Moët & Chandon Impèrial Rosè. And on your dining room table you have a beautiful red cut-glass vase which depicts the world and is covered in gold leaf – your husband bought it for you when you honeymooned in Venice.'

'How do you know all these things about me?' she asked, surprised.

'Let's just say I've had a vision, and if we don't move straight away, Alice is going to die.'

Looking at her cameraman she said, 'I'll be back shortly.' Alexis sat next to Slider and spoke firmly. 'I hope for your sake this is not some kind of fucking joke!'

'No, it isn't. It's no joke at all.'

As the car accelerated along Windsor Road, she screamed as a bus coming towards them decided to overtake a lorry unloading its goods. Slider, though, was unmoved by it; his sixteen years as a driver was being put to the test and calmly he dodged the cars, with Alexis staring at him in disbelief. As the car flew across the large roundabout and into Windsor Terrace the road dropped away into a steep descent, with Slider saying, 'If I'm right we should see HMS *Deacon*, which is a Royal Navy Destroyer, as we go around this sharp bend.' And sure enough, there it was, but only for him to shout, 'We're way behind where we should be!'

As his Skoda thundered down the hill, Alexis screamed and hung on tightly as the car hit a large pothole. 'You fucking idiot, are you trying to kill us?'

He was impassive as the car screeched to a halt outside the entrance to Penarth Pier, and the smell of burning rubber perfumed the air. Slider was out like a shot and screamed at Alexis to follow him. 'Come on, run!' he yelled at her. As they ran onto the pier, time strangely seemed to move very slowly, and people's movements were also strangely slow. As they rounded a corner, there she was. Alice had placed her shoes on the cornice in between the railings and was standing much higher than anyone else. Both ran like hell to get close to her, but try as they might, time seemed to stand still and hold them back.

A large gathering of schoolgirls blocked their way, and they watched in horror as girls started to move slowly backwards, forcing Alice to wobble. Somehow, Slider wriggled his way through and in a desperate last measure flung himself forwards towards the little girl. Miraculously he was able to hook his right arm around her tiny waist. For a few seconds they both seesawed over the handrail and then with a last-ditch effort he was able to pull her back over the rail, causing himself, Alice, and several schoolgirls to fall in a heap on the decking.

It seemed to take an age to uncoil themselves and get to their feet, and after checking that everyone was OK, Alexis, with tears flowing down her flawless face, hugged and kissed Slider and cried, 'Thank you, thank you for saving the life of my daughter.' After they had composed themselves, they began the slow walk back towards the entrance of the pier. Still breathing hard, she said, 'Why don't I buy you a coffee and you can give me a full account of everything that's happened to you?'

Slider, who was still panting for breath, replied, 'Thanks, I'd like that, but I'm afraid I don't drink coffee – I drink tea.'

Stephen Martin Miles was born in Cardiff in 1954 and resides in the Vale of Glamorgan. Like Slider, he suffers with a tension headache. This is his first novel.

The Piano Teacher.

She stands beside the seat,
she's calling out the beats.
A sudden smile enlightens her face,
as the tune is captured.
At last, there is a meaning to this grace.

ഗ്ഗ

Like floating on a raft of air,
she can only stand and stare.
His fingers glide back and fore,
like waves that crash, and ebb and flow.

ഗ്ഗ

The tune is good, but not that good,
she says as he seems pleased.
His fingers shake with fear.
And then the tune he had just disappears.

ഗ്ഗ

It's gone for now it's been reclaimed,
but subconsciously it still remains.
Thoughts of quavers demands behaviour.
Gone for now, but, not for long.

ഗ്ഗ

She's pleased to see him at his ease,
he plays the tune for her again.
The flavour of the tune she hears,
is buried deep within his ears.

ഗ്ഗ

She stands in silence at the seat,
nervously, she can't retreat.
He plays the tune for her again,
she marks it down, a perfect ten.

Stephen Martin Miles (1993)

Printed in Great Britain
by Amazon